Birds of a Feather Flock Together

By

Clare Gallagher

First Published in 2023 by Clare Gallagher with Temple Woman Publishing

Edited by Temple Woman Publishing

www.templewomanpublishing.com

ISBN: 978-1-7394811-9-3

From the Author

Cat is a fun-loving, free-spirited Irish girl who enjoys pints with the lads and is very much a city girl who has experienced the bright lights of Dublin but has never experienced America before and is set to embark on a year's study in an American college. Alex is an all-American blonde-haired Californian who lives in a small town just outside San Francisco and has never been out of her own County before.

Both girls, from very different backgrounds, are living away from home for the first time. The two quickly realise how much they have in common and soon get stuck into college life and all the drama that goes with it! For Cat and Alex, college is the beginning of a new, exciting chapter in their lives and they surely live life to the full.

They experience the college dating scene and discover that love is hard to find for both girls but for very different reasons! For Alex, love is the scariest thing in the world. And for Cat, love just doesn't know her name.

Very much a modern-day tale of friendship, it's a quirky look at girls transitioning from their teens to their twenties and dealing with life, love and finding their way in the world. Luckily, they have each other – true birds of a feather that always flock together!

Dedications

To Genevieve, my dear friend and soul sister. You have given me my wings to fly high and write this book. Thank you for all the memories and fun times we have shared over the years. No matter the miles between us or the time apart, we are always there for each other - true birds of a feather.

To my son, Riley. Thank you for all your love, hugs and “You can do this, Mum” reminders. I love you to the moon and back.

To my Mum, Dad and sisters. Thank you for all your support and encouragement. I am so very lucky to have you all rooting for me. To all my family and also my American family, I love you all.

To all my close friends - you all know who you are! They say if you’re lucky to have a friend, you’re lucky enough. I’m so grateful to have you all in my life. Thank you for being there for me.

Finally, this book is dedicated to all the birds of a feather who flock together; friends who are there for each other, no matter what!

Contents

Chapter 1

College Girl

As I stepped off the plane, jet-lagged from a 9-hour flight from Ireland, I could feel the blistering heat overwhelm me like a thundering furnace. The temperature was unbelievable! Then it hit me - I was in the sunny State of California - me, an Irish girl from Dublin, all the way over the Atlantic and ready for a year of American college!

My goodbyes to my parents at the Departure Gate in Dublin Airport only 12 hours before seemed such a long time ago. My heart felt so heavy remembering their sadness at leaving their little girl. All I had ever known was their constant presence in my life.

As the only child of two doctors, I had always felt safe and secure. My dad was one of the top surgeons in Ireland and my mum was a GP who headed up the local doctors' surgery; both busy professionals but they always had time for me.

I kept thinking back to what my parents had said before I boarded my flight to America. With tears in her eyes, my mum told me, "Darlin', just think of this as an adventure. You go out there and have a ball, enjoy every bit of American life and show them what you're all about - and remember to study, okay?" My dad, who is always such a strong man, looked sad at the thought of not seeing me for a year. "Kitty Cat (which was what he always called me), you stay safe and, as your mum said, enjoy your adventure." As much as my dad was an expert in heart surgery, nothing could have prepared him for the heartache of missing his daughter. "Come on now, Helen, we must let her go!" my dad reluctantly told my mum. "I know, George, just one last hug." My mum held me so tight and then they watched me until I disappeared through the Departure Gate.

Now standing at the Arrivals Gate at San Francisco Airport, for the first time in my life, I was all alone and it felt scary to be so far away from my parents. The city streets of Dublin were a far cry from California. This would be my home for a year.

Looking around, I frantically tried to catch a glimpse of anyone who might be looking for someone else. The problem was that this was Arrivals and everyone was looking for someone; parents waiting for their children, children waiting for their parents, chauffeurs waiting for that all-important high-powered suit to come down the gangway and friends waiting for friends they hadn't seen in a while. I, on the other hand, had no idea who was meeting me.

Then, just as an expression of fear and panic came over my face, I noticed a short, stocky lady in a pink business suit, standing in the corner and holding a sign with my name on it. Relief! Someone knows I'm here! As I walked to the lady who was waving her hand in my direction, she shouted, "Yoohoo! Are you Catherine? Catherine Kennedy from Ireland?" As I nodded, she burst into laughter. "I just knew it was you - a lovely Irish girl. I just looked for the palest girl in Arrivals and I guessed it was you - a lovely Irish rose if ever I saw one. Well, hi there. My name is Melanie and I am the Recruitment Officer for Deacon College. I'll be looking after you during your stay so, anything you need, just ask me." I could tell right away that Melanie was one of those lovely Southern women, so American and super friendly as if she would just burst with excitement at the slightest thing.

"Thank you, Melanie. I'm Catherine but everyone at home calls me Cat for short. It's so wonderful to finally be here and it's so hot!" "Yes," Melanie chuckled. "You will have to get used to this California sunshine and know that sunscreen is indeed your best friend." Melanie attempted to help me to her car with my luggage but, with her tight-fitted pink suit and matching pink stilettos, hauling my heavy backpack was just not something she was able to manage. Bless her heart - she was just so nice to try.

My excitement skyrocketed as Melanie talked about Deacon College on the drive there. “Oh, you are just going to love college life here in the States. All exchange students have a wonderful time. What is your major in your college back in Ireland?” “Business Management,” I replied and began to tell her about my life back home in Ireland. Melanie was enchanted with my description of the sights and sounds of Dublin, the beautiful landscapes, the lush rolling hills and the breathtaking scenery of the Irish coast. “Oh my goodness, it sounds just divine. Darlin’, you are just going to blossom here, I can tell you that, coming from a beautiful country like Ireland. Most of our students have never been out of their State.”

For some reason, she just loved the fact that I was different from all the other students she was looking after this year. I was from another country. “Melanie, how many other exchange students will you have at Deacon College this year?” I asked. “You’re the only one this year but don’t worry dear, you will fit right in with all of us folk here. We are a very small school and a really tight student community."

As we arrived at the College gates, I saw a huge banner that read, "Welcome Deacon College Students - Class of 1998/99." I could feel the excitement building in my stomach but, at the same time, I felt a little nauseous. What if American college life wasn't for me? All I knew of America was from the movies and the TV shows I had watched. As Melanie parked her large station wagon, she looked over at me and smiled a sweet smile which helped calm my nerves. "Cat, welcome to Deacon College. This is us. I'll take you to the Student Affairs building. You can meet the Head of Student Affairs, Brad Anderson. He will be looking after your accommodation and showing you the Halls."

Walking towards the Student Affairs building, I couldn't help but be amazed by the beauty of the Deacon College campus. With lush greenery and crisp, finely cut, manicured lawns, meticulously trimmed palm trees lining the pathways and each building displaying that modern, Spanish-style brick and slate roof architecture, it looked like a hotel in Barcelona rather than a student campus.

Walking around the campus, I noticed numerous lecture theatres, a library, science labs and a spacious quad - all sitting beside a stunning lake. With a modern athletics recreation centre which included a large outdoor pool, football field, softball and baseball field, soccer field and athletics track, Deacon College had it all.

As Melanie dropped me at the Student Affairs building, she said her goodbyes and I headed to the main office. I gently knocked on the door and heard a strong, warm and friendly voice call out, "Come in!" As I walked into the office, I was greeted by a very attractive man in his mid-thirties. "Hello there, I've just arrived on campus and I was told that Student Affairs was going to sort me out with a room. I'm not sure if you can help. I'm not sure of anything really, bit jet-lagged, just got in from Ireland this morning. Shut the hell up, Cat!" I thought to myself. I knew I was gabbling which was what I tended to do when I was nervous.

"Ah, you must be our overseas student, Catherine, right? I'm Brad Anderson. You have come to the right place. I'll show you to your room. Let me first check to see where we have you located. Ah yes, you're in Daisy Hall. The dorms are named after flowers. Girls are in Daisy Hall while the guys are in Rose Hall."

Taking in all that Brad was saying, I could not help but take him in too. He was extremely good looking and, if the students were anything like him, I knew I was going to enjoy the scenery at Deacon College for sure.

"Okay," he said, "Let's see who your roommate will be. This damn computer takes forever and a day to load up. Okay, let's see. Ah, I have a name. Your roommate is Alexandra, yes, Alexandra Garner. It says here she is a local girl from just outside San Francisco. She is a transfer student and this is her first year at the College also. So, you have something in common already. You're both new to the College." I could tell Brad was trying to set my mind at ease. I was really nervous about meeting the person I would be sharing a room with for a whole year. What if she was a freak of nature, a sadistic devil worshipper or something? But, as Brad spoke, I knew he was assuring me that she was okay, no devil worshipping or offering Irish girls up as a sacrifice or anything like that.

"Alexandra already got her key about an hour ago and is getting settled in as we speak. So, let me give you the key to the dorm and you can get settled in." "Thank you kindly for your help, Brad. I appreciate it." Okay, I was babbling again! "You're welcome, Catherine," he replied. "Oh please, call me Cat. That's what my friends call me." I was really flirting with the Head of Student Affairs. What was I thinking? "Okay, Cat it is and I'm quite happy to listen to that charming accent of yours all day long," he said with an endearing smile that just totally melted away my worries. I was so hot - both with the heat of the Californian sunshine and with the way Brad looked at me. He was a babe. "Maybe he's doing a little flirting himself and would like to have a student affair," I thought. However, that hope was shattered when I looked down and saw a gold wedding band on his finger. Figures!

The campus was a hive of activity as I walked towards Daisy Hall. Students were arriving with what looked like half of their house with them. Parents were helping their kids out of their large SUVs with all their luggage. Others were leaving and saying their goodbyes to their beloved son or daughter and friends were meeting up again after their summer break. I felt so new – and so being watched. As Deacon College was such a small school, everyone seemed to know everyone else but that was fine with me. I was an unread book full of wonder and mystery. I could be anyone I wanted to be in America. This was my adventure!

I walked up the first flight of stairs to my room and, on the way, passed several guys carrying boxes into the dorm. I realised they were going my way and were walking into my room! Holy shit, have I got the wrong dorm! Then I saw a girl standing by the window. "Must be Alexandra," I guessed. Thank the Lord, she looked normal. With blonde shoulder-length hair and gleaming white, perfect post-braces teeth, she looked like a true all-American girl. "That's the last of the boxes now, Alex. Is there anything else we can help you with?" "I think I'm good. Thanks for your help, guys. Sorry, I didn't quite get your names," she replied politely. "I'm Rob and this is Josh and Brett. Anything to help our new students." These guys clearly had a bit of a thing for her. As they pulled their tongues off the floor and turned to leave, I met them at the door. "Why hi there!" the first one said to me in an *'I haven't seen you before, fresh meat, new girl'* kind of manner. But I was so unbelievably jet-lagged and tired from a full day of travelling, all I wanted to do was flake out on my new bed. I really wasn't ready for any *"Hey, how you doin'?"* chat-up lines. So, I smiled and made my excuses.

As I walked into the dorm room, Alexandra greeted me with a pretty, shy smile and said hello. “Hello, you are Alexandra I’m thinking. I’m Cat, your roommate for the year. Fuckin’ hell! I was so nervous about meeting you, I have to tell ya. I’m from Ireland and I’ve been on a 9-hour flight to get here so I’m a bit jet-lagged, to say the least.” She looked at me with an expression that said “What the fuck did you just say to me? I didn’t understand a word with that accent of yours.” I knew I had started babbling again. “Cat, shut the fuck up and let her have a chance to respond!”

“Hi Cat. Yes, I’m Alexandra but everyone calls me Alex. I hate Alexandra. It’s such an old lady’s name. Cat - what is that short for Catherine or something?” she asked. “Yes, you got it in one. I know what you mean. I hate being called Catherine. Only my mum calls me by that name now,” I laughed. “I hear ya on that one,” Alex smiled in agreement. “So, you’re from Ireland. That’s really cool. I’ve never met anyone from Ireland before. Shoot, in the piss-ass town I live in, I’d be lucky to meet anyone. I’m from a little place just outside San Francisco, about two hours from here. Thank goodness. It’s my first time away from home so I’m feeling a little weird.”

“As I looked at Alex, I noticed her lip tremble a little and it was clear she was missing home already. I, on the other hand, was trying not to think about home or I would be on the first plane back. Just then, a middle-aged couple came into the room. “Hi sweetie. Well, it’s time for us to go. All the paperwork is sorted out and you’re officially registered,” the lady said as she came over and hugged Alex. I guessed it was her mother. Then, looking over to me, the lady said, “Why, hello there!” with a motherly smile. “We are Alexandra’s parents. I’m Jean and this is her father, Pete.” “Hello, it’s very nice to meet you,” I said in a timid Irish voice. Pete looked at me the same way Alex had and he laughed. “You sure aren’t from around here with an accent like that and skin as white as snow. Where are you from little lady?” he chuckled. “Hi, I’m Cat from Dublin, Ireland. I’ll be Alex’s roommate for the year. Just came off my flight this morning so everything is a little new. I hope you can understand my accent. I’ve learned in a short space of time to talk much slower. I know I can go off on one really quickly.” I was doing it again! “Yes, I can see that,” Pete smiled.

Alex’s mom gave her a big hug and said, “We’d better be hitting the road, honey. I don’t want to leave you at all. I’m so very proud of you going to college.

Now Cat, I want you to take real good care of this little lady." I smiled at Jean and, as the tears began to flow, mother and daughter held on to one another for what felt like an eternity. I, myself, felt quite emotional; it was less than a day ago that I had said goodbye to my family. It's hard to let go of a family that loves you and cares for you but, at the same time, the prospect of starting a new adventure at college in California was so exciting and exhilarating.

As Alex said her goodbyes to her parents, I could tell she was going to miss them a lot and they were going to miss her. Now that we were alone, I felt completely at ease with Alex. She wasn't the type of American girl I had imagined, all so into their looks and shit and, although she was very pretty, she was very natural. She seemed to have the same personality as me and she loved to talk, which was a favourite pastime for me.

"Alex, I'm really glad to have met you at last. Brad Anderson told me that you have just moved here this semester. Have you met Brad Anderson?" Alex and I gave each other the same look and both shouted "Babe!!" "Totally, I thought I was just gonna melt when he was talking to me." "I know," Alex laughed. "Hell, I think I'm in love!!"

We both laughed at the fact that we were fantasising about a member of the faculty. "Well, at least we both have good taste." "Definitely," Alex replied.

We unpacked and settled into our new surroundings. I, with my one suitcase and backpack, took only moments to unpack. It took Alex a little longer. With her fridge, TV, CD player and microwave to install, along with her entire wardrobe from home to arrange, she was going to be busy so I offered to help.

The dorm room was equipped with two beds, two study desks and chairs, two closets and two storage drawers. It was functional and looked like a blank canvas with whitewashed concrete walls which made the room feel cold. Luckily, Alex had brought a few posters to hang on the walls which brought a bit of colour to the room.

"Cat, I'm sorry I brought so much stuff but you can use whatever you like. You don't need to ask." "That's great," I said. "Unfortunately, the airline wouldn't let me bring a damn thing over on the flight as my luggage was way overweight as it was. Going to another country for a year, I thought they would at least let me take an extra bag or two but that's airlines for ya." "I really wouldn't know," replied Alex. "I have never flown before in my life. I'm shit scared of flying."

I was amazed. "Are you serious?" I loved the feeling of flying and travelling to places I had only dreamed of. "I'm serious as a heart attack, Cat. There is no way I could ever get on a plane - not even if you paid me a million dollars!" "Shit Alex," I said. "Just throw a load of alcohol down your neck, knock yourself out and, before you know it, you've landed! It's as easy as that!" Somehow, I don't think Alex was convinced.

"This wouldn't be difficult for me. Shit, I've only drunk alcohol once. I'm still 19," Alex said with a pissed off, 'sucks to be me' tone. Then I realised, "Holy shit, you have to be 21 over here right? I miss Ireland already. I've been going down to my local since I was 18 and a bit before that too. What the fuck! I'm not 21 for another two months!" "Welcome to my world," laughed Alex. "Isn't it lucky that we have the lovely Duty-Free that I brought over on the plane," I laughed as I produced a few bottles of vodka and rum. Alex smiled, "You are going to have to ration yourself." "Don't I know it!" I laughed. "Fuck me! I'm going to have to get used to this American way of life."

"Cat, tell me more about your life in Ireland. What's it like living in Dublin?" I began to tell Alex all about my life back home, with its rich heritage, traditional pubs and lively music scene, there was plenty to do and see in Dublin.

"I live on the outskirts of Dublin so we have to get the train into the city. My dad would always take me to watch his favourite football team and then go for a pint afterward. I'm an only child and I think my dad was hoping for a son so that's why I was thrown into sports as a child. He was the classic "soccer dad" as you call it and he would seriously watch paint dry if it was a sport. He just loves all sports! I take after him in that. My mum loves to go walking up the mountains and, as Ireland has a shit load of mountains on our doorstep, she takes me walking all the time. I love being out in the countryside and taking in the views of the Irish landscape."

Alex listened intently, her eyes lighting up with excitement. She was fascinated to hear all about Ireland. Living in such a small town in California, Alex could only dream of being in another country like Ireland. The hours flew by as we sat talking about our lives back home. We were both in the same boat; away from home for the first time and looking forward to the college experience but at the same time feeling a little homesick. Just then the phone rang. It was Alex's parents calling to see how she was doing. I think they missed her just as much as she did them. Her tanned face lit up when she heard her parents' voices and she told them how we had been talking since they left. I excused myself and gave her some privacy. Venturing out to view the campus, I felt that I could become good friends with Alex. She was just like me. She loved to talk and was easy to get along with. Thank goodness she wasn't at all the nightmare roommate I was expecting.

When I got back to the dorm, I could tell Alex had been crying. I didn't know what to say. I guessed she was a little homesick. "Are you okay there, Alex?" I asked. "Yeah, Cat. It's just hard hearing from my parents. I'm going to miss them so much, especially my mom. I'm actually an only child too and she is my best friend. We do everything together and I can tell her anything. I'm really going to miss that."

Trying to lighten the mood, I jokingly reminded her, "Hey Alex, it's okay. You will see them soon and I'm sure they will be over to visit. Shit, at least your parents are only 200 miles away by car. Hell, mine are 5000 miles away by plane!!" With that, she laughed, "My dad thought you were a devil worshipper with your skin being so white and all." "Oh yeah, That's right, did I not tell you? But I only go out and bite the heads off chickens when there's a full moon!" We laughed. "I'm so white over here, I'm gonna stick out like a bloody bull's backside!!" Alex chuckled, "Cat, you are hilarious with your Irish talk!" At least I got her laughing again but I knew her mind was on her parents and home. For me, at least for the year, this would be my home.

Chapter 2

Girls Just Wanna Have Fun

Early the next morning, I was awoken by an almighty bang on the dorm room door and the most annoying voice coming from the other side. "Wakey Wakey! Rise and shine! Come out, come out whoever you are!"

As I slowly got out of bed, I turned to see that Alex had also been woken up by the goings-on outside our dorm door. "Cat, what the fuck was that?" Alex asked as she rubbed her eyes. I moved to see what was outside the door and, as I opened it, an energetic girl came bounding into our room.

"Well hi there! What a great day it is today! It's orientation day!" This small, somewhat annoying person was looking at us as though we should have been up already and enjoying orientation day. Alex and I gave each other a look like we gave a flying fuck about orientation day. "It's Saturday – go away." Of course, neither of us said this to her.

"I'm Carla by the way. I'm your dorm team leader. Any issues you have with the dorm or anything, just come and see me and I'll sort everything out for you. Now, I have everyone assembled in the downstairs leisure room for my presentation and you two lazy heads are late. Did you not get my note about orientation yesterday? Anyway, get dressed and be down in five minutes," Carla demanded in a friendly but very bossy manner.

Carla was small in stature but evidently had a very large opinion of herself. With long blonde hair and olive-bronzed skin, she was very pretty and immaculately dressed in a pencil skirt and jacket. She looked like she was dressed for a job interview rather than a college orientation day meeting.

The leisure room was a large lounge on the ground floor furnished with lots of sofas, a pool table and a TV in the corner. As Alex and I entered the room, we were met by all the other girls waiting for Carla's presentation to start. We felt like two naughty school kids as we slipped into the back seats. We evidently hadn't made a good impression on our first outing together if the glaring looks from girls in the front row were anything to go by. They were looking at their watches and puffing out their cheeks as if they had been waiting forever for us to arrive. I turned to Alex and whispered, "Is it just me or are we getting a few dirty looks? Fuck, are we the only ones that didn't get her stupid orientation day letter?" As Alex laughed, Carla gave us a stern look, "Okay, now that we are *all* here, I will begin by welcoming you all to this 1998/99 college year."

Carla began to give us a blow-by-blow account of her previous two years at Deacon College and how, this year, she had recently been made dorm team leader to which a little applause came from some of the girls in the front row. Alex and I looked at each other and rolled our eyes. Alex leaned over and whispered, "Who the hell are they - the Carla Fan Club?" I tried not to burst out laughing and replied, "It might be a while before we get our subscription to join." We started sniggering but stopped when Carla gave us another razor-sharp look. She was clearly not impressed with our behaviour.

We reluctantly listened to Carla's life story, and how we were going to have a wonderful time with her as our dorm leader, with the Halloween party, the Christmas Party and the DVD nights she had planned for us and how much fun we were going to have together. I could feel the boredom setting in already just thinking about it.

"Okay everyone, that's about it for this morning. It's lunchtime and I have reserved a table in the cafeteria for all of us girls to sit together," she said so proudly. "Just a little getting-to-know-everyone lunch." So, Carla marched us all to the cafeteria.

Neither Alex nor I had visited there yet and there was one thing in my thoughts. College food! What should we expect - a slap-up lunch or a pile of trash that had been deep-fried to its last end?

We all entered the cafeteria together, as part of Carla's clan, as she strode in front making sure we were all singing from her hymn sheet. The cafeteria was a buzz of activity, just as I had imagined a college cafeteria to be. The flavourful aroma of hot food wafted in the air. There was a variety of food stations such as a salad bar, a hot food area that had pizza, pasta, burgers and chips, rice and noodle dishes, a sandwich bar and a dessert bar with every kind of dessert imaginable. It looked more like an "all you can eat" buffet and was nothing like the old dining halls back home. At my university, we had the choice of chicken or roast beef with potatoes – that was it! This cafeteria had a bright, modern look to it. There were colourful murals on the walls and plenty of round tables to sit and eat with friends. The sound of chatting, laughter and hard plastic trays slamming down on tables was all around. There were groups of students hanging out together, catching up after their summer break and checking out the latest gossip; who was dating who and who wanted to be dating who. This was the height of college conversation. It didn't change no matter what continent you lived on.

As we were hustled along the line, I could feel people staring at me like I was some sort of alien from the forbidden planet with five heads or something. Alex must have felt the same as she turned to me and said, "Ever get the feeling we're being watched? It's the fresh meat, new students effect. We are the unknowns. I bet that's why they are checking us out. That or they are thinking we are sad bitches putting up with Carla for the day!" As we laughed, we heard voices calling for Alex. It was her moving-in guys, Josh, Rob and Brett. They seemed to be a bit of a trio; one was never seen without the others.

"Alex, it's your fan club there," I whispered. "Alex, why don't you guys come and sit with us?" Alex looked at me and asked, "What do ya think?" "Sure as hell better than sitting with Carla and listening to how wonderful she is." So we both slid our trays onto the guys' table and sat down. "Thank you," Alex smiled, "We were supposed to sit over there with our dorm team leader but she is a bit of a pain in the ass." "Who is your dorm team leader?" Josh asked. "It's Carla Clarke, that perfect-looking girl over there," I moaned. "Perfectly annoying, you mean," Josh smirked. "Bad luck girls. She is one pain in the ass alright!" "Yeah, we've sort of gotten on the wrong side of her already and we thought, what the hell, we've already pissed her off once today so twice won't matter!"

As Alex started to fill the guys in on our bad timekeeping for the dorm meeting, I looked over sheepishly to Carla's table. She was frantically looking around the cafeteria, no doubt looking for Alex and me. Sitting next to her were the other girls on our floor as they had just returned from raiding the salad bar. I noticed that they all looked exactly the same; all very pretty, shimmering blonde hair with immaculately bronzed tanned skin. It looked like Carla had cloned each one of them but had given them the height that she never had. There was Tiffany, quite a tall girl with sun-bleached blonde hair; Pattie, another tall, thin, attractive girl who looked picture perfect; and Stacey, yet another Carla clone who had a guy sitting with her. He was incredibly handsome and extremely fit, wearing a tight tank top that showed off his large worked-out biceps and perfectly toned pecs. From the long lingering kiss he gave her as he left the group, I concluded that he was Stacey's boyfriend.

At our table, Alex had been chatting with the guys and they seemed to be totally captivated by her conversation. She surely had a fan club alright. Alex was very different, in terms of personality, to the

Californian girl I thought she was going to be. However, she was every bit the California girl in looks, with long blonde hair, perfectly tanned bronzed skin, blue eyes and a perfect figure. I, on the other hand, was definitely not a California beach babe – more a bony beanpole that was sticking out like a sore thumb, skinny, with a pale white complexion and mousey brown hair. No wonder the guys were so attracted to Alex.

"Hey girls, what have you got planned for later tonight? A bunch of us are heading over to the Lake House for a bit of a get-together to start off the college year. Would you like to come along?" Both Alex and I asked in tandem, "What's the Lake House?" "Oh sorry," Josh apologised. "I forgot you guys are new to these parts. It's our college house. Each year, the house is passed down to new students. Five guys live there. It's such a cool place and the parties are famous or should I say infamous," Josh explained. "You have to come along." Alex and I looked at each other. "Well Alex, if you're up for it, I am." "Beats Carla's movie night!" Alex replied and, with that, we had our first college social engagement already planned.

Later that evening, we were frantically trying to decide what to wear to our first college party. After emptying the entire contents of her wardrobe that she had only yesterday so carefully put in place, Alex screamed, "Fuck me, I have absolutely no clothes!" "Are you serious, Alex? You have an entire wardrobe there and here am I with one suitcase of clothes for the entire year!" "I know, Cat. I'm just so nervous about tonight. I hope there are some cute guys here." "Yes, and hopefully some of them might understand my accent!" I smiled. "Now Alex, show me what you have to wear. We will find you something in this heap of clothes on your bed!"

After about two hours of trying on outfits, Alex asked me to curl her hair with the heated rollers she had brought from home. "Sweet Jesus, Alex. You really did bring the entire contents of your house with you." "No shit right? Could you do my hair, Cat?" I had never used heated rollers before but I thought I'd give it a try. Taking the first heated roller in my hand, I quickly realised why I had never used them. They were fuckin' hot as hell! I let out the loudest scream and ran to the sink to cool my fingers down. "Shit Cat, are you okay? I tried to warn ya that they can get kinda hot!" "No way, really?" I laughed back sarcastically.

After curling Alex's hair, and a few burnt fingers later, we were good to go. We caught a ride with the guys, “the fan club” as we nicknamed them, and arrived at the Lake House at just the right time as the party was in full swing. The excitement was showing on our faces. I looked at Alex and whispered, “What a bit of eye candy we have here, Alex.” “Yeah, I know Cat. I think we are gonna have some fun,” Alex replied with a smile.

The house was located on the other side of the lake from the college and was very much what I thought a fraternity house would look like. It had a pool table in the corner and a games console hooked up to the TV, not to mention the sports memorabilia hanging from the walls and beer bottles lining the hallway. It had man cave written all over it. Mingling through the crowd, we were given a plastic cup and directed to the keg. Just what I needed - a nice cold beer. Since it wasn’t long until my 21st birthday, college party beer would do well. I noticed that Alex was already in full socialising mode and was chatting with a very attractive guy. I decided to leave her to it and check out what was going on outside the Lake House. The music was banging out a hip-hop R’n’B sound that was new territory for my musical ears. Then I heard a warm, deep voice behind me, “Would you like to dance?” Turning around, I saw a cute, friendly-looking guy offering me his hand to lead me out onto the dance floor. “I’m not very good at dancing to this type of music," I said. "I guess coming from Ireland, it's not your scene. I'm Mike by the way. It's Cat, right?" "How did you know my name?" I asked, "And how did you know I was from Ireland?" "I have my spies. So, what about it – fancy a dance? I can teach you some moves." Mike was extremely sweet but not in a drop-dead gorgeous way. He was a little shorter than most of the guys I was attracted to but there was something about him that I was drawn to. So, I accepted his kind offer. We danced for a while and chatted about life in California. I soon discovered that Mike's parents were Italian which I had suspected given his dark hair and dark eyes.

About an hour into the party, I felt a tap on my shoulder. It was Alex. "Hey Alex, how's it going?" I asked excitedly. Then, when I looked at her a little closer, I realised that she was surely drunk off her ass. "Alex, are you okay?" Looking at her wandering eyes and her unstable posture, I could tell she was clearly not as she started to slur her words, "Cat, I think I'm a bit drunkededed. I'm sorry to bother you, please don't hatedededed me. Oh, I think I'm really drunkededed!" "Yes Alex, I think you're drunkededed." I laughed at Alex's drunken language which she seemed to have created. "How did this happen? I just left you not that long ago!" She was quite giddy in a drunken, happy way. “Come on, my little one-pint wonder, let’s go sit down,” I said. ”Cat, I think I need the bathroom!” I could see a throw-up was on the horizon so I helped her inside and, after a few stumbles and falls bringing me down with her, I eventually got an apologetic Alex to the bathroom.

Sitting her down and running a glass of water, I tried to make sure that my little drunken friend was alright. I felt so guilty. I shouldn’t have left her beside a keg of beer on her first college party experience. “Alex, are you alright? I should have stayed with you.” “That’s okay. I loovvee this party. I loovvee this bathroom. I loovvee this beer!” “Yeah Alex, I think you loovvee it a little too much.” Turning around to get her another drink of water, I quickly returned to see her slipping off of the toilet seat. This was going to be hard work. I felt really guilty. This was probably Alex’s first real party with alcohol involved and she hadn’t handled it very well.

Suddenly there was a knock at the door. A girl called out, “I think I left my purse in there. Can you please hand it out?” I noticed a purse sitting by the sink. As I picked it up, I looked at Alex and she put her fingers to her lips and in a drunken whisper said, “Cat, let’s fill the purse up for her.” So, we emptied the contents of the bathroom cabinet into her bag –

soap, razor, toothbrush, shaving cream – the lot. "Let the girl get a lovely surprise when she opens up this sucker," Alex whispered. "We are bad, Cat." "Yeah, but it's fun!" I handed the purse to the girl and quickly closed the bathroom door, as we laughed with each other like two naughty schoolchildren and stayed hidden in the bathroom until the coast was clear.

I talked to Alex to try to sober her up. "So Alex, tell me, who was that attractive guy you were talking to when we arrived? Quite cute, I may add." "Yes, very cute!" Alex replied excitedly. "His name is Jonny. He is on the college tennis team and I have a date with him next week. I asked him if he would teach me some tennis moves!"

Just like that, Alex had a date. I was impressed. I always wondered how some girls just seemed to get a date with absolutely no effort. I, on the other hand, was too much of a chicken shit to ask a guy anything. I was always the guy's best buddy or the girl guys would ask to help them go out with my friends. I was really fascinated by how at ease Alex was with guys. Even at lunch earlier in the day, she had the fan club eating out of her hand and hanging off of her every word. I so wished I could be like that.

Alex turned to me as if she had a revelation, "So Cat, what about you? I saw you getting up close and personal with that guy on the dance floor! Tell me the story, girl." "Nothing really to tell," I said coyly. "His name is Mike and we just had a dance." I tried not to make a big deal of it and let Alex talk about Jonny. She seemed really taken with him even though they had only just met. Sometimes, that's the way it goes.

When Alex had finally sobered up, we decided to rejoin the party and were greeted by the fan club. "Hey guys, are you enjoying yourselves?" Josh asked as he danced around us. "Come on, let's dance!" He took Alex's hand and pulled her onto the dance floor. Alex grabbed hold of my hand and took me with her as she whispered, "Stay with me – this time I may need some help." I could tell Josh was very attracted to Alex. She was looking around frantically and then whispered to me, "Cat, I hope Jonny doesn't see me dancing with Josh. I just met him and I don't want to give him the wrong impression." I had a look around and told her that he may have left already. I was also looking for Mike but, to my disappointment, he was nowhere to be seen.

Josh's attraction to Alex was very evident and, as he caught her eye, he leaned in for the all-important kiss. Unfortunately for Josh, Alex was not feeling the attraction at all. "Sorry Josh, I really don't think this is a good idea. You're a really nice guy but I don't want to be in a relationship right now. I'm just settling into college here. I'm sorry." Alex was trying to let him down gently as she had already agreed to a date with Jonny but that was not what Josh had wanted to hear. He had built his hopes up on getting the kiss returned in a passionate embrace but it didn't turn out as he had hoped. As the party came to an end, we caught a ride back to college with the guys. The fan club was reduced to two, as Josh was not really in a sociable mood after getting the unexpected knockback from Alex.

We were glad to get back to the dorm and away from the disappointed Josh. Unfortunately for us, we were still rather happy from the beer. We tried so hard to be as quiet as possible but, as much as we tried, there was no missing the trash can which was placed by the door. Falling over the trash and landing on my ass seemed to be the funniest thing in the world to Alex. She burst into hysterical laughter which led her to slip and go belly up on the floor with me.

We were both rolling about with laughter but quickly stopped as we were confronted by a stern-looking Carla. She was standing by our heads as we looked up from the floor. I could see the disapproving look on her face. With her sleek, silk bathrobe and her sleeping eye cover lifted to her head, we had clearly disturbed her beauty sleep. “Guys, it’s 4:30 in the morning. This is not the way I want my floor to run with people laughing and screaming at this time of night.” “Sorry Carla,” we both replied trying not to laugh. I bit my lip holding back a smile. We dragged ourselves up from the floor while attempting to fix the trash can that didn’t seem to want to stand up and that led to Alex and me laughing and Carla giving us both another hush.

As we got into our dorm room and crashed, Alex looked over and whispered, “Cat, are you awake?” “Yeah, what’s up?” “Thanks for looking after me tonight. I’m not very good with beer.” “That’s okay, you did good for your first party but you were quite drunkededed,” I said, reminding Alex of her new drunk language. “Apart from having to turn Josh down. I think I broke his heart.” “Oh Alex, I think he will get over it. You probably just dented his pride.” Alex laughed, “Yeah, you’re right. Night Cat.” “Nite Alex.” After talking for most of the night, we both crashed out.

Chapter 3

Little Miss Sunshine

The following Monday was the first day of college. I had been at Deacon College for three days and, having recovered from the Lake House party, I was ready to tackle student life. College well and truly had started with the hustle and bustle of students rushing to and from class and others hanging out enjoying the Californian sunshine.

I had chosen my subjects in business before leaving Ireland so I knew what to expect and, within the first few days of class, any fears I may have had were laid to rest when I realised that I had completed all the work in my college in Ireland the previous year – so I was laughing.

The first week of college went even better for Alex. She had settled into her classes, studying a History major, and even had a tennis lesson with Jonny. Alex and I were inseparable from day one. It was so good to have a roommate like her. We got on so well and, with both of us being away from home for the first time, we relied on each other for support. I knew we were going to be good friends.

As we sat in the cafeteria, having just finished another bagel sandwich, which had become our favourite choice of food as the selection was not tickling the taste buds, Jonny came by. “So Alex, how’s that forehand going?” “Great, I think I need a bit more practice though.” As Alex and Jonny flirted, I made my excuses to leave for dessert. I headed straight for the ice cream which had become my daily ritual. The fact that I was skinny as a rake had its advantages.

As I was taking my final scoop of ice cream at the dessert bar, I looked up to see Josh standing in front of me. I felt bad about his rejection by Alex. I could tell that he really liked her so I decided to make some polite conversation. “Hi Josh, how are things going? How are your classes?” “Fine,” he snapped back with an ice-cold expression that would have frozen the entire Antarctic. “What’s the matter Josh, aren’t you talking to me?” “You’re friends with Alex, right?” “Yeah, of course, she’s my roommate,” I replied, confused as to why that had any bearing on Josh not talking to me. “She wants nothing to do with me so I want nothing to do with her. She told me she didn’t want to be in a relationship but I see her all over Jonny over there.” “Josh, she just didn’t want to hurt your feelings, that’s all. So, what, because I’m Alex’s friend you don’t want to talk to me either?” I was becoming quite annoyed with his childish behaviour. “You know what they say, Cat. Birds of a feather flock together. If you’re her friend then you're no friend of mine." I couldn't believe what I was hearing. What a complete arse! I was going to dump the entire tub of ice cream over his head but thought better of it. What a waste that would be. I turned to him and replied, "Are you fucking serious, that's just bad craic." "Cat, what do you mean bad crack? I didn't crack anything? I just don't understand your English language," Josh snapped back in a condescending tone. "It's the Irish language, ya dumb fucker! It means that's just not right. Josh, you may wind yer neck in because, if you act like that, you are going to be one lonely guy. Grow up, Josh!" And, with that, I turned and walked away.

Still fuming at what Josh had said, I returned to Alex by which time Jonny had left. As I repeated the story to Alex, she became really angry. "What an asshole!!" "Cat, I'm sorry if he is not talking to you because I rejected him." "Don't worry, Alex," I replied. "I'm sure I'm not missing out on anything if that's the way he is." "Cat, his behaviour is so high school. I thought that, going to college, I would get away from jerks like that who are only interested in a girl for what they can get. So, when he can't get any, I'm the bitch!" "Don't worry Alex, we have guys like him back home too. I guess guys can be complete bastards globally." I smiled at Alex to reassure her that I was still her friend even though Josh didn't want anything to do with her or with me for that matter.

"I think I totally confused him with my Irish slang though. I told him it was bad craic and he hadn't a baldy notion what I was saying." "Jesus Cat, I haven't a notion what you are saying. When you talk about crack in America, it's something ya put up your nose don't you know." Alex looked at me with a blank expression on her face.

"So when we say it's bad craic in Ireland, it means it's not good, like it's not on. When we say, 'What's the craic?' it means 'How's it going?' If we say, 'The craic was 90,' that means we were having a great time. It's spelt CRAIC."

"Holy shit Cat, that's a lot of craic!! I love it. You Irish sure do have a lot of fun. What's Irish for 'Josh, you're a fucking ass hole?' Alex laughed. "I'd say that's the same in any language Alex but, if I was back home, I would definitely call Josh a complete and utter wanker." "A what?" Alex asked getting that confused look on her face again. As I gestured the universal hand sign, Alex quickly realised exactly what I meant and we doubled over with laughter and shouted out in unison, "Jerk-off!!" Then I taught Alex more Irish slang while we finished our lunch.

As we walked back to the dorm, which we had begun to loathe due to our wonderful dorm leader, Carla, catching us out at every chance she got, I tried to take Alex's mind off the jerk, Josh. "So, my friend, how are things going with Jonny? Are you playing anything more than tennis?" "Cat, he is really nice but… I don't know. It's hard for me. I've had a couple of bad experiences and I just don't know if Jonny is what I'm looking for. He is really nice but do you ever get that voice in the back of your head that says he's the one or he's not the one?" "Yes, Alex it's called love. Look don't fret. You don't have to fall in love on the first date. Give the guy a chance and see what happens." "You're right, Cat. I'll do that. You always know what to say to make me feel better about things. Thanks for that. Maybe it's because you're not from here. All my American girlfriends just bitch about all the shit of the day but you listen." "Thanks Alex. I guess being Irish has its advantages."

The next few weeks went by pretty quickly. My college schedule was working well. Morning class, afternoon study and plenty of time for enjoying student life and the beautiful Californian sunshine in the evening. I had totally fallen in love with the weather. No more rainy days in Dublin for me – for a while at least.

With a bit of free time on my hands, I decided to look for a job, as did Alex. Looking through the student job vacancies on the notice board, I found one that was right up my street. Pool lifeguard. I had some experience lifeguarding back home and I knew I'd be perfect for it. "Girl, you'd better put on some sunscreen if you're going to be working at the pool every day. That pale Irish skin will fry." "I know. I'll be fine. I should be a walking commercial for sunblock." "Anything takes your fancy there, Alex?" I asked. "Here is one for the Coffee House. Sounds easy enough. Make a cappuccino or two, I can do that." "Nice one and I can come over and drink them." Suddenly, a voice came from behind us, "Oh, I really think you should go for that job too." We turned around to see a tall, very handsome, familiar face smiling down at us. I knew where I had seen him before. It was Stacey's boyfriend who I had seen sitting with her and Carla's clones at lunch.

"Hi, I'm Tom and you're Alex, right?" Tom looked directly at Alex and smiled alluringly at her. Alex just seemed to have that way about her. Guys just couldn't get enough of her. Alex gave him a big, warm Californian smile and replied, "Hi Tom, do I know you from somewhere?" as if to say, 'How the hell do you know my name there buddy?' "You're in a few of my classes. I've seen you around. Oh, and my girlfriend, Stacey, lives in your dorm. She told me your name. I didn't want to introduce myself without knowing who you were first." Alex looked relieved, "Ah, that's where I recognise you from, History and Algebra right?" "So, you think I should take the job at the Coffee House? I've never worked in a place like that before but I figure how hard could pouring coffee be, right?" "You would be surprised," Tom replied knowledgeably. "I work there, so don't worry if you get confused between the mochas and lattés. I'll share my expertise in the art of making coffee." "Man, I didn't know I needed such training," Alex laughed sarcastically. "You can learn from the master." Tom bowed his head as he joked about being the king of coffee brewing. "Well, with such a fine teacher, how can I refuse the opportunity to learn such a skill?"

As Alex and Tom were exchanging playful banter, I stood eyeing the job board but couldn't help being amazed at how easy it was for Alex to get on with the opposite sex. I was always a bumbling idiot when it came to flirting with guys. "Oh, this is Cat, my roommate. She's from Ireland." Alex always seemed to want to tell people that I wasn't American. She would always introduce me as Cat from Dublin or her roommate Cat who is Irish. I guess it made her feel as if she had something different to tell people.

Tom looked over and gave a charming hello. “So Cat, how are you enjoying college life in California?” “I really love it. Just getting used to all this sunshine though,” I replied as I looked at my pale skin against Tom and Alex’s immaculately bronzed arms. “So Alex, has Tom convinced you to work at the Coffee House then?” I asked playfully. “Yeah, he has,” she smiled. “I just hope I don’t poison the customers!”

So, we both had part-time jobs. My job required sitting by the pool in the heat of the Californian sunshine while Alex was working up a storm in the heat of coffee making. The Coffee House had a chilled vibe. With large sofas, oversized chairs and lava lamps in the corners, it was a really cool place to relax with friends away from the study halls and libraries.

Tom did as he promised and helped Alex, training her in the art of coffee making. He was on a number of her shifts and, when they were not busy, they helped each other with the dreaded algebra class they both had to take. Our nights soon became busy hanging out at the Coffee House with Tom, his buddies and Stacey, of course, who appeared to be in a serious relationship with Tom. Stacey was indeed living on our floor in the dorms. We had seen her a few times but, unfortunately, she was always with Carla who thought we were the devil incarnate. However, Stacey was always pleasant to us when she was on her own or with Tom.

Alex and I became good friends with Tom. He was tall and very good looking but not one of those guys who knew it and thought their shit didn't stink. With floppy dark hair and an athletically toned body, I could tell that Tom liked to take care of himself. After three years of dating Stacey, their relationship had the classic feel of a Prom King meeting a Prom Queen and everyone expecting that they would marry. Tom came from the beaches of Malibu and enjoyed surfing and all things outdoors. He was really funny and great to be around. He would always call to see us if he was visiting Stacey.

It was good to have a really nice guy friend who already had a girlfriend and wouldn't get all heavy like Josh had done. Alex was dating Jonny and seemed to be getting on very well with her tennis lessons.

We had settled into life at Deacon College and had become great friends in the process. Maybe it was being away from home for the first time but Alex and I were each other's family, we were friends, sisters and sometimes even each other's mother.

My job at the pool was working out great and it was a godsend to be able to sit under a large umbrella, protecting my pure white skin from the blazing Californian sun. The crystal-clear blue water of the pool shimmered and looked so inviting and, as the sun's rays became stronger, I wanted to dive into the deep water to cool down. Although it boasted a 50-metre Olympic-sized swimming pool for the swim team to train in, the pool area was mainly taken up by sun worshippers. There were red terracotta brick tiles on the ground surrounding the pool which were scorching hot for many who had run in their bare feet from their lounger to the pool. It was really easy money as most of the students would go to the pool solely to lay on the sun loungers and top up their tan and, if anyone was going to swim, it was usually to just cool off and then get back on to their loungers. What better way to spend the afternoon after a morning of classes?

One afternoon as I was getting set up for my afternoon shift, a familiar "hello" came from behind me. I turned around and clumsily dropped the large umbrella I was holding. Unfortunately, and to my horror, I had dropped it right onto Mike's foot! "Oh My God, I'm so sorry! Are you okay?" "Yes, I think so," Mike replied as he hopped around on one foot trying to ease the pain.

"I swear, I'm such an arse. I hope it's not broken." "I think I'll be okay. Might not be dancing for a while though," Mike said, smiling through the pain. "I was hoping to see you again after the Lake House party but I didn't think it would hurt so much." "I'm so sorry, Mike. Please don't think I did it just to get out of dancing with you," I joked back, trying to apologise for nearly taking off his big toe.

Mike recovered from the fallen umbrella but, unfortunately, I had done too much damage to my lifeline – the umbrella was broken beyond repair. "I'm going to fry without my umbrella. My saviour from the sun has fallen. Thank goodness I always have sunscreen with me," I moaned. "I understand. Shoot, I've lived in California all my life and I still can't get used to the heat. Don't worry, it's quite overcast today anyway. Can I help you with that sunscreen?" I looked at Mike as if suggesting he was being a bit forward which I think he could tell from my expression. "I didn't mean to be too much of an ass. I just know how much you need that sunscreen on your back if you're going to be working at the pool today," I smiled and relented as I needed his help. For some reason, I always missed half my back or half an arm and ended up completely burned on one side.

Mike stayed at the pool and we chatted for a while. "So Mike, tell me more about you. You know all about me and, from what I remember at the party, you had my name and where I came from already. I do know that you are a great dancer." Was I really flirting with Mike? I was never one to flirt but I felt like I could be a totally different person here in California – a new flirty me! "There's nothing much to say. I'm pretty much your typical guy, ya know? I love to travel, watch movies and, of course, go dancing." "So, what movies do you like? Maybe we could go to the cinema sometime?" Oh shit, was I actually asking him out on a date? "I love anything with Tom Cruise in it. He's my favourite actor," Mike replied. "No way, me too! I love Tom Cruise!" I screamed excitedly. "I have all his DVDs in my dorm room. You must come over and have a movie night with me." As Mike was talking, I could tell he wasn't your typical guy. He was very sweet and sensitive and I really enjoyed his company. He was really easy to get along with and I found myself letting go and talking, even flirting with him. Maybe hanging out with Alex gave me the confidence to take a leaf out of her book and just be cool. After Mike left to go to class, the shift dragged on, especially since my replacement hadn't shown up so I ended up working a double shift – four hours instead of two! Just what I needed without my umbrella to protect me.

When I got back to the dorm, I was tired, sweaty and feeling uncomfortably hot. As I walked into the room, Alex looked at me in horror. “Oh my God, Cat! What the fuck happened to your face?!” I looked in the mirror and, to my horror, I looked like something that had been deep fat fried within an inch of its life. “Fuckin hell Cat, your face looks like a red lobster! Did you not use that sunscreen I told you about?” I put my hands on my face and it felt so very hot. “Fuck Alex, ring the dinger and stick a fork in me – I’m fried! I can’t believe it. We put half a tube of sunscreen on me but, holy shit, I think I totally forgot about my face!” Alex began to laugh. “It’s not funny! I look horrific! How can I show my face outside!” Trying to hide her smile, Alex asked, “What do you mean WE put on sunscreen? You mean you had help with the sunscreen and you still managed to fry?” “Well, to cut a long story short,” I explained, “Mike, the guy I was dancing with at the Lake House party, came to say hello at the pool today. I dropped the sun umbrella on his foot and broke the damn thing so he helped me with the sunscreen.” “I bet he did,” she smiled back suggestively. “Nothing like that! We just talked and, well, I guess we did too much talking and not enough covering up." "Cat, I hope he uses better protection for other things if you know what I mean!" "Oh, behave yourself, you dirty bird," I laughed "We're just good friends." "Right Cat, that's how it starts. I'll be keeping an eye on this Mike." "Okay Mom," I joked.

"Cat, are you ready for dinner?" "Hell no, Alex! There's no way on earth I'm going out looking like this. I'll get picked up by the X-Men or aliens will come and get me and claim me as their long-lost cousin or something." "Stop overreacting, Cat, you look fine." Alex looked at me as if to say 'Well, I'll tell her what she wants to hear. I want to go eat.' "Alex, are you looking at the same face I am? I look like a frikkin' freak." I couldn't help but laugh as she was trying so hard not to but we couldn't help it. My poor face was red raw and, to add insult to injury, it hurt when I laughed.

I drowned myself in Aloe Vera gel that made me look illuminated and sticky-faced but at least it soothed the pain so off we went to the cafeteria. I hid my face under a baseball cap for fear of putting everyone off their food. I quickly dug into a delicious bagel sandwich and drank a gallon of water on Alex's orders to rehydrate myself from the effects of the sun.

When we got back to the dorm room, I felt much better. The gallon of water and food had helped to bring some life back to my face. It sure as hell didn't need any more colour! "Cat, are you feeling okay? Can I get you anything?" Alex asked, looking sorry for me. "Cat, I'm so sorry. I have a date with Jonny tonight. He's taking me to the movies and it's the first time we have done anything other than play tennis but, if you really want me to stay, I will. I can reschedule the movies."

Now I felt sunburn and pangs of guilt. "No Alex, you go to the movies with Jonny. I'll be fine." I didn't want to be a wet blanket about her big date. What kind of friend would I be? "Okay, Cat. I promise I'll be back early to make sure you're alright. Just drink plenty of water and don't worry, you will be fine. Sunburn sucks, just get some rest." Alex patted my forehead with a wet cloth and tried to make me feel better. Soon after, Jonny called to pick Alex up to go on their hot date.

My hot date consisted of more Aloe Vera and water. Having slept for a few hours, I woke up in a pool of sweat. I plastered my face with aloe vera for the hundredth time and practically used the whole tube. For a split second, I felt like I was back in the land of the living. Then, suddenly, I became dizzy and I was barely able to see straight. I didn't know what to do. I knew Alex wouldn't be back for a while so I reached for my phone and called Tom. He would know what to do. But my call went straight to voicemail. What should I do? I couldn't ask the girls in the dorm as most of them were not on speaking terms with Alex or me as we had decided not to go to Carla's DVD night and they totally let us know that she was not impressed.

"Okay, okay," I thought "Who can I contact? Holy shit, definitely not Josh!" Then I remembered that Mike had given me his number but did I really want to contact him and ask him to come over and see my face looking like this? I had only met the guy. I didn't want to scare him away completely! "Needs must!" I thought. I was getting to the last drop of aloe vera and rapidly running out of bottled water, so I took the plunge and called. "Hello, Mike speaking." His warm, friendly voice was music to my ears. "Hi Mike, it's Cat," I said in a weak voice. Having explained my delicate state, and the fact that I had almost passed out just a moment before, he immediately dropped the phone and came right over. I was so relieved when I heard the knock on the door five minutes later. I opened to see Mike with a bag of provisions and a shocked look on his face. "I know it looks bad doesn't it?" I moaned. "No, it's not so bad," Mike replied reassuringly. "I can't believe we forgot to sunscreen your face!" Mike joked, trying to put me at ease. I looked at him and we both smiled but for me, it hurt too much and I let out an "Ouch!" "Please don't make me laugh. It hurts so much. I look like Frankenstein's bride or something. I can't believe I'm letting you see me like this." I was so embarrassed but Mike was the perfect gentleman. "Don't worry, Cat. I've seen worse. I have the complete collection of the Friday the Thirteenth movies… I'm just kidding, I promise!" I gave him a playful nudge in the ribs to which he pointed over and ordered, "Okay there Miss Cat, let's go to bed." I looked at Mike and joked, "Now Mike, I've only met you!" I knew what he meant but I was getting him back for making fun of me. "Oh, I didn't mean that the way it sounded!" Mike smiled, embarrassed.

As I got into bed, Mike opened the shopping bag and lifted out a six-pack of water, some aloe vera and a large tub of ice cream. "Cat, this is for medicinal purposes. There's nothing like a bowl of ice cream to soothe a sunburn. I promise it's not for your face. "But you never know! You should try it - it just might work!" As he talked, I noticed how cute Mike was with his dark Italian skin and dark eyes. There was just something about him that I found attractive. He was not the type of guy I would usually go for as he was a bit short but he was such a good listener and was kind, considerate and easy to get along with. The perfect guy – what's height got to do with it?

Time flew by as we sat eating ice cream, watching the movie and talking for hours. Mike and I were getting on great guns. After a short while, the door opened and Alex walked in. She seemed quite startled to see Mike there with me. "Cat, how are you feeling? Are you okay?" She looked worried. "Yeah, I'm fine. I just felt a little faint earlier and I gave Mike a call just to hang out with me." "You fainted! Oh my God, Cat, are you okay? I'm so sorry. I shouldn't have left you to go on a stupid date," Alex said concerned. "It's okay. How were you to know I was going to pass out? It's just a little bit of sunburn, that's all. Besides, I want to hear all about this date." Alex rolled her eyes and said, "Oh, you know." It didn't sound too promising but I didn't think she wanted to go into detail with Mike there and neither did he, so he got up to leave. "Cat, I'd better get going now. I need to study for class tomorrow. Okay Alex, now you take care of Little Miss Sunshine here!" Mike joked and they both laughed. "Hey, I hope you're not laughing at my face! It's not a laughing matter. Sunburn is very serious!" But I couldn't keep from laughing at myself. I really did look like something from a horror movie.

After Mike left, Alex and I lay in our beds and talked about Alex's date with Jonny. "Cat, I'm so sorry for leaving you. I really should have stayed. I feel awful. I should never put a dumb ass date before you." By the way Alex was talking, I sensed that the date hadn't gone as well as she had hoped. "So girl, what happened with Jonny? From the expression on your face when you came in, it didn't go too great, huh?" I asked. "Cat, I just don't know. He is really nice. When we were playing tennis, he was just so excited but when we went to the movies he had nothing to say or talk about apart from tennis. Tennis is his life. It's getting a bit, well a bit…" "Boring?" I guessed. "Yeah, just a bit but maybe it's me, Cat. I'm so mixed up when it comes to guys," Alex sighed. "What? No way, Alex. You're the most confident person I know around guys. They just seem to want to know you and talk with you everywhere we go. I even get guys coming up to me saying, 'Hey, who's your friend?' What you said, Alex, couldn't be farther from the truth!" I exclaimed.

"Cat, I have never had this amount of attention from guys before. I swear, I don't know why they want to talk to me now but it might have something to do with the fact that I'm 40lbs lighter than I was six months ago. I think it's given me a little more confidence. Look, here is a picture of what I used to look like." Alex showed me a picture of a girl who looked nothing like her at all. "This is not you!" I denied. "Oh, it's me alright. See what you can do when you go on a diet and highlight your hair? I'm one of those high school nerds who, if you take their glasses off and let their hair down, actually looks quite pretty."

I couldn't believe it was the same person. Alex looked stunning now. I guess that was why she was enjoying all the attention from the guys and why not, she deserved it! "So, what are you going to do about Jonny boy?" I asked. "Oh Cat, if I have to listen to his explanation of the overhead lob one more time, I think I'm gonna scream!" I think that answered my question. It was game, set and match with Jonny on the losing side.

Chapter 4

We all have a story to tell

The weekend came and went pretty quickly and I had spent my entire time staying out of the sun with a baseball hat covering my now peeling face, which looked worse than the sunburn. I had a few double takes in the classroom and, if one more person said to me, "Oh, you got the sun!" I was going to have a fit.

One night, I sat in the Coffee House while Alex was working with Tom. When I say working, it usually consisted of Alex pouring a few cups of coffee but mainly Tom, his guys, Alex and I just sat talking and joking around. When Tom worked, Stacey would always be there waiting for him to finish. They were the perfect couple. He was tall, strong and incredibly handsome and she was tall and totally the Californian beauty. The only thing was that, when we were hanging out at the Coffee House, Alex and I were two of the guys but Stacey wasn't. She tried to be but her femininity just didn't fit into the hanging out with the guy's persona that we had going on. For Stacey, it was all about hanging out with Tom and that meant putting up with his friends.

As we settled down to play a game of cards, I saw the most beautiful specimen of a man walk in my direction. “Oh, sweet suffering Jesus, Alex, look who’s just come in,” I whispered. “Holy fuck, it’s Brad Anderson!” As we looked at him with our tongues hanging on the floor, Tom looked round to see what had caught our eye. “Are you two okay?” Tom asked. “Yeah, we’re great. Cat, look at that face!” Alex and I were drooling at the sight of Brad. “Seriously, do you guys have the hots for Brad Anderson? He’s like 30 years old!” Tom winced at the thought of it. “Come on. He’s seriously gorgeous. Look at him!” Alex joked.

As Brad turned to leave with his take-out coffee, I prayed he would go straight out the door but, to my embarrassment, he headed straight for our table. “Fuck, Fuck, Fuck!!” I thought, “He’s coming this way!” “Hi everyone!” Brad smiled as he looked around the table and then he saw me. “Oh my, Cat. You caught some sun,” Brad said, stating the obvious. I was mortified. “Yes, Brad. I need to remember the sunscreen, right?” I had so many people telling me that lately that I thought I’d finish Brad’s sentence for him. “Well, be careful. The sun is hot out there,” Brad advised. “You’re fucking hot in here,” Alex whispered to me as we smiled and said our goodbyes to Brad.

A short time later, a guy walked into the Coffee House, turned to me and said, "Man, you got some sun, didn't you?" This was the final straw so I sarcastically shouted back, "Noooo, really, ya think so? Can't imagine where the hell you got that impression!" The guy was blown away by my outburst but it was just one remark too many. When the poor guy left in total shock and with his latté in hand, everyone burst into tears of laughter. "Holy shit, Cat, that was so funny! The guy really did say the wrong thing to ya. I was gonna ask how the sunburn was but I won't now! Not ever!" Tom joked. I did find it funny myself "Shoot me in the head. I got sunburned. The guy didn't have to remind me and point it out, ya know? Poor guy. I don't think I'll be on his Christmas card list!"

The next day, after morning classes, Alex and I met in our dorm room to go for lunch which had become our daily routine. We would always go together as neither of us liked to hang around the cafeteria on our own. It made us feel like loners. As we made our way from the bagel bar to a table, Alex looked uneasy. "What's up with you, Alex? Are you okay?" I asked concerned. "It's Jonny. He is looking over at us. I haven't returned his message in about four days. I just don't know what to say to the guy apart from, nice serve."

"Alex, you're right. I think he's serving up a few looks this way." Jonny made his way over to our table and sat down beside Alex. "Hey there, beautiful. Where have you been hiding? I was wondering if you wanted to come and see me play tennis today. There's a big game against our rival college and I'd love for you to come along." Alex looked at Jonny trying to prepare him for a big letdown. "Look Jonny, I really don't think this is working. I'm just not that into the whole tennis thing and I know it's your life and, well, I just think there is more to life than tennis."

Ouch! I could feel Jonny's pain. Hearing someone say that they were not into tennis was like a kick in the teeth to him. He couldn't understand why she had suddenly changed her mind. "But what about the past month? We have been getting on so well and your forehand has been improving so much!" "Ya see, right there!" Alex exclaimed. "I don't want a relationship that's all about frikkin' tennis!" "Tennis IS my life and if you are not going to be there to support me then I guess I am going to have to break up with you." How quickly the tables had turned. Now Jonny claims to be breaking up with Alex? I think his ego couldn't cope with rejection. "If that's how you feel then it's goodbye, Jonny!" Alex said as she started to walk away.

"Alex, I'm outta her
want my tennis racquet b
"Yeah well, guess what Jon
to want? You told me I cou
correctly," Alex quickly rep
at Alex's sarcastic response
racquet. Even though relation a month,
there are always possessions that have been left with each other. Both parties think the relationship will last forever but, unfortunately for Jonny, that was not the case.

As Jonny turned on his tennis heels and left us, I could hardly hold in my smile remembering what Alex had said. "Alex, what does it feel like to want? That was a classic." "Well, ya know Cat, what can I say? My father has a sharp tongue and so do I. Hey, at least I got a tennis racquet out of it." "You're not gonna give it back to him, are you?" I smiled. "I'm not going to keep it, just hold onto it for an extended amount of time!" "Alex, what's the difference?" I asked. "There is no difference, that's the thing." We couldn't hold back the laughter as we walked out of the cafeteria. People looked at us as if we were crazy but that was beginning to be the norm for Alex and me. No one really got our bad sense of humour except for Tom and he was as bad as us. Josh really did have it right. We were birds of a feather.

unchtime class, I had a lifeguard shift to keep me out of trouble for the rest of ernoon. Making sure I had the trusted umbrella and all-over sunscreen protection, I was pretty much 'chillin' out' as they said in California. The pool was quite deserted as many kids were still in class so the afternoon shift was quiet during the college week.

As I began to do my hourly check on the pool, making sure all the loungers were cleaned down, I heard a mysterious rumble in the lifeguard's office. No students were allowed in there and, fearing that someone was about to steal the contents, I rushed in to capture the thief. To my surprise, I found another lifeguard looking back at me and smiling. "Oh hello, I wasn't aware that anyone else was working today," I said, a little startled. "I'm sorry, I didn't mean to freak you out. I've just got out of class and I'm taking the next shift but I thought I would just catch a few laps of the pool first. You don't mind me changing in here, do you?" he asked with a smile. In that moment, he had stripped off his T-shirt to reveal a perfectly toned, tanned not to mention washboard abs body which totally made my face turn beet red, if I wasn't red enough already. He was to die for! With short, wavy blonde hair, a perfect body and a cheeky self-assured look, this guy was a dream. I think I was in love or maybe lust. I wasn't sure.

"That's fine, go right ahead. Oh well, you already have," I laughed nervously as I always did around cute guys. "I haven't seen you working here before. I'm sorry, I didn't quite get your name. I'm Cat by the way." I was trying to get as much information about this guy as possible. Hopefully, he was going to be working with me more often. "Hi, I'm Rick. I've just started working here this week. Cat, short for Kathleen, is it?" "No, the other one, Catherine. You were close but no cigar." Look at me flirting, I thought. I was trying to act cool and not make too much of an arse of myself.

"So Cat, you're Irish right? I was over in Europe on vacation a year or so back. It's a cool place. We went to Ireland for a few days. Have you been to the pub for a few pints yet?" Rick tried an outrageous Irish accent which sounded like a mix between Australian and Scottish but was a good attempt. "No, not yet," I replied disappointed. "With this whole 21 rule here, it's sort of killing me. But it's my birthday in a week and I'll soon be 21! Thank fuck for that!" Rick smiled. "Yeah, I know how much you guys love your pints of beer. When I was over in Ireland, I was 19 and I just loved the over-18 rule you guys have going over there. So, where are you going for your birthday? If you're looking for some good pubs, I'm your man! I know a cool Irish bar you would love for your birthday. It would be just like home."

Rick stood talking with me for a while and was so excited to have met an Irish person. He really fell in love with the country when he was over there and loved the Emerald Isle's forty shades of green. I, on the other hand, was turning fifty shades of red and blushing as he stared straight into my eyes, burning my skin with just the slightest look. "Boy, I wish he would fall in love with me," I thought. At least I had something in common with him. Ireland was my saviour.

Rick went on to tell me how he was from Chicago, the Windy City, and had won a scholarship to Deacon College in track and field. I could tell he was an athlete as he was one pure solid muscle. Mind you, most of the guys at Deacon College were the athletic type. Maybe it was the sunshine but there weren't too many fellas who didn't play sports. Not like in Dublin where most of the guys I knew had a daily walk to the local pub and back again as part of their exercise routine.

"Hey Rick, I'm sorry. Look at the time. It's almost time for your shift to start. I've been gabbing away like a mad thing about home and you were looking to get in a few laps of the pool." I tried not to make Rick feel like I was boring him. "I'm sorry too. I'm sure you need to get away from this pool soon. I just love your accent. I could talk to you all day." "Oh please do," I thought to myself. "I'd better get a few laps in, like you say. I don't want to get a beer belly just yet. Let me know about the whole birthday thing. My buddies are always up for a good party. I'd love to organise something for you." With that, Rick dove into the water, not a beer belly in sight. I was so excited, with a rip-roaring body and personality to match, he was too good to be true.

Later that evening, as Alex and I drove to the mall which was about 30 minutes from campus and I filled her in on the babe at the pool. "Alex, you should see this guy. He is just gorgeous and great fun at the same time! Do you think I should call him about the birthday bash? He seemed pretty up for planning a party." As I gushed about Rick to Alex all the way to the mall, she suddenly gave me a reality check. "So Cat, what about your friend Mike? He seems pretty interested in you." I thought about Mike and how kind and considerate he was to me but, at the same time, I thought he just wanted to be friends. I didn't really know where I was with him at that moment. "I don't even think Rick would go for me.

He would be way out of my league. He just has the total package if you know what I mean, jellybean. This is definitely lust, not love," I joked. "Oh Cat, I totally know what you mean. I had a guy with the perfect credentials once." Alex looked sad and teary-eyed. She was definitely thinking about someone in her past and I could tell she had been hurt. As we walked around the mall for a few hours, making way too many purchases, we made a pit stop for coffee and a break. It gave me enough time to question Alex about the perfect package relationship she had mentioned earlier.

"I think I might let this latté settle for a bit. The last time I had one of these, I burned my mouth and couldn't speak for a day. Hey, might not be a bad thing" I joked. "So, while we're waiting, Alex, tell me the story about your perfect package guy. You never told me about him before." She looked down as if she was thinking of a way to start the conversation or to find the words to tell me what she had been so upset about. "Okay Cat, so this is my story. This is why I'm so fucked up when it comes to guys. Now, this is a bit of a long story, Cat, so you might want to get comfortable. Do you see this ring?" Alex pointed to a beautiful diamond ring on the third finger of her right hand. "This was a promise ring given to me by my boyfriend of three and a half years. His name was Jake. He was my High School sweetheart, my first love and my everything. We were inseparable throughout High School, so much in love and we were planning on getting married once we finished college. I loved him so much, Cat. We were so comfortable with each other and we went everywhere together." Tears were beginning to well up in Alex's eyes as she told her story. It was obvious that she was still really hurting. I was intrigued by her relationship with Jake, as she seemed to be confident and perfectly at ease around guys but at the same time she claimed she had no luck with the opposite sex. From what I could see, she had it all together. What happened between them to make it all go so horribly wrong?

After a few sips of coffee, Alex continued her story. "Cat, we had it all, the perfect relationship, everyone at school would say how perfect we were for each other and I bet you're wondering what happened, right?" "Well yes, why did you guys break up?" I was puzzled. "Yes, that's the million-dollar question alright. I'll tell you the biggest bombshell ever to have rocked my world was when I found my beloved Jake in bed with one of my friends." "What? Are you fucking serious?!" I gasped. "Holy shit, it's bad enough to hear about him doing the dirty but you actually caught him at it! Oh Alex, you poor thing."

"Yeah, that's about the height of it. Cat, I was devastated. I couldn't believe that he had done that to me and what's worse, it was with a so-called friend of mine." At this point, Alex could not hold back the tears and, as they streamed down her face, I gave her a reassuring smile and squeezed her hand. "Cat, that's why I wanted to move away to college. I could have stayed at my community college but Jake was there and there was just too much to remind me of him - too many memories. I just had to get away."

"Well, you know what I say? It's this guy Jake's hard luck. If he could only see you now with all these guys after you! Josh, Johnny and I see the guys looking at you, girl. You're gonna be fine. You have a great personality. You're incredibly funny and understand my Irish sarcasm which most Americans don't. Alex, trust me, it will get easier. You never know who you might meet in college. And, hey, you've already met a freaky Irish girl who is just so glad to have met you and doesn't know where she would be without you! Ya see, things happen for a reason. If you guys had stayed together, you wouldn't have met me!" I was trying to make Alex feel better and she smiled at me and threw her arms around me. I think it worked.

“So Cat, what’s the story with you? You’re bound to have had some perfect package guys over in Ireland?” Alex was quizzing me and, with a deep breath, I plucked up the courage to tell her about my so-called love life. “Alex, if we are going there, I do have a perfect package back in Dublin but the story of my life is that we are just friends. Well, a bit more than just friends. “Really?!” Alex got excited. “No, nothing like that; more like brother and sister,” I added. “Oh, all sounds a bit incestuous there, Cat, do explain,” Alex laughed. “If you can believe it, I’ve been in love with the same guy for about fifteen years,” I confessed. “What? Wait. Cat, that means you have loved him since you were five years old?” Alex asked.

“Okay, this is my story. So, my mum and dad met at medical school when they were studying to be doctors. They had a whirlwind romance and got married only six months after they met. At their wedding, my mum had her best friend as her maid of honour and my dad had his best friend as his best man and, guess what, they fell in love with each other at my parents’ wedding. I think my parents really pushed them together,” I explained. “So your mom’s best friend married your dad’s best friend?” Alex checked. “That’s correct and it was perfect as they actually got pregnant at the same time too. I really think my mum and her friend planned it to a tee." "So my mum's friend, Kate, gave birth to a boy, James, and two days later I arrived. My mum and Kate were both in the same hospital at the same time."

"So basically, James and I grew up together and we were practically brother and sister. We had our birthdays together, went on holiday together, went to the same school and played the same sports together. I think my dad was banking on having a son so he had me playing all the same sports as James. We played what you call soccer together and I was pretty good. I turned out to be a real tomboy. Then…"

"Then what, what happened Cat?" Alex asked, excited to hear what the rest of the story had to offer.

"Then I grew out of my tomboy phase and grew more and more fond of James if you know what I mean. Alex, I fell in love with him but it's all in my head. He still sees me as his sister and he's my brother from another mother as James always likes to joke," I explained sadly.

As I opened my purse to show Alex a photo of James, I felt relieved that I could talk to someone about him. James was the classic young Irish gentleman. With short brown hair, blue eyes and a charming smile, he had a wicked sense of humour and was the one person who could always make me laugh. "He's cute and he's almost as white as you!" Alex joked. "What is he doing now, does he go to college?" "Yes, he is at university in Dublin studying Law," I explained. "Fancy!" Alex seemed impressed.

"Cat, have you ever told him how you feel?" Alex asked. "Fuck no, Alex! This is the first time I've said anything about my feelings for James to anyone. I felt awful for so long. My mum and Kate joked when we were young that James and I would get married but James always screwed up his face as if that would be the worst thing in the world. We are best friends and I think that's just the way we will always be. James talks to me about everything. I know him so well and I also know what type of girls he likes. He always asks me to hook him up with my friends. He is a bit of a, what you guys call, player."

"What? I'm sure you felt like someone was pulling your heart out when he was hooking up with your friends. What bitches would do that to you?" Alex said angrily. "Oh Alex, it wasn't my friends' fault. They didn't know how I felt about James and I didn't want anyone to know. As far as everyone else knew, James was like my brother, my best friend. We were mates." Suddenly, I felt so relieved to be talking to Alex about James. For some reason, I felt so at ease letting all my emotions out. It was good to finally talk to someone about my feelings for him.

"So, have you been saving yourself for this guy James?" Alex asked. "Oh no, Alex. I have had my share of relationships but none has ever lasted. There was one guy, Daniel, who I was pretty serious with but it didn't work out. Besides, James absolutely hated him. They never got on," I confessed. "So James didn't like your boyfriend. Cat, it seems to me that James wants you as his best friend but just doesn't want you to be with anyone else! Fuck him, Cat! You deserve to be with someone who loves you and not just as a friend. You are amazing, Cat. You're kind and generous and you're so beautiful inside and out. James doesn't deserve to have you pining over him," Alex declared. "You know what? You need to fall in love with a great American guy, then get married and stay here! We can have babies at the same time too!" Alex laughed. "You're right," I smiled through the tears. "Things happen for a reason. Now, we'd better get back to shopping before this mall closes with us in it and besides, there is nothing like retail therapy for getting your mind off guys!" "Absolutely!" I smiled and agreed.

Ch

The Ca

When we got back to c
we slumped onto our be
totally taken it out of u
exclaimed. “Retail thera
you.” Alex went to ch
answering machine as she always did. She was very much the phone girl. She was either calling someone or someone was calling her. Usually, it was Tom calling to chat or catch up on homework.

“Cat, I got a message from my parents. They want me to go home for the weekend, this weekend!” I could tell she was excited at the prospect of seeing her mom and dad but she looked quite sullen and worried. “Alex, that’s great. I know you’ve been missing them so why the long face?” “Cat, I do miss my folks but you know what, I’m gonna miss this place and I’m gonna miss you.” “Ah Alex, don’t worry. It’s only a long weekend and I’ll fill you in on all the gossip when you get back.”

I was trying to put her mind at ease but at the same time, I so wished she would stay. Four days on my own without my best buddy to get into trouble with - what was I gonna do with myself?

...nt the phone rang. "Oh, hi mom!" ...d. "Yes, I got your message. I would ...to come home and see you guys but what ...Cat?" Alex made me sound like a lost puppy ...o had no home or who needed to be looked after. A sudden smile came over Alex's face, she was relieved to hear news from her mom. "Thanks, Mom. I knew you wouldn't mind." Alex then hung up the phone.

"Cat, pack a bag for the weekend. You're coming with me! My mom and dad totally made sure that I asked you too." "I don't want to impose or anything. You should go and do stuff with your folks." I didn't want to put her parents to any trouble. "Hell no, Cat! My mom said to tell you that you're welcome to come. She knows how much of a good friend you are to me and, besides, where would I be for four days without my wee Irish pal to go shopping with!" Alex was so excited. I think she was looking forward to going back to her roots and showing me a part of where she was from and part of me was looking forward to seeing her in her own surroundings. "Well, as long as your mom and dad don't mind…" I said, happy to accept their invitation.

The weekend came pretty quickly and Alex was really looking forward to seeing her parents.

We packed our bags into Alex's trusty Ford, along with the entire contents of her washing hamper. She figured she could kill two birds with one stone and get the laundry done while she was at home - saving on quarters which was a smart move.

As we drove the 200 miles to Alex's home, we listened to our favourite music, the funky hip hop and R'n'B vibes that Tom had got us both hooked on. We were two crazy birds off on a road trip. Getting a few truckers to honk at us on the way kept us amused and, as we talked about life, love and college gossip, the journey went by in no time.

As we arrived at Alex's house, her mom and dad came running out to greet us. Alex was just as excited to see her mom and dad as they were to see her. Her mom threw her arms around Alex as if she hadn't seen her in ten years! "Jean, let go will ya? You're gonna smother the kid and besides, I need a big hug from my girl," Pete joked.

"We missed you so much, sweetie. I know it's only been two months but I have been so lost without my baby girl. Are you okay? How's school? How are your classes? Are you working hard?" Alex's mom asked excitedly. "Oh Mom, I'm doing fine. Cat is looking after me well and teaching me a few Irish traditions." Alex looked over and smiled. "I bet there's a bar or two involved, right Cat? I know what college life is like. It's wonderful to see you too, sweetie. You're more than welcome here and please make yourself at home, will ya." Pete smiled and, with that, he gave me a huge bear hug. Alex's parents were so kind and welcoming - just what I needed, as seeing them with Alex was making me miss my own parents terribly. They totally made me feel like part of their family just when I needed it.

The weekend with Alex and her family was so much fun. The house was a charming beach-style property, only a block away from the ocean, with plenty of large windows to capture the natural light and beautiful coastal views. There was a quaint little front porch with patio chairs which was perfect for sitting out at night and enjoying the warm evenings while listening to the waves lap up against the shore.

Each morning, Alex and I would take a walk along the shore and chat about just about everything. "Mom, we're away to the beach for a walk, okay?" Alex called out to her mom. "Alright, darling. You want me to go?" "It's okay. Cat is coming along for a walk too. We won't be long." And with that, Alex was speed walking down to the beach.

"This is what I used to do every day to get in shape after the whole Jake break up. Every day, my mom and I would go power walking. It's so exhilarating and a way for me to tune out everything in my head." I sort of had a feeling Alex was thinking about Jake now that she was back in her hometown. "Alex, are you thinking about him?" I asked, concerned. "Who? Slime ball Jake? Nooo, not at all. Well, maybe just a little," she confessed. "It's just weird coming back home. It's like I've a whole new life back at Deacon College with new friends and a new me and I can be different. I can be the Alex I want people to see. But when I'm home, it's like I'm the Alex people always expect me to be. I mean, I get noticed at college, guys notice me and I never got that here and I guess, because I was in a three-year relationship with Jake, I never took any notice of other guys that much. But now I'm popular which I never was before. People don't know me and I can be whoever I want to be. Does that make sense, Cat?"

"Totally. I understand when you go to a new place like college, it's like you're a new book with nothing written in it. You can be whoever you want to be and open up a brand-new chapter of your life. I know that you have bad memories of here with Jake but this is your home so don't let memories of him freak you out. You look wonderful and, if he could see you now, I'm sure he would realise that he's the one who is losing out." I said firmly. Alex was such a wonderful friend to me, taking me to her home and looking after me. I hated it when she put herself down so much.

As we made our way back to the house, Pete shouted from the door, "Come on in girls, lunch is just on the table!" We sat down to a beautiful roast dinner which I thought I was going to just inhale - it looked so delicious. College food was taking its toll on me and I missed traditional home-cooked meals. As Pete started to serve up the food, he took my plate and with a smile, he laughed, "Extra potatoes for you, Cat? Girl, you are too skinny! I'm gonna have to fatten you up!" Pete was such a jolly guy. Alex called him a smart-ass and always joked that was where she got it from. As I finished my third helping, I sat back and thanked Jean for a wonderful dinner. Again, Pete joked, "Holy shit girl, where do you put it all? Do you have hollow legs or something?!" "I must be like you Pete and talk it off!" I laughed back. Pete smiled. He was impressed that I was just as much a smart ass as he was. He enjoyed the banter.

After lunch, Alex got a phone call and stayed in her room while she talked. I stayed in the kitchen with Jean who was showing me the family album. "This is Alex when she was a baby. This is her at gymnastics. Alex playing softball. Oh, and this is so cute. Here is one of her cheerleading at only six years old," Jean gushed. I could tell she was so proud of Alex and was totally devoted to her daughter. I flicked through the album with hundreds of pictures of Alex through the ages, from bubble perms and braces to short hair, 90s baggy jeans and tie-dye T-shirts.

"Jean, who is the girl in this picture?" I asked, noticing a girl who didn't look familiar. "Cat honey, that's Alex. This was taken last year. She was a lot different back then." "Shit, I totally didn't recognise her! The other picture she showed me in college was totally different. When Alex told me she lost a bit of weight, she wasn't kidding!"

"Alex was dating that Jake guy then and, when that awful thing happened, she became terribly depressed. I was so worried about her." "Yes Jean, Alex told me what happened with Jake. I'm sure it was a total shock for her." "Cat, I just didn't know what to do, apart from beat the crap out of Jake and that so-called friend of hers! Alex wouldn't eat or see her friends or even go out of the house. I was at my wit's end. It was like she had lost all confidence and trust in people," Jean explained.

"Cat, I'm just so glad she got away from him and, although I miss her terribly because she is my everything, she needed to get a complete break and find new people. And she found a lovely, skinny Irish girl." Jean laughed and hugged me. "You don't need to worry, Jean. I'll look after Alex for you. She is looking after me too. We look after each other," I said, smiling reassuringly.

A few moments later Alex came jumping down the stairs. "Oh Mom, are you showing Cat that album? You do this all the time with my friends." "I know, sweetie, but you were just so cute when you were a baby and pretty too." "I'm sure as hell not cute now, pretty maybe, pretty ugly that is!" Alex laughed. "Hey girl, don't say that about yourself. What have I told you about putting yourself down? You look great especially now that I have seen these pics!" I showed Alex her picture from last year and she laughed with a real grimace on her face. "Bird, you look great now - I'm telling you that!"

"Yeah, Cat. You tell me what I want to hear." Alex said again, trying to put herself down. "Now, Miss Alexandra, what did I tell you before." I wished so much that she didn't always focus on the negatives. Alex seemed to focus on the one thing she didn't like about herself over the million things that she was amazing at. "Now put those pictures away 'cause we are going shopping! We're meeting my friend, Kim, at the mall." I was so excited. Shopping was my favourite pastime and, as I had barely any clothes with me for a whole year, I took every opportunity to go shopping. "Alex, you know me, I'm not one to turn down a trip to the mall."

As we drove to meet Kim, I started to wonder who this friend of Alex's was when Alex said, "I bet you're wondering who Kim is." I swear we were becoming telepathic twins or something. "I was wondering a little bit," I confessed. "Kim is my oldest friend. Don't get me wrong, I love her to bits…" I could feel a "but" coming on. "…but Cat, she is such a rich fucking bitch!" "Holy shit, Alex, don't hold back or anything! Tell me what she's like why don't you!" I laughed.

"I know that sounds like I am jealous but, I kid you not Cat, I have never met anyone as spoilt as Kim. She is beautiful and totally knows it." "Okay Alex, how are you guys friends again?" I joked. "I know, right? But I guess I've known her since we were in kindergarten and she is harmless really. Trust me, you will like her," Alex assured me but for some reason I became nervous. What if she doesn't like me? This was Alex's oldest friend and I guess, in a way, I was her newest friend. I had only known Alex for two months but I felt like I had known her my whole life with our late-night talks about our lives, loves and our dreams. What would it be like to see an old friend of hers?

We arrived at the mall which was the size of a small city. I still couldn't get over the size of those places. With Dublin having all the stores on the High Street, I had never seen one building that had so many stores under one roof. As we made our way towards the food court where we were meeting Kim, I kept my eyes on all the stores that I wanted to check out. There were so many of them. Alex suddenly screamed and I looked round to see a girl running towards us. It had to be Kim and, just as Alex had described her, with bleached blonde hair, perfect size zero figure and perfect, olive-tanned skin. She was just about perfect.

"Oh my God girl, it's so good to see you!" shrieked Kim. "It's been so long. You have to tell me what's been happening. What's college life like? Dad has been at me to go but you know what I say, why spend four years getting an education when you can buy one!"

"Hey Kim, this is my friend Cat from Ireland." Alex smiled as she introduced us. Alex started to tell Kim all about Deacon College and that we got up to all sorts of trouble and how wonderful it was. Yes, college life sure was great. Alex really wanted to show Kim that she was different and that she was having so much fun away from her hometown. “Kim, you should see the guys at College - totally gorge! I get asked out like all the time. It’s crazy!” As Alex excitedly filled Kim in on the Josh and Jonny conquests, I wondered what it would be like to be as confident as Alex and Kim. I really wished I could be like them. Instead, I was the skinny, white Irish girl who couldn’t get a date for love nor money. Hopefully, that would change with working so closely with Rick.

As Kim and Alex chatted and caught up on the gossip, a sudden exasperated look came over Alex’s face. “Alex, are you okay? You look like you have just seen a ghost!” I exclaimed. “Holy shit, Jake is walking in this direction!” Alex sat motionless hoping that either the ground would swallow her up or that she could overdose on “invisible juice” and Jake would just walk on by, oblivious to the fact that she was calmly having a heart attack. “That fuckin’ asshole. Alex honey, you are so better off without him!” Kim shouted. “Kim, shut the fuck up. I don’t want to draw attention to myself. Holy fuck, has he seen me?” Alex looked as if she was about to slide off of her chair in an attempt to hide from the ex. Unfortunately, she didn’t succeed. Jake had spotted her. “Hi Alex, how are you?” Jake asked quietly, not sure what the response was going to be. “Hi Jake, I’m doing well,” Alex replied politely but I could tell she just wanted to rip his head off with her teeth in a sort of dream sketch.

“Wow, Alex you look great. I’m glad you’re doing good. How’s college? You’re at Deacon College, right?” “Yeah, it’s wonderful. I’m loving it!” After a few minutes of ‘How are you?’ polite conversations and awkward silences, Jake left, much to Alex’s relief. “Oh my God, guys. I’m trembling! I never thought I would see him this weekend. I swear this town is too small. You can’t move without bumping into someone, and someone that you so don’t want to see!” “Kim, we’d better be going. We are heading back to college tomorrow morning and it’s a bit of a long journey. I’ll call you the next time we’re back in town, okay?” Alex then made her escape with me in tow.

I could tell that seeing Jake had totally freaked Alex out. She was quiet in the car on the way back to her parents’ house so I left her to her thoughts. “That fuckin’ piece of mother fucking shit!” Alex screamed. “Okay bird, just let it out. I think you needed that. What are you thinking?” I knew Alex was ready to let her feelings out.

"You know what Cat? He just comes over and is like, 'Hi, how are you, Alex?' How the hell does he think I am? He totally breaks my heart to where I just don't know how it will ever get back together again and then he comes off with that friendly shit!" "You know what Cat? I think that's why I can't commit to guys like Josh and Johnny. I'm scared to get hurt again. I just find it so hard to trust. Jake totally dicked me over so much that I don't think I'll ever fall in love ever again."

Alex was becoming so upset just thinking about Jake so, trying to lighten the mood, I said, "Kim seemed nice! Bit of a rich bitch but a nice rich bitch." Alex smiled, "Yeah, she's great but did you hear her tell me all about what's been going on here? It's like she is the fountain of all knowledge and I'm missing out on so much. I made sure she knew how wonderful Deacon College is though." "Yeah, I was picking up on that," I smiled and we laughed.

The next morning, we got up early for our road trip back to College. Jean and Pete, who were up for hours beforehand, made us a cooked breakfast and a hamper filled with water and snacks for the journey. Another hamper was full of groceries. Jean was worried that we were going to waste away on college food and wanted to stock up for us. They were such wonderful people and just adored Alex. I felt so welcomed by them like I was part of their family and, even though I had only really known them for a short while, it was like I was at home.

Before we made our way out of the house to the car, Pete stopped us to make an announcement. "Cat, it was a real pleasure to have you stay. Any time Alex comes back home, you're more than welcome to come with her. From now on, this is your home too. You have a set of American parents. Oh and by the way, I hear that it is someone's birthday next week!" Pete and Jean smiled at me. "I wonder who could have told you that?" I smiled and pointed to Alex who was standing with an innocent look on her face. "Jean and I have a little something for you."

Jean produced a box tied up with a red ribbon and handed it to me excitedly. "Oh goodness guys, you shouldn't have! You have done so much for me already." I felt so touched by their kindness as I opened their present to see a beautiful handmade bed quilt. "I made it myself," Jean smiled. "It's so beautiful, thank you ever so much," I said, giving them both a huge hug.

"Hey guys, remember me, your daughter?" laughed Alex. "I think you are gonna adopt Cat. Can we? Then she can be my sister!" "Guys, I'm very lucky to have my family back in Ireland but you're definitely my American family." And with that, Alex joined in the hugs.

"Okay girls, I guess you'd better get going and hit the road." Pete sounded sad at the thought of us leaving. "I really enjoyed the fun of having a pair of crazy girls in the house." "Hey, less of the crazy! Thanks for everything dad, mom. I love you guys and we'll see you real soon." "Don't leave it too long sweetie. Okay, now get going or you will get stuck in that highway traffic," Jean sighed and gave us both a hug. "Okay, okay, we are going," Alex smiled and blew a kiss to her parents then headed out of the driveway and we were off.

The road back to College seemed longer than before but we managed to keep our spirits up with a few songs which, fortunately for us, were confined to the car. Neither Alex nor I were blessed with the gift of song but we enjoyed belting out a good tune or two from the radio. "So Cat, what did you think of Chez Garner?" asked Alex. "I so love your parents - they are the best! Thank you so much for taking me home for the weekend. I just don't know what I'd have done at Deacon College without you. I might have had to give Carla a call and see if she wanted to hang out." "Fuck Cat, you wouldn't get that desperate, would you?" Alex joked.

"Thanks for coming. I don't know if I could survive a weekend with my parents without you for company. And with the whole Jake encounter, I'm so glad you were there." "Anytime sister. I think it's official, your parents have adopted me." "Yeah, I know. They loved you and I love you too, my bird of a feather!" "Ah, you had me at hello," I gushed back jokingly.

"The folks aren't too bad as parents go but sometimes I feel so suffocated when I'm at home. I was so nervous about leaving home for college but now I love my freedom. I can do whatever I want now without the 'Don't you think it's time you went to bed sweetheart?' or any of that." "I hear what you're screaming, Alex! It's like you miss home but you miss your freedom. Your folks seem pretty cool though."

"Yeah, they are. My mom works a lot," explained Alex. "What do your parents do?" I asked. "They're both cops. That's how they met, at work on a big case. My dad doesn't work anymore though. A few years ago he got shot on the job and he was never the same since, so he can't work out in the field. He works at the station a bit but he says it's not the same.

I think he really misses being in the thick of it and getting out and catching criminals. My mom is a sergeant and works crazy hours but she is really dedicated to the job," explained Alex. As she went on to tell me how her parents met and about growing up in a cop house, I was fascinated. The stories told at the dinner table must have been unbelievable. Pretty soon, we were back at college after our road trip. Back to the craziness. It was quite late so all we were fit for was to unpack the car and crash into the dorms.

"Holy shit Cat, we have been away for two days and we have like twenty messages on the answer machine. I feel so special!" Alex listened to all the phone messages, most of which were from Tom wondering when we were getting our silly asses back to see him. Some were from guys in Alex's classes looking for homework and to hang out with her. None, as usual, were for me.

Suddenly, the last message played and a familiar voice came on the line. "Hi Cat, it's Rick here. Just wanted to say hey and see if you had made any plans for your birthday. It's next week, right? Well, I'm always up for parties especially a twenty-first. I'd love to plan something special. Give me a call, my Irish lass!" Oh my God, I was so excited. A call from

Rick. I tried not to let Alex see that I was just bursting inside. Does this mean he is interested in me - the skinny funny-looking Irish girl? I couldn't wait to find out!

Chapter 6

Happy Birthday to Me

As the school week began, Alex was pretty quiet. I could tell she wasn't herself and was thinking about her weekend back home. Seeing her slimy ex-boyfriend, Jake had taken its toll.

When I finished class for the day, I made my way to the pool to start my shift. But first, I had to make sure I was looking my best as I had the lovely Rick working with me. "Why are you putting on the old makeup to work today, Cat?" Alex asked, "You should be putting on sunscreen instead!" Alex was trying to tease me and it totally succeeded as my fair skin turned sunburned red again. "I just wanted to make an effort to try and hide this damn sunburn," I replied casually, trying to explain myself.

The pool was pretty quiet when I arrived; just a few sun worshippers, lazing on their loungers as usual. As I looked over towards the office, I noticed Rick standing there in all his glory smiling back at me. His bronzed tan pecs and abs were just to die for!

"Hey Cat, I was hoping you were going to be working today. How's things, did you have a good weekend?" From what I could see, he was just as glad to see me as I was to see him - this might be a good sign, I wish! I filled him in on my adventure with Alex at her parents' house and visiting her hometown.

"You know what Cat? I could just listen to your accent all day. I love it. I'm sure you enjoyed it but it's nothing compared to Dublin. Do you miss Ireland much?" Rick seemed to be fixated on everything I said which was lucky for him as, of course, I talk a lot when the nerves got the best of me.

"I do miss Dublin. I love to go shopping up Grafton Street, that's our main shopping area, what could be better?"

"And, of course, the good old Irish pubs to go to?" laughed Rick. "You're not kidding there, mister. You can't beat Temple Bar. I do miss my friends but I've made such a wonderful friend over here. My roommate, Alex. She is the best. I really don't know what I'd do without her over here."

"It's great to find a good friend. She'll have to come out with us this weekend. I'm still organising your birthday, aren't I?" Rick asked like he was looking forward to it so much that he was going to burst with excitement. He was taking his job as party organiser very seriously. "Of course you can still organise my birthday. I'm so looking forward to it. I can't wait to be of legal drinking age over here."

As we chatted, I was thinking the same thing Rick was about me; I could sit and listen to him all day. I was ready to go jump in the pool and miraculously get a cramp in my leg so that Rick would have to jump in and save me. Oh, what a thought!

I was brought back to earth by a loud shout in my direction. “Hey you, Irish girl, I hope you have that sunscreen on!” It was Alex heading in our direction. “Hey there, American girl! Did you get out of class early?” “Na, I didn’t quite make it to class,” Alex replied in a naughty schoolgirl tone.

“Alexandra, what were you up to or should I say whom were you up to!” I laughed back.

“Tom and I decided to ditch class and go for a drive instead. We ended up at the mall as it’s Stacey’s birthday soon and Tom wanted me to help him pick out a nice gift for her. We just got back as Stacey was calling Tom on his cell looking for him - again. I told him to turn the damn thing off.”

“I swear that girl is a real stalker; she never lets Tom out of her sight. He has to tell her what he’s doing and where he’s going all the time. He had about ten calls from her while we were at the mall. It’s all a bit much if I’m honest. I really don’t think he’s happy but it’s none of my business. Whatever floats his boat. She was standing waiting for his return with her Carla clone posse. If Tom ever went to church, Stacey would be calling him and asking him to put Jesus on the phone just to make sure he was there. "

Alex had just finished her sentence when she looked up and noticed Rick. "Hello there, sorry did I disturb anything here?" Alex asked in a very alluring manner, looking right in my direction. The sunburned face was coming back again. "I'm guessing you're Rick, right? Cat has told me so much about you."

"Yes, I'm Rick and I'm guessing you must be Alex. Cat has told me a lot about you too," Rick joked. "It's very nice to meet you. You're held in high esteem by your roomie here." "Watch out, she is going to get a big head over there," I warned.

"Alex, Rick has kindly offered to organise my birthday party which will be at a club in the city. How exciting is that!" "Cool, we'll have to get Tom and the guys along from the Coffee House." "Do ya think we should invite Josh there, bird of a feather? Or maybe even Carla? Our favourite friends!" Alex and I laughed at the prospect. "Something tells me you girls are being rather sarcastic with your invitations," Rick said. I guess it was our private running joke.

We began to fill Rick in on our encounters with Carla and Josh who Rick thought was an asshole and agreed that Alex had a lucky escape.

"Well girl, have you finished your shift? I'm starving so let's go for dinner." Alex rubbed her stomach as if she hadn't seen food for days. "You go Cat, if you want. There are only fifteen minutes left of the shift and all the Sun Gods have pretty much gone for the day." Rick smiled and handed me my bag. "Besides, you guys have plenty of planning for this invitation list of yours."

"Thanks Rick, I owe you," I replied. As we made our way to the cafeteria, Alex couldn't help but quiz me about Rick. "Cat, that Rick is pretty hot. Did you see the body on that guy?" I already knew everything that she was saying. She saw the same attraction as I had the week before – the abs! Just then, Tom sat down beside us. "What are you ladies talking about?" "We are talking about perfectly toned abs and pecs if you must know," replied Alex. "Ah, so you guys are talking about me again then. I told you, if you want to feel my perfectly toned body, all you have to do is ask." Tom was so funny in a totally perverted kind of way. He had such great confidence and loved himself so much but at the same time, he did have the goods to back it up.

"Well ladies, what are you up to later? The college is selling tickets to a baseball game tonight. You guys fancy going?" Alex was not too keen on the idea. "I don't know. I'm not really down with the old sports. Movies yes but sports, I don't know." "Oh come on there, girl, you gotta go. It will be great fun. Cat, tell this Miss Sports Phobia that it will be a blast!" Tom was really putting pressure on Alex to go.

"Ah, go on Alex, it'll be a change from campus for the night anyway," I said, trying to help Tom. I was really into sports which I think was the only difference between Alex and me. "Why not get Stacey to go with you?" Alex replied. "Alex, if you're not keen on sports then my dear Stacey is surely not into sports! It's totally not her thing at all." I did wonder about Tom and Stacey's relationship because, in many ways, they were the perfect couple. They were both tall, beautiful and extremely popular but they seemed to have nothing in common. But hey, if it works, I guess don't knock it.

Tom managed to drag Alex to the game and, in the end, she really enjoyed it. To my delight, I did too. It was my first ever baseball game and after a million questions to Tom, I finally got the hang of it. The whole experience was amazing; the smell of the crisp cut grass in the open-air ballpark, the cheer of the crowd and the aroma of hot dogs and roasted peanuts floating in the warm evening breeze. I loved it – it was a real American experience. As we drove back from the ballpark, Tom wanted to make a stop at the ice cream parlour which was greeted with total agreement from Alex and me.

"So then Miss Alex, go on admit it! You had a good time at the baseball, right?" Tom teased. "It was okay I guess." Alex gave a slight smirk as if to admit defeat. "Okay? Oh come on, I heard you cheering and rooting for the team. You loved it out there. I'll have to get you back to the ballpark if it kills me." Tom had a winning smile on his face. For someone who wasn't really into sports, Alex had a great competitive streak and she loved to win, just like Tom. Together, they acted as if they were in competition for the Olympics.

The days went by so quickly that week that it was no time until the weekend arrived and, of course, the birthday that I had been waiting for with bated breath. I was twenty-one, legal and over the moon! I woke up to see a great big balloon tied to my bedpost and a large banner that read "Happy Birthday Bird". I looked up to see Alex sitting at the edge of my bed. "Hey birthday girl, I was ready to wake you up. I thought you were going to sleep through your birthday. Come on girl, let's get to the liquor store. You're legal now!" "Holy shit I am, hell let's go!"

I threw on a pair of old jeans and a shirt and we headed out to buy the all-important alcohol. The beer kegs at the frat parties were okay for a while but now I was ready for a good old pint of beer just like I used to have in the pubs back home. When we got to the liquor store, Alex stayed in the car for fear of getting asked for ID. As if we were going to rob a bank or something! I was like a kid in a candy shop. I stocked up on beer, wines and spirits and, as it was my birthday, a few shot glasses were purchased also. Making my way to the store clerk, who looked over his eyeglasses at me, I could feel butterflies in my stomach. What was I worried about? I was legal. They were not gonna call the cops and throw me in jail!

The store clerk looked at me and asked, "Can I see your ID, missy?" "Sure, no problem at all," I replied confidently, producing my Irish driver's licence out of my back pocket. The clerk looked at it for what seemed like forever and then announced, "I'm sorry, miss, what kind of ID is this?" "Oh, I'm from Ireland. It's my driver's licence from over there." I wasn't sure if he even understood what I had said because of my accent and I could tell he was like 100 years old. “Sorry miss. I can’t accept that. Have you any other form of ID?” What the fuck? This old-timer store clerk was surely not going to deny me my booze, especially on my twenty-first birthday!!

Trying to stay calm, I could see his name badge on his shirt and replied, “Hal, is it? I’m from Ireland and I’m going to Deacon College just up the road. Look, here is my college ID. It’s my twenty-first birthday today and I could really do with a celebratory drink.”

As Hal inspected my ID like he was the head of forensics at the FBI, I stood there with a huge, hopeful smile on my face. “Well, I guess this looks real to me. I’ve seen so many of you kids from Deacon trying to forge these college ID cards, I am a master at detecting a fake, you know.” Holy shit! “What the fuck is he, Columbo or something?” I thought. But I was glad that he believed me and I thanked him for being so stringent. “I’m sure you have had to deal with plenty of those students trying to catch you out. You’re very thorough, I have to say.” I was babbling again but this time I was totally sucking up so, next time, he wouldn’t give the third degree. “I’m Cat. I hope to see you again soon, Hal.” “Why thank you, Miss Cat. What a pleasure to meet a charming young lady." I quickly said my goodbyes and headed out the door to the waiting Alex in the car.

"What the fuck were you doing in there? Drinking half the shop before you bought it? I know it has been a while but holy shit, Cat, you were forever in there!" Alex exclaimed. "Jesus, Alex don't even go there. I just had a close encounter with what felt like the FBI." As I told Alex about having to convince the old guy of my age, we both had a good laugh about it. "Cat, it's so ironic that when you get to the right age and show your ID, they still don't believe you! I guess we'll have to be sixty with grey hair and false teeth to be believed."

That afternoon, we had a liquid lunch which consisted of a couple of beers finished off with two shots of vodka for dessert. We were getting quite happy and I was indeed getting into the party mood. Rick was picking us up at 8:00 pm so that gave us five hours to get ready and, for Alex to decide what to wear, she needed five hours. I wanted to look fabulous. To start with, it was my twenty-first and, more importantly, Rick was going to be there. To think that he wanted to plan my birthday gave me goosebumps. Does that mean he really likes me? What if he tries to kiss me? "Okay," I thought, "easy tiger, that's just the drink kickin' in. I must make sure he notices me." So I got my most prized commodity out of the drawer, my totally fabulous, life-of-its-own Wonder Bra! This Wonder Bra was my best friend for so many first dates. Well, it got me a first date at least!

Moving on to the bottle of wine, Alex and I totally pampered ourselves. We did each other's makeup, painted our nails and, of course, I curled Alex's hair with my trusty cold bottle of what used to be ice water but, today, was a nice cold bottle of beer so my fingers would not get burned.

Pretty soon, it was almost 8.00 pm and Rick was due to arrive at any minute. Before I had time to fantasise about him anymore, there was a knock on the door. It was Rick looking like Prince Charming. His blonde hair was wisped back from his face and his bulging biceps were rippling out of his T-shirt. Sex on a stick if ever I saw it. "Let's go, birthday girl. Your carriage awaits!" Rick smiled as he led Alex and me down the stairs to the stares of Carla and her girls. The only one who was not there was Stacey as she was actually defecting to the other side and heading out on the town with us as Tom's date, of course.

As we got to the car park, Rick pointed us in the direction of a minivan that he had ordered for the night. When I got in, everyone was there and a big surprise shout was heard from them all. Tom was on board along with the ever-present Stacey, the guys from the Coffee House and Rick's buddies who he introduced us to. There was Dave who looked extremely attractive and very much Alex's type, I thought. I could see a bit of double dating going on there. Rick with me and Alex with Dave - perfect. Maybe Alex was right. I had longed for James for so many years that I never really let myself fall too much for anyone else. They were just not James. Maybe falling in love with an American guy was just what I needed. Why not enjoy a little bit of foreign relations?

Just before I began to pick out the colour scheme for our wedding, Rick turned to Alex, produced a driver's licence out of his wallet and gave it to her. "Here Alex, you might need this since you're not of age yet." We had a look at this Californian driver's licence which, to our horror, looked absolutely nothing like her!

"Rick, where did you get this? This person looks nothing like me!" The lady in the photograph looked forty years old and had bags under her eyes. The only similarity to Alex was that she had blonde hair and a bad blonde bottle job at that. Alex and I laughed at the thought of giving the security guy a driver's licence that looked absolutely nothing like Alex. "Don't worry guys, it will be fine, as long as you have some sort of ID the security guys don't give a shit, trust me," Rick replied confidently.

The van got to the city pretty quickly, too quickly actually as I was having such a fantastic time with Rick. As we pulled up to the side of the road, Rick got us all out of the minivan and we walked the boardwalk where all the cool clubs were at. My eyes totally lit up. It was amazing. I felt as if I was back in Dublin again, making my way through the streets to the hustle and bustle of Temple Bar. There was line upon line of nightclubs and each one was as busy as the next.

"Cat, I could listen to you talk for like forever. You're so easy to get along with," Rick smiled. "Rick, thank you so much for organising my birthday bash. It was really sweet of you." I looked into his sea-blue eyes and felt like I could just jump right in and totally lose myself in his lashes. Rick gave me that perfect smile again and chuckled, "Anything for my fellow lifeguard."

At that moment, Rick stopped me as everyone else walked a few steps ahead. "Cat, can I ask you a question?" I thought this was it, Rick was going to ask me out! My heart raced and I felt like my birthday and Christmas had come at once. Then Rick leaned over and said, "Cat, do you think your friend Alex would be interested in me?" Boom! I came down to earth with a crash! My heart sank. I should have known that a guy like Rick would never be interested in a girl like me anyway. Of course Rick would be interested in Alex and not in a skinny, pale, funny-looking Irish girl.

"Cat I've been watching her in the van. She's amazing and I'd really like to ask her out. What do you think, my Irish buddy?" Rick asked hoping that I would help him out. "Buddy, Buddy," I thought, well that was that. All the fantasising was just in my head. Once again, I was just a buddy. The story of my life. This was like James Part Two. "Well Rick, Alex is single." Rick was clearly delighted with my response. "Excellent! Cat, will you put in a good word for me?" Rick pleaded. "Of course I will, sure that's what buddies do." The words came out of my mouth so quickly that I didn't have time to think.

As we walked along the row of nightclubs, we suddenly stopped. "Okay this is it, THE club of all clubs on the Strip. You will love it!" Rick announced proudly. "Look Alex, you go in with me and make sure you act confident. You are that woman in the ID and make sure the security guys know it." "Holy shit, I hope not, she looks ancient!" Alex cringed.

Rick had us all in line as if he was the sergeant of an army regiment and this was a military operation we were undertaking. I never thought getting into a club would be so challenging. Well for me, at least, it was easy. I was twenty-one and loving it. Alex, on the other hand, was becoming worried. "Oh my goodness, Cat, I'm going to pee my pants I'm so nervous! This ID doesn't look like me at all!" As Alex hesitantly gave the security guy the dodgy ID, she gave him a great big Californian smile which totally melted his hard persona and he laughed back, "Here ya go darlin' and here is your cup. Ladies drink free all night tonight."

Thank goodness Alex got in! "Cat, I'm going to the bathroom! I'll see you at the bar!" Alex looked at me with two thumbs up and a triumphant smile on her face. I hung back a bit and made sure all was well then, I made my way up to the door and proudly produced my driver's licence to the security guy. "Sorry little lady, what kind of ID is this? This is not a proper ID." He gave it back to me a little confused by what he saw. Then, remembering Hal's expression at seeing my Irish driver's licence earlier, I should have known that he would be confused. "Oh, it's an Irish driver's licence. I'm Irish, don't ya know, and it's my twenty-first birthday, see?" I showed him the date on my licence but he was not convinced. "Look sweetie, I don't give a damn if it's an English, Irish or Scottish licence, it's not ID that we accept." "Okay, here is my College ID, look it shows my date of birth." Thinking back to Hal, it totally did the trick for him.

"Sorry miss, I don't accept College ID. You got a passport or something you can show me?" Like I frikkin' carry my passport everywhere I go, mother fucker, what am I, James Bond? "No sir, I don't," I replied more calmly. "Well then, I can't let you in. Move aside." And that was it. He shushed me out of the way on my own birthday. The dumb ass let Alex in on a forty-year-old's ID but would not accept my Irish ID. What discrimination! What an injustice! But I was not about to argue with him. The last thing I needed was to be rejected from a club and thrown into the county jail.

As I sat on the sidewalk, I heard a warm, familiar voice behind me whisper, "Hey birthday girl, what's going on?" The voice wasn't Rick but to my delight it was Mike. “Hi Mike, I’m so glad to see you. I didn’t think you would show up! I haven’t seen you around in like forever! What are you doing here?” I was ecstatic to see him. “I did get a cute invitation in my post box the other day from your sweet self and, if there is a twenty-first birthday party going on, I’m there honey! Now the only thing left to ask is why the hell are you sittin’ out here on the sidewalk?” It was at that exact moment that I saw Alex running out to join me. “Cat, what are you doing out here? The party is inside, don’t ya know! I went to the bathroom and waited for you at the bar. Rick and I have been looking for you for the past ten minutes!” “I can’t get in! That fuck nut of a security guard won’t accept my ID! He accepted your piece of shit forgery but not mine, what’s that all about?” I sat back on the sidewalk feeling totally dejected.

Alex was not impressed at all. “Well, this is a load of SH1T if ever I heard it! It’s your twenty-first birthday for Christ’s sake and you are sitting outside when you should be in there havin’ fun!” “Thanks for pointing out the obvious, Alex.” I was getting so upset but I didn’t want to be a wet blanket and make Alex feel bad. After all, it wasn’t her fault that the security guard was a prick. As she attempted to make her way to the security guard and give him a piece of her mind, I had to rugby tackle her back to the sidewalk. “Easy on there, tough girl. What ya doing? There’s no point in you getting thrown out too!”

“I’m staying out here with you. You’re not staying here on your own,” Alex declared. She was such a sweetheart for saying it but I didn’t want her to have to suffer, besides, she was so looking forward to a good party after seeing the shit face, Jake, the weekend before.

As I pulled Alex aside, away from Mike for a moment, I told her, “No Alex, you go on in and enjoy yourself. Drink some for me, will you? Besides, I have Mike here to keep me company. I want to hang out with him for a while. Alex, go back inside and, besides, I think Rick wanted a dance with you.” Trying to put in that good word for Rick, I gave Alex a reassuring wink suggesting I think he might be interested in her. I ordered Alex back to the club with strict instructions to have a drink or twelve for me! “Okay Cat, I’ll go in just to tell Rick that you are out here as he was wondering where his Irish buddy went to. Will you be okay for a minute or two?”

As Alex went back in to tell Rick the situation, I turned to Mike and smiled.

For some reason, Mike always seemed to be there at the right time whether it was my first frat party for a dance or my sunburn experience and now he was there when I really needed him. Maybe my infatuation with Rick, which was clearly in my head since he made it quite clear we were only buddies, had clouded my feelings for Mike. I had a guy who was always there for me. Why did I not see it? Maybe Mike was just the guy to end my run of 'let's just be friends' reactions.

"Mike, I'm sorry you have to sit out here with me. You should be in there having fun with everyone." I felt so guilty and I was sure the last thing he wanted to do on a Saturday night was sit on the sidewalk with a skinny Irish girl.

"Don't worry about it at all Cat. I don't like those types of clubs anyway," Mike said, trying to make me feel better. "What too loud or something?" I asked. Mike smiled and said, "Yeah, something like that. There's a little coffee house across the street. Fancy going for a latté or something?"

Mike was so kind and considerate - not like the average guy at all. As we sat talking over two lattés, I got to know Mike better. Why was I not giving the guy a chance? Was I blinded by my lust for Rick? Suddenly, a knock at the coffee shop window startled us both. It was a slightly drunk Alex and Rick looking as beautiful as ever. I noticed he had his arm around Alex. However, it was probably to hold her up as she had surely had plenty of drinks for herself and me! “Hi guys! What are you two love birds up to?” Alex joked. Mike was clearly embarrassed as his face started to go like mine at the pool – red lobster.

“Hey bird, you might need a strong cup of coffee to sober you up.” I tried to change the subject as I could see Mike was becoming quite uncomfortable.

“Yes, indeed my lady, I’ll get the coffees in. Would you guys like the same again?” Rick asked. Both Mike and I declined as, after our fourth latté, I think we could have turned into a pot of coffee.

While Rick was getting the coffees, Alex slipped in, slouched beside me and drunkenly tried to whisper but it was more a shout, “Cat, I have a secret to tell you!” At this stage, Mike got up as he could tell that Alex was looking for a girly chat. “Okay then,” Mike declared, “I guess I gotta go to the bathroom. I’ll be back in a bit.” With that, Mike got up and winked at me as he left. He was so very sensitive and knew when to be there for me and when to make a quick exit.

While she placed her finger on her lips to hush herself, Alex proceeded to let me in on her secret. “Cat, I didn’t want to ask this question in front of Mike but tell me, do you have feelings for Rick?” After my conversation with Rick earlier, it was clear that my feelings for Rick were not reciprocated. “Oh no Alex, sure Rick and I are just lifeguard buddies, that’s all. We are just friends and, besides, I’ve had a wonderful evening with Mike.” I tried to reassure Alex that Rick was of no interest to me as I had heard those four words I always got from James, we are just friends!

“I have to tell you, Rick asked me out on a date!!” Alex said excitedly. “Cat, I really like him but I don’t want to be one of those friends.” “What friends, Alex?” I asked. “One of those friends back in Ireland who dates James and rips your heart out. I know you never told them but please tell me, I don’t want to hurt you Cat, you mean so much more to me than some guy. Jonny taught me that, remember?”

“Alex, you’re not one of those friends and I am definitely not interested,” I declared. Or rather, Rick was definitely not interested in me. “You should go for it, bird. I think you would be perfect for each other.” Looking at Alex and Rick, they would actually be the perfect couple.

“I really like him, Cat. What should I do?” Alex looked at me for advice with hope in her eyes, firstly for reassurance that I was not mad at her and secondly that I’d be happy as she obviously was. With the heartache of the ass hole, Jake, behind her, maybe Rick was just what Alex needed and I was happy for her. Besides, this was the story of my life. "Cat, your such a great pal, who's your friend?" That was what James had done my whole life. Rick was obviously into Alex and liked her a lot and I wasn't going to be one of those friends who would say, "If I can't have him, then no one can." Who was I to stand in the way of true love?

As I gave Alex a big, convincing smile, I reassured her that she had my approval. "You go for it girl. Yes, he is gorgeous. I get to see him at the pool, remember? Alex, you are my best friend and if you're happy then I'm happy." Alex gave me a huge hug, "Cat, I'm so happy. I never would have thought Rick would be into me. Anyway Cat, what about you, spending all night with Mike! He really likes you Cat, I can tell. I'm picking up these vibes from him." Alex gave me a playful nudge on the shoulder as I smiled. Alex always had a way of making me smile.

Mike was a wonderful guy. Maybe Rick was just not meant for me and there was a great guy who sat outside on a sidewalk with me for half the night. Maybe he did like me. I started to wonder. "Alex, Mike is such a wonderful guy. I have never met a guy who is so sensitive and caring. I feel like I can talk to him about anything but I don't know, he seems quite distant when it comes to showing his emotions," I confessed. "Cat, I wouldn't worry about that. I think he is just shy. He likes you I can tell. I can feel that vibe, trust me!" Alex gave me a reassuring nod just as Mike got back to his seat and Rick returned with the coffees.

"Sweet Jesus, how long does it take to make a cup of coffee? I thought they went to Columbia to go pick the fuckin' beans, mother fuckers!" "Here ya go babe, a latté for you." Rick sat by Alex and stretched his long muscular arm around her waist. She smiled with delight, so widely I thought she was going to burst. I looked at Mike and smiled suggesting he could put his arm around me, but Mike looked embarrassed and his face began to redden again. Did he like me and was too shy, as Alex had thought?

As we made our way out of the coffee shop and headed back to the minivan, Alex and Rick walked ahead. In that moment, I decided to throw caution to the wind. I was convinced Mike was just the type of guy I needed and I wanted to let him know there and then. I stopped and turned to him, his warm dark eyes looking back at me.

"Mike, thank you so much for looking after me tonight." "Cat, it was nothing. I would…" Before Mike could finish his sentence, I planted a warm and lingering kiss on his soft lips. Once I had released him, he looked at me in surprise. I was not expecting a surprised look and he seemed upset with me. My heart sank again. He doesn't like me! Oh great, my night was just getting better and better.

"Mike, I'm sorry. I shouldn't have done that and, by the looks of it, you're mad at me. I really like you and I just thought that, because of the way you looked after me tonight, you liked me too and, well, I've just had the worst birthday anyone could possibly have and now, to top it all off, you're mad at me! I'm sorry if I over-stepped the mark." As I went off on another verbal diarrhoea moment, due to the embarrassing position I had put myself in, Mike took my hand and put his finger to my lips, probably to shut me up and to try to explain his reaction.

"Cat, I'm not mad at you. It was a bit of a surprise and I'm truly flattered, I am, but I'm..." "You're not interested in me, it's okay, you can say it, I'm a big girl and I can take rejection." I was trying to convince myself that I was able to take rejection but twice in one night? A girl's got to have a bit of pride, ya know! "Cat, you're right. I'm not interested in you," Mike replied. As I turned to walk back to the car, Mike took my arm to stop me.

"Not so fast there, my Irish beauty. Look Cat, the reason that I'm not interested in you is that I'm not interested in any girls. I'm gay!" Mike confessed. "What? You're kidding, right?" I exclaimed. "No Cat, I'm not kidding. It's true. I'm totally 100% gay and, right now, I so wish I wasn't. To have a hot lady like you coming on to him would be every guy's dream come true but the only thing is that I'm not like most guys. Cat, I truly haven't told anyone at all. I just thought you would understand. Please do not tell a soul, not even Alex. I'm not ready to come out yet." His face was as serious as a judge and he was shaking. It was as if he had been waiting his whole life to tell someone and that someone was me!

"Fuck me, Mike, how long have you been holding this in? It makes a lot of things clear. No wonder you looked like I had just shot you when I kissed you!" We began to laugh and then I gave him a warm hug and kissed him on the cheek. His shaking began to ease and he looked at me with a friendly smile. "Mike, I promise this is just between us. I feel so honoured that you felt you could tell me about this." "Cat, you are a very special person. Maybe it's your Irish charm but you're not like the American girls out here," Mike complimented me. "What, you mean because I have a personality?" I joked. "I swear, I think Alex is the only girl I talk to over here.

I think she was Irish in a past life." "The way she was drinking tonight I think she is definitely a little Irish." Mike was always so very funny and made jokes about things even when he was pouring his heart out to me. "Cat, thank you for understanding. There is so much I want to tell you but let's leave it for another time. We'd better get back to the minivan."

As Mike and I walked back to the car, he held my hand and gave me a little wink as we caught up with Alex and Rick. Alex looked down at my hand firmly in Mike's hand and raised her eyebrows to check if we had got together. I gave her a little shake of my head. We had our own sign language these days.

On the way home, I had my head on Mike's shoulder which, I think, was a lot lighter after the load he had been carrying was lifted. I smiled as I thought about Alex and how she had such strong vibes coming from Mike. Little did she know they were gay vibes! So, tonight my Prince Charming happened to be a Queen… just my luck!

Chapter 7

There's No Crying in Baseball

The next morning, I woke up early feeling very fresh and totally sober. I had visions of me hugging a toilet seat after my drunken twenty-first birthday but, then again, since I was downing coffee all last night, I think I was still wired. At least I can thank the security man for something - no hangover! I turned to wake up Alex but she wasn't there!!

I jumped up and headed to the bathroom thinking the poor thing was probably hugging the toilet bowl but she was nowhere to be seen. Now I was starting to get worried. She did come home with me last night, didn't she? As I threw on my jeans and a top to go look for her, I looked out the window to see Alex dancing across the campus as if she was in Swan Lake or something.

"Holy shit, she's still drunk," I thought. If any of the campus security caught her, they would call her mum and dad. As I ran out to get her, the lovely Carla came out of her hovel… I mean room. "Hello Cat, where's your friend Alex this morning? Are you guys not joined at the hip these days?" she snarled.

"Hi Carla," I growled back. She was like the Wicked Witch of the West on a bad day. "I'm just about to go meet Alex for breakfast right now but why am I telling you that? You probably already knew," I smiled. "Oh, I can see Alex is up and at it. She seems to be singing outside. What is she, auditioning for a musical or something?"

Fuck, now she was singing! She must be more drunk than I thought! As I dismissed Carla's jibes, I ran downstairs to save my friend from the ever-vigilant security guards. As I ran to catch up with the all-singing, all-dancing Alex, she saw me from a distance and ran to meet me, only to fall on her ass by my feet.

"Jesus, Alex are you okay? I was so worried. Where have you been? You didn't even go to bed - it hasn't been slept in!" I exclaimed. "I'm so sorry Cat, I really am but I have had the most amazing night of my life!" Alex shouted excitedly. "Shit, I wish I did. I had the exact opposite," I thought. "So, where have you been?" I asked. "Cat, you're angry with me. I'm so sorry. Please forgive me, do you forgive me?"

Alex wasn't making any sense at all. "Alex, what's wrong, what happened?" Now I was getting angry. "I spent the night at Rick's and Cat, I totally, completely absolutely think, no, I know I'm in love!! Please don't be angry with me!" Alex was bursting like she had won the lottery.

"Alex, I'm not angry. I was just worried about you. I woke up and you were nowhere to be seen. You could have left a note to let me know where you were, ya know!" I was beginning to sound like her mum! Alex looked exhausted. She needed to get some rest as I didn't think she got much sleep last night.

"Come on Juliet, tell me about your night with Romeo while we get back to the dorms." Alex began to tell me how Rick called her and asked her to come over to watch a DVD. "Cat, how funny, Rick didn't even have a DVD player if you know what I mean! We sort of had to make our own entertainment. We…" "Okay there, hoochie, that's enough information. I think I can let my own dirty imagination fill in the rest." We laughed as we headed home. Alex yawned. "Okay sleeping beauty, you have a rest. I gotta go to the library. I have a paper due tomorrow. I'll meet you on the second floor of the library." "Shoot Cat, is there a second floor in the library? Hell, if I know! I don't think I have ventured past the computers to check my email," Alex confessed. "You're too funny missy. Get some sleep. To make it easier for you, I'll be on the first floor of the library in case you get lost with all those books and shit." I kissed her on the forehead and left her to sleep off her night of passion.

A few hours and a couple of drafts of my business paper later, a rejuvenated Alex came through the library doors. "Hey there whore, what ya doin'?" Alex joked with a smile as warm as a hot day by the pool. I had never seen her like this before. It was as if nothing could get her down and she was destined to have a constant smile on her face the rest of her life. To be honest, it was great to see Alex so happy. Last weekend's heartache at meeting the slime ball, Jake, seemed a million miles away.

"I'm just finishing off this Business Studies paper. It's gotta be in for tomorrow," I explained. "Are ya done yet? I wanna go to Walmart; we need provisions. We need beer." Alex sat like an impatient kid. "Sure we got a shit load of beer yesterday, didn't we? Are you craving more, my little alcopop?" I joked. "No, it's not for me. I promised Rick you would get some beer for him now that you're twenty-one and all," Alex smiled. I was beginning to become an alcohol pimp, hooking guys up with beer. "Yes, I guess I wanna go and get some stuff too. Let's go. I'm done with this place. I swear, libraries give me the shits." "I know what you mean jellybean," Alex agreed "There are actually three floors in this place! I checked for ya, Alex." "Man, I gotta get into this thing called study," Alex said as she jokingly picked up a book and flicked through it. "Work? The only thing you will be working on these days is Mr. Rick."

"Oh shut up Cat, what about you and Mr. Mike?" I smiled and walked on as if I didn't hear her. After Mike's confessed to me last night, I didn't want Alex to see my expression. She was beginning to know me too well since we were together 24/7 and she knew me better than anyone ever had.

On our way to Walmart, Alex was flying down the highway but came to a stop as the traffic began to back up due to what appeared to be an accident. Yes, we were stuck on the highway travelling at like 10 mph. "What the hell's going on, Cat? Can you see anything?" Alex was beginning to get frustrated. She was the ultimate driving freak. She loved to get out there driving and never gave a hoot about speed limits; another trait that she got from her dad.

"Looks like a bit of an accident up ahead. It's over to the side now so it's just these cars in front slowing down to have a look at what's happened, that's what's going on. What's the American word for people who slow down and stare at an accident?" I knew there was a word for it but just couldn't remember it. I needed my American dictionary. "I don't know Cat. Nosey fuckers, is that the word you're looking for? Just kidding, they're called rubberneckers."

"Rubberneckers, yes, that's it." I was beginning to learn the American lingo quite well. As we got to Walmart an hour later, we were ready for a beer right there, right then! Traffic jams were not the best thing in 30-degree heat.

As we did our ritual walk around the store, which usually meant covering the entire area of Walmart, I spotted something that I had wanted since I went to the baseball game a few weeks back, a baseball bat and glove! "Oh Alex, I want one of these!" Alex looked at me as if I was crazy. "Why in God's earth do ya want a baseball bat? You planning on hitting me with it?"

"No, I've always wanted one and you can teach me how to play!" "Do I look like Babe Ruth?" Alex replied sarcastically. "Come on Alex, let's play baseball later!" I pleaded like a little kid to her mum. "Okay, I will get you the baseball bat for a belated birthday present but we have to get the glove and ball." I was so excited as I got my baseball bat and picked out a ball. "Jesus Alex, these balls are huge and rock hard!" Alex replied "Girl, that's what all the ball players say." She always had a funny, and usually dirty, comment. It made me laugh so much.

Once we walked the length and breadth of Walmart and bought a brewery full of beer, we decided to hit the road. The drive back to campus was a lot quicker as the traffic had cleared from the accident and, of course, Alex's need for speed kicked in and we were feeling the warm breeze on our faces. "I tell ya, Alex, you are a real speed demon. Have you ever had a ticket? The way you fly, it's a wonder you haven't!" I joked. "I know I love to drive fast but I'm an accomplished driver. My parents are cops, remember? They taught me all I needed to know. God help me!" Alex went on to tell me about how wonderful Rick was to her last night.

"Cat, that's the only thing that concerns me about Rick. I can see myself really falling for him but I just hope he doesn't break my heart, ya know? He just seems too cool to be in a serious relationship." I could tell Alex was really concerned. The last thing she wanted to do was fall in love and get her heart ripped out again. That guy Jake really had done a good job on poor Alex. She was looking for love but she didn't want to get hurt again.

"Alex, just see how it goes for now. If you guys are getting serious, you gotta let him know how you feel and that you don't want to get hurt again. Just enjoy it for now, bird. I can tell you really like him because you have not shut the fuck up about him all way home!!" I said jokingly. "I know Cat, am I obsessed or what and I've only met the guy!"

As we got back to campus, I was getting excited about my baseball purchase I wanted to get out there right away and play ball. "Come on Alex, let's go out to the playing field and hit some balls, is that what the ball players say?" "Cat, I can't be getting all hot and sweaty. I gotta see Rick later and, besides, what if he sees me running like a possessed freak around that field? Oh, I would be mortified!" I couldn't believe it. My best friend was turning into a Carla clone! "Alex, it's only a little play about! You're sounding like Stacey talking about Tom or something! Come on, burn your bra! So what if he sees you sweaty? It might be a turn-on!" I joked.

Alex came to her senses and realised she was acting like one of those needy, perfect girlfriends that we made fun of. "You're right, Cat, I'll let him see me as me!" "You go girl!" and with a high five, we headed out of the dorms to the ballpark.

As we made our way outside, we were stopped by the bitch troll from hell, as Alex and I so fondly named her, Carla. She was with her usual posse of Susan, Pattie and Stacey. When she was with Tom, Stacey was cool but, as a Carla clone, she was under the troll's spell. Today, there was an extra member of the posse, a girl called Susan.

Susan was the manager of the Coffee House where Alex and Tom worked, which is why we knew her so well. If Alex was working, I was there too and she joked that I might as well have had a job in the place too. Susan was such a nice person. What the hell was she doing talking to Carla? I hoped she hadn't taken Susan to the dark side!

"Hi Alexandra! Hi Catherine!" Carla snarled. She was the only person on campus who called us by our full names which, of course, we hated. "Ladies, can you please come over here? I need to talk to you about something." Alex and I looked at each other. Fuck! What did we do now?

"Alex, I was in the Coffee House last night and Susan here was in a bit of a bad situation. You were apparently scheduled to work last night, correct?" Carla gave Alex a razor-sharp look as she tried to catch her out.

Alex was slightly taken aback by the accusation but then, thinking back, she thought she might have been scheduled to work last night. Not acknowledging Carla, Alex turned to her boss, "Susan, gosh, was I supposed to work last night? I'm so very sorry. It was Cat's twenty-first birthday and I just couldn't miss it. Sorry Susan."

Susan was a very shy girl and, not wanting to make a big deal about it, was completely fine about the whole thing. Carla, on the other hand, was not.

"You know Alexandra, the way you have been treating Susan and your job in the Coffee House is really not on. As a Residence Association member, I really have to say that you are not taking your job very seriously. Susan was rushed off her feet last night and, from the way you were this morning, you were downing drinks and having a good time." Coming to Alex's defence, Susan replied, "Alex, don't worry about it. I'm sorry, I didn't mean to make you feel bad. Of course you had to be at Cat's birthday." Susan was the type of girl who you would let down but then she would apologise for you doing that to her!

Susan seemed happy enough about the situation but Carla was not going to let it lie. "Susan, you have to be firmer with your employees. Did you not tell your employees that the staff handbook states missing too many shifts constitutes a dismissal? Now Susan, I'm not trying to tell you how to do your job but…"

The bitch troll was unbelievable. She was bullying Susan just to get at Alex. "Why don't you shut the fuck up, Carla! What has this got to do with you anyway?" Alex exploded. "Susan, don't worry about it, you don't need to fire me. I know you wouldn't do that you're too nice a person unlike some people," Alex said, looking in Carla's direction. "I'm quitting the job anyway. Are you happy now, Carla?" Alex and I then turned on our heels and left Carla and her clones behind. We could tell that she was shooting daggers at us; we could feel them ripping into our backs.

As we got to the ballpark, Alex let out a huge scream, "Fuck that fucking bitch fucking annoys me! What a fucker!" Alex let rip. I could tell Carla had really gotten to her. "Okay Cat, let me see what kinda pitch you got. I wanna get rid of some of that bitch troll frustration!!" Alex hollered. "I take it the pitch is me throwing it at your face, right?" I was getting the terms right. "Okay Alex, here it comes!" I yelled back. As I turned to throw the baseball, we heard someone shouting to us from across the field. It was Tom. Alex turned to look at him at the totally wrong moment as I had just thrown the ball in her direction. I could see, in slow motion, that it was going to hit but there was nothing I could do to stop it! Clunk!

The baseball hit Alex directly on the side of the face and, on impact, she fell off her feet and was out cold!

Tom and I ran to her as fast as we could. "Alex, Alex!" I screamed "Are you okay? Are you alive? Say something! I'm so sorry!" I could see her coming round and, eventually, Tom and I managed to get her to sit up. "Gosh, I always knew I could sweep a girl off her feet but I never thought they would faint just from hearing my voice! You okay there, sweetie?" Tom, always the joker, managed to get a smile from Alex. "I think I'm okay guys. Good pitch Cat!" "So sorry bird. I didn't mean to literally hit you in the face! We might have to get you over to the nurse just to make sure you're okay." I could see a large lump forming on the side of her head already. Tom scooped Alex up in his strong arms and carried her to the student association building where the nurse's office was located.

As we sat outside waiting for the nurse to see us, I heard a familiar voice call me and I looked around to see a waving Melanie teetering over to me in her high heel stilettos. I had not seen Melanie since the day she picked me up from the airport. It seemed a lifetime away from that day. "My Cat, don't you look great. How's my Irish Rose doing? I hear you have really settled into life at Deacon College. Now, watch that lovely fair skin of yours!" Melanie chatted for a short while and we filled her in on life at college, the annoying Carla and her interfering but mostly how well Alex and I have been enjoying College life. As Mel left us, Alex was beginning to feel the effects of the baseball collision. "Holy shit Cat, that Melanie woman can talk. I thought you could talk for the Olympics but she takes the gold. How come she called you the Irish rose?" "It's just an Irish expression that people call a girl over there," I explained. "If you're the Irish Rose on campus, what the fuck am I the American thorn? Probably, if Carla has anything to do with it! Fuck my head hurts like a mother fucker! I tell ya, it's karma for me taking Jonny's tennis racquet. He has cast a spell on that racquet until he gets it back!" Tom and I laughed at Alex's conspiracy theory. "Come on bird, remember, there's no crying in baseball!" I tried to make Alex smile as I could tell she was in pain.

"Alex, I also have a bone to pick with you. What's this I hear about you getting fired from the Coffee House? You can't get fired! What am I going to do without you? We're a team!"

Tom was kidding with Alex to go and get her job back. "Oh, I guess Stacey told you, right? Well Tom, for your information, I didn't get fired. I quit. I didn't want to give Carla the satisfaction of making poor Susan fire me so I quit. I don't need the job anyway and it will give me more time to spend with Rick," Alex explained.

At that point, Tom's eyebrow rose up. "Rick, Rick who? Not Rick the lifeguard?" Tom looked quite surprised. "Yes, we are dating now. So you know Rick?" Alex asked excitedly. "Yeah, I know him a bit from hanging out at the pool. I didn't know you were dating anyone, Alex," Tom answered as if he was Alex's father. He was becoming quite interested in her love life.

"So we hooked up last night at Cat's birthday. It was after you left, I think, Tom. I had the most amazing night." Alex began to fantasise again and momentarily forgot about her injury but it quickly came back to her as she began to stand up and almost fell down again on top of Tom and me. "Easy there, tiger, don't be getting too carried away by Mr. Rick. You have a concussion or something like that so you'd better stay seated," I advised.

After a while, the nurse came out to see us. Alex sat, her head throbbing in pain with her hand over her eye and, when she took her hand away, she revealed a large bump below her eye. "Oh, it's gonna be a big one," the nurse exclaimed. "Now dear, how on God's green earth did you manage to get a shiner?" I explained that I had accidentally thrown a baseball in her direction and that Alex was looking the other way. Simple – a complete accident.

"So, your friend threw a baseball at you? Shoot, you have a nice friend there! Alexandra honey, are you seeing stars or anything? I'll go get you a glass of water." The nurse went to get the water and looked at me like I had intentionally tried to kill Alex or something. What a bitch! "Are you seeing stars? What the hell, it's not frikkin' Looney Tunes! How about having a glass of water? Never mind a frikkin' glass of water, get an ice pack!!" I exclaimed. Tom began to laugh. "Tom, it's not funny. I think she is going to arrest me under the charge of being a terrible friend or something."

Alex laughed, "Cat, don't worry. I still love you, birds of a feather, right? It wasn't your fault. If someone hadn't shouted over to me, I wouldn't have turned and you wouldn't have hit me so it's Tom's fault." Alex looked jokingly at Tom. She knew I felt terrible about what happened.

"I see the way it is, blame the guy for it all!" Tom defended himself. "Damn sure blame the guy. I blame guys for everything," Alex retorted as if she was the founding member of the women's rights movement. Just then, the nurse came back with that water and, to my relief, an icepack. She ordered Alex to rest and to stay away from baseballs while looking at me when she said it. "Come on tough girl, you need a man to help you back to your dorms, don't you?" Alex relented. She couldn't get to the dorms with just skinny me. Sometimes a guy does come in handy. Tom lifted Alex up in his strong arms and carried her across campus to the dorm rooms where, of course, the bitch troll and her clones were standing guard at the door and taking note of all the comings and goings.

Stacey was, of course, with Carla and was quite surprised to see another woman, especially Alex, in the arms of her boyfriend. "Tom, can I ask what you're doing?" Stacey asked. "Relax babe. Alex had an accident so I'm helping her back to the dorms. She was finding it hard to stand up so I'm just helping a friend out," Tom tried to defend himself. Alex and I looked at each other and smirked. We had started a domestic, just what we needed, especially since we were in the clones' bad books already.

Tom carried Alex upstairs to our dorm room and gently laid her on her bed. He was so wonderful and I was glad he was there. I was always terrible in an emergency. "Now missy, you take care now and have a rest and Cat, make sure she doesn't go out raving tonight! Doctor's orders!" Tom smiled and winked at Alex then left to calm down his jealous girlfriend.

Just as Tom closed the door, Alex tried to get out of bed. "Yo, sick girl! Where do you think you are going?" I shouted. "Cat, I gotta get ready. I have a date with Rick later and I don't want to look like I've done ten rounds with Rocky. Can you put some concealer on this shiner?" "Hey there missy, you must have hit your head harder than I thought! You're not going anywhere tonight. Loverboy will have to just wait until you can actually stand up without keeling over!" It was amazing. Alex was hardly able to stand up but here she was, walking on air when it came to Rick.

"I tell you what, I'll bring the phone over to your bed and you can call him and tell him what happened." Alex smiled and relented. It was as if she had taken Rick cocaine last night and needed to get her fix. Alex called Rick and began to tell him what had happened and, no sooner had she told him about the baseball accident than he was over in the dorm room.

"Hey Hun, are you okay?" Rick rushed into our room and sat by Alex's bed. It was amazing. Alex had Tom taking care of her and now Rick!

Remembering my collapse from heat stroke, I wished that I could have a guy who would drop the phone and come rushing to me. At least I had Mike there to look after me and, even though he did bat for the other side, I could always say I had a guy who cared for me. When I stopped daydreaming and came back to reality, I realised that three was a crowd so I tried to say my goodbyes.

"Hey Irish girl, where are you going?" asked Alex. "Mike wants me to watch Top Gun with him. He knows I love that movie." I tried to act casual and not for one minute think of it as a date or Alex would get suspicious. But, of course, she saw right through me. "A movie with Mike? Is that what they call it? You'd better watch out; Rick asked me to watch a DVD last night and he doesn't have a DVD player!" Alex winked at me suggesting I should go for it with Mike. If only she knew there was no chance of anything like that. "Top Gun! Man, that movie is so gay!" Rick joked. I smiled as Rick had no idea. Then I left the lovers alone so that Rick could give Alex the fix she was craving.

Chapter 8

Happy Hump Day

The next day, I woke up in very unfamiliar territory… in a guy's bed, Mike's to be exact. "Good morning Sleeping Beauty, how's it going?" Mike smiled at me as I rubbed the sleep out of my eyes. "Holy shit Mike! Did I stay here all night? Why did you not wake me?" "You were so peaceful sleeping during the movie and I didn't want to wake you. Besides, you enjoyed the movie so much you were out like a light only 30 minutes into it!" "Gotta love Top Gun," I joked. "Mike, I'd better get going. Alex will be wondering where the hell I am!" I remembered how freaked out I was when she didn't return from Rick's the night before. "Alex called last night looking for you, so I told her you were here with me. She was very pleased and I think Rick stayed at your place last night." I smiled. Well, at least one of us is getting some.

Mike was so sweet and kind and he would be perfect boyfriend material. He was the type of guy who would really be there for a girl. He was smart, funny and really cute. Too bad he was gay. I was dreaming again. Getting back to reality, I smiled at Mike and thought about how much he had had to hold back. My so-called love life entailed a guy who thought of me as a sister. I wondered if Mike had ever experienced unrequited love.

"So Mike, now that we have shared a bed together, you know you can tell me anything! How long have you known you were gay? Does your family know? Have you had any relationships?" I was fascinated by Mike's circumstances and, in a way, could totally relate. It was like I never came out, so to speak, to James and told him my feelings. That would have just wrecked our friendship.

"Slow down there on all the questions," Mike laughed. "I honestly can't believe that I told you the other night. I've never told anyone," Mike said. "Well Mike, maybe you had to tell me as I was throwing myself at you. I gave you no choice."

"Cat, I really don't know how long I've known I was gay but I guess I've always known it. When I was a kid, my dad, the all-rounder sports star, wanted me to play football and baseball but all I ever wanted to do was dance. You know how much I love to dance," Mike laughed.

"I really wasn't the macho guy that my dad wanted in a son. I tried so hard to be a sports jock but there was a dance studio near my neighbourhood and I begged my parents to let me join. Well, that went down like a lead balloon. My dad declared that no son of his was going to be a pansy ass dancer. From then on, I knew I was never going to be able to live up to my dad's expectations." Mike looked so sad as he remembered his childhood.

"So, you never got to go to dance school then?" I asked. I was intrigued listening to Mike and how he had to hide who he truly was. "I did go to dance school. I got a job and worked in a local store to pay for my classes. I signed myself up, forging my mum's signature of course, and went to my dance classes. I loved it. It was like I was in a place where I belonged. I felt like I was at home on the dance floor and not on a football field. It was at the dance studio that I met Matty."

"Matty!! Oh Mike, do tell me more." I was now sitting up in bed. I couldn't wait to hear the next chapter in Mike's story.

"Cat, Matty was my first love although, at the time, I didn't know what all these feelings were. I just knew that when I saw him or I was around him my chest would pound like I was going to burst. It was a really confusing time for me. I was sixteen and going through all the changes that young guys do at that age. I didn't know what was happening. I had such strong feelings for Matty but I didn't know what to do. We actually became really good friends. We were the only guys in the dance class and we struck up a really close bond. One night, we were both leaving the studio and I swear Cat, I thought this was it, Matty was going to tell me he had feelings for me. I really thought he felt the same but then nothing. I was too scared to tell him how I felt. I guess it's hard for you to understand."

"No Mike, it's not hard at all," I said, thinking back to James and how I had suppressed my feelings for him for so long.

"So, Mike what happened to Matty?" I was dying to know if Mike's story had a happy ending. "Nothing happened. I was too chicken to tell Matty how I felt. Not long after our close encounter, he left the dance studio and I never heard from him again. I always wonder about him and where he is and if he thinks about me like I've been thinking about him." Mike was so sad but I could tell he was relieved to have been able to talk to someone.

I thought about how Alex had her High School sweetheart broken relationship; Mike had his Dance Studio bromance and I had my best friend's fantasy to tell. Everyone comes to College with a story to tell and with a past they want to forget. College was a way to find new people, to essentially start over.

“So Mike, I take it your parents don’t know about your situation. Did they ever find out about the dance studio?” I asked. “Oh hell no, Cat, to this day they think I was working overtime in the local store. I just loved it though. It was a place where I was free to be me. Dancing was a way for me to express all the crazy emotions that I had built up and I was also able to be with Matty.”

“Mike, do you know where Matty is? Have you ever tried to contact him?” I asked. “I’ve thought about it a lot. He still lives in our hometown but I just never had the balls to call him. What are we like? We are a right pair or rather we need to grow a pair!” Mike laughed. He was right. We were so scared to let out the feelings that we both had kept inside for so long.

I hugged Mike before leaving to go back to the girls’ dorm room. Leaving the guys’ dorm, I felt like a two-bit hooker as the guys saw me come out of Mike’s room at 7:30 am. “Not a good look,” I thought. Not bad for Mike’s reputation though. At least I was giving everyone the impression that he was the tough guy heterosexual that Rick claimed to be.

As I climbed the stairs to the second floor, I looked in my bag for my key and opened the dorm room door very slowly as I was expecting to see Alex waiting for me and wanting to know what I had got up to with Mike. What I didn't expect to see was my best friend, buck naked, having sex with her boyfriend!

"Ahhhhh, oh holy fuck, I'm sorry. I, err, didn't realise you were busy doing… oh fuck!! I'll see you later. I gotta go to breakfast!" I headed for the cafeteria and I tried to totally blank the image of Alex and Rick going at it like bunny rabbits in our dorm room, not to mention the look on their faces when they saw me!

As I sat with my coffee and bagel, trying to keep the food down, I looked up to see a now fully clothed Alex heading towards me looking completely embarrassed. "Sorry about that one bird!" Alex smiled awkwardly. "Alex, who was the grossest thing I have ever seen - you two bangin' away at each other."

As I screwed my face up, Alex began to crack a smile. I did start to see the funny side of it too and then both of us started laughing hysterically at the whole situation.

"You should have seen your face, Alex, when I walked in. It was like your mom had just walked in and caught you." The tears were running down my face with laughter. “My face! Did you see Rick’s face? He is so funny - he is not embarrassed at all. It’s like he has something to tell the guys now!” Alex Joked. “No, I couldn’t see his face just saw his butt cheeks. Very tight butt cheeks, by the way, Alex!” We laughed so hard that other people were beginning to look at us as if we were crazy. Just then Tom came into the cafeteria for breakfast. After loading his tray up with everything on the menu, he waved over to us. As Tom came over, Alex and I were trying desperately not to laugh but it was too late, we just couldn’t help it. “Man, did you guys get up on the right side of the bed or what! What’s so funny?” Both Alex and I knew this story was one we were keeping to ourselves. It goes to the grave with us. However, the more we tried to act natural, the more we laughed. Alex and I were always laughing about something and it was as if we had our own language or something that no one else could understand.

“Tom, stand up a second will ya? Okay, now turn round, okay great. Now Cat, how does this butt compare?” Alex asked while laughing uncontrollably. “Oh Alex, Tom is bootilicious up there on the Ricktometer!” I joked. Tom was looking at the two of us as if we were from another planet. “What the hell are you two on some kind of happy pill or something? Because I sure as hell want some of it! I want to be part of the, what do you call yourselves 'Chicks' club?" "Tom we are not Chicks, we are birds and we fly high, mother clucker!" Alex laughed and gave me a high five.

"So what's with looking at my ass? Although I have to say I do have a pretty fine ass. You guys wanna see it?" Tom pretended to moon his ass at us but we quickly screamed out not to bother. Seeing Tom mooning in the middle of the cafeteria was not the best move first thing in the morning. Tom was always so confident and cocky. He knew he looked good and was not afraid to show it as we were soon to find out. At that particular moment, Brad Anderson, the faculty stud, walked by. "Hi girls, how are you getting on this year at Deacon College? I was hoping to run into you both. Being at college for the first time can be quite daunting but it looks like you are both getting along well as roommates. Cat, I see you're using the sunscreen," Brad joked, after our last encounter when he saw my flesh peeling off of my face. I cringed at the thought.

"Yeah Brad, they're getting on too well. I tell ya, these girls are real firecrackers!" Tom joked as both Alex and I smiled alluringly at Brad. "You know, what can I say, we are just two birds of a feather, so I'm glad you put me with Cat. Thanks Brad.

Although I am the butt of a lot of her jokes." Alex smiled at me and we burst out laughing again remembering the butt naked scene I had witnessed earlier. Brad looked at us in exactly the same way that Tom had but no one got the joke except us. As we left the cafeteria to go to class, we said our goodbyes to Tom. Alex and I then agreed on our daily rendezvous time to meet for lunch back at the dorms and then headed off to class.

Rushing back to the dorms to meet up with Alex for lunch, I knew she would be waiting for me. Her class only lasted an hour and she was done for the day. "Great you're here, let's get out of here and head to the mall for lunch. I need to get away from this place. I just had Carla inform me that it is unacceptable to have male friends in the dorms after midnight. She spotted Rick leave this morning, fucking bitch!"

I could tell Alex was fuming. "Alex, don't worry about it. Bitch troll is probably just jealous that she is not getting any booty." I tried to calm Alex down. "Hell yeah, you're right Cat. She wishes she had a hot boyfriend like I have. Oh, speaking of hot boyfriends, I so have to grill you about Mr. Mike!"

"Okay, okay!" I conceded as Alex looked quizzingly at me. "But I'll tell you over lunch. Come on, let's get to the mall before my stomach starts to talk back to me. I'm so fucking starving I could eat the arse off of a scabby cat." So Alex and I hit the road. At least Alex's concentration on driving gave me time to come up with a logical explanation as to why I had not done it with Mike - other than the fact that he was gay! It was hard to concentrate though as Alex was doing her usual 100 miles per hour along the highway.

"Holy shit, Alex, you gotta slow down there, tiger! You're way over the speed limit. I swear it's a miracle you haven't been given a speeding ticket!" Alex's driving was beginning to worry me. Although she was very confident, there was definitely a little speed demon inside of her.

"Don't worry Cat, I know what I'm doing. Look, we are almost at the mall and I feel the need for speed when it comes to eating. The food court has to be our first stop-off point because I'm ready to eat that scabby cat of yours too!"

Having purchased the family-size meal at the local burger joint, Alex and I sat happily eating lunch and we hardly said anything to each other for five minutes. We were too busy digging into our lunch as if we had never seen food before! However, after our feast was over, I was ready for Alex to grill me about my so-called night of passion.

"Okay Miss Catherine, spill the beans. What's happening with you and the lovely Mike then? So, are you guys together or what? Did you get to see a bit of booty last night? What was he like? I'm so excited you have to tell me all!" Alex was like an excited child who had just been told she was going to Disneyland.

"Alex, honestly, there is really nothing to tell. We watched a movie and I fell asleep halfway through. Next thing I know, it's morning and I'm walking into our dorm to find you with sweet cheeks Rick." I tried not to make such a big deal of it but Alex was having none of it. "Oh come on, it's me, remember? You don't fool me for a minute! I bet you if I had called over to Mike's dorm last night, I could have seen a bit of butt action." Alex was so desperate for something juicy that I wished I had something juicy to tell her but, the more I tried to be relaxed about it, the more Alex thought Mike and I were doing more than watching a movie. It was the hardest thing as Alex was the closest person in the world to me. All I wanted to do was tell her the truth - that there was no way on God's green earth that anything was going to happen between Mike and me.

After an afternoon of interrogation from Alex, she was eventually distracted by a voice message on the answering machine when we returned to College. It was Rick so she called him right away and was beaming from ear to ear. I could tell Alex was completely smitten with Rick as her face totally lit up when she spoke to him. After she got off the phone an hour later, Alex grabbed my arm and shouted, "Right, let's hit the shower. We're getting ready to go out! Rick and his guys are going out drinking and he wants us to go with them!"

"Oh shit, that means Cat getting her fingers burned on those frikkin' hot rollers again right? I hope we have a few cold cans of beer in the fridge!" "Yes, we surely do have the cold ones in the fridge for you my little sensitive friend," Alex teased. "You will probably be able to numb the pain with drink. Rick says it's hump day so we have to go out drinking!"

"What the fuck is hump day?" I asked "Is that an American ritual or something? I'm not too familiar with that one. In Ireland, we don't need an excuse because every day is hump day back home." "According to Rick, it's Wednesday so we are sort of over the hump or we are closer to the weekend, see it's hump day!" Alex tried to explain as she rushed to get ready.

After a few hours, several burned fingers and cold beers later, Alex and I were ready to hit the town. We met Rick and his boys in the car park. The plan was that Alex would drive to the club and Rick's non-drinking friend, Dave, would drive us home. He was a teetotaller who never touched the stuff so, much to our appreciation, we had a designated driver. Now that Alex had a fake ID, she wanted to use it every chance she got.

"Hey babe, you look amazing!" Rick gave Alex a long lingering kiss before getting into the car. "Hi Rick, ass to see you… oh sorry, I mean nice to see you!" I couldn't resist making a joke about that morning especially as I thought he would have been embarrassed about it but, to my surprise, he was cool. "Hi Cat, yeah sorry about this morning. We'll have to put a white handkerchief or something on the door to warn you next time," Rick smiled and winked.

"I think Mike might have something to say about you. Yeah, my little Irish buddy, are you guys an item or what?" Rick joked. "Don't even go there, Rick. I've tried to ask and all I get is a 'we're just good friends' bullshit answer." I could tell that Alex was getting fed up with me constantly denying things but what could I do? Mike had sworn me to secrecy but Alex was my best friend so how could I keep something from her, especially as she knew I was hiding something? "Why not ask Mike to come along with us? We can ask him what's going on with you guys!" Alex suggested. "He can't make it. He has a student council meeting to go to tonight." Thank goodness, I didn't want Mike getting the third degree or Alex asking what his intentions were towards me.

As we drove to the city, Rick had the music pumping in the car. He was a really cool guy and I could tell he really was into Alex. He had his arm on her seat while she was driving, implying that Alex was his girl. Alex was cruising the Interstate when suddenly a strange noise and flashing lights came from nowhere, right behind us and riding our tail. A cop car was behind us!

Alex began to panic. "Holy fuck, I have a cop car behind me and he's flashing his fucking lights. Is that for me?" "Na, don't worry about it babe," said Rick in his cool as ever tone. "Oh, let's worry!" Alex screamed. "He's flashing his lights and indicating to me to pull over. I think I'd better stop." So Alex pulled into the side of the road and the cop car pulled in right behind her. The cop got out of his car and walked up to Alex's side of the car.

As Alex rolled down the window, she said the old line, "Is there a problem officer?" "Ma'am, please step out of the car," the cop asked sternly. "Licence please." Alex rummaged in her bag to find her ID, making sure she did not show the cop the fake one. "Do you know how fast you were driving there, little lady?" The cop was one of those condescending kind of cops. He was not going to be impressed by Alex's sweet voice and batting eyelids. "I might have been driving about 75, I guess, Officer," Alex said, trying to be as polite as possible and trying not to upset the asshole cop. "Missy, try 90! Here's your speeding ticket. Have a nice day!" And with that, the cop returned to his car, leaving Alex with her mouth open and a speeding ticket in her hand.

"Oh fuck, I got a fucking speeding ticket! Oh my God Cat, what did you say this morning!!" "Holy shit, I know but I was only kidding. I'm never going to say another word ever again!" I couldn't believe it. Alex was so upset. She didn't know how she was going to tell her parents that she got a speeding ticket on the highway in the middle of the week!

Needless to say, after the ticket incident, Alex was not in the mood to party and pretty much just wanted to go back to College. So, the ride home was a very quiet, slow ride. No one wanted to say anything as Alex couldn't laugh about it. She was too scared to think about the conversation she would have to have with her parents.

As we got closer to College, Alex turned to us and shouted, "Fuck this shit, let's drink!" as she turned left to Bob's, the local dive bar watering hole, instead of taking the straight road back to College. Rick smiled and said, "That's my girl, don't let this bullshit ticket get to you. Besides, it's Hump Day." Alex smiled and threw the keys to Dave. "Dave, you are the honorary designated driver. It's hump day, let's celebrate!"

A few tequila slammers later and Alex had almost forgotten about the ticket. "I can't believe that cop didn't even let you off with a caution. What a total fucker!" Rick lambasted. Alex began to laugh and whispered to me, "I'm sorry for shouting at you in the car earlier Cat. I love you, my bird of a feather." Realising that Alex had forgotten that I had cursed her with a speeding ticket, I replied, "We always flock together!!"

We hugged each other and realised that we were both extremely drunk at this point. I had just downed my fifth shot of tequila and was feeling a little shaky on my legs. "Bird, you know I like this hump day thing. I should start this over in Ireland." "Easy bird, you're acting a little drunkededed." Alex was actually beginning to build up a very good tolerance for drink - even more than me. "Any more drink and watch out, Mike might be getting another good night! Are you going to go over to watch another "DVD" tonight?" Alex started to tease. "No, Alex, I told you we are just good friends," I said, trying to sound convincing.

"Here's to good friends and Cat, you're the best," Alex laughed as we toasted with another tequila. We smiled and knew that we were okay. We had each other and a huge speeding fine.

Chapter 9

You Drive Me Crazy

The morning after our hump day experience, Alex and I sat in the cafeteria with the biggest hangover ever. I was sipping a strong Americano while Alex hugged her bottled water trying to re-hydrate herself.

The reality of the speeding fine hit Alex as she wondered how the hell we were going to tell her parents. "Cat, I'm so screwed. This fine will be on my record and I'll probably get a big fat letter delivered to my house. Mom and Dad will not be impressed." I could tell she was very worried about it especially since we were due to go home to Alex's in a few days for Thanksgiving. But also, a big part of her worry and frustration was the fact that she would be going home for a long weekend and leaving Rick. They had become quite an item and I could tell Alex had fallen hard for the lifeguard.

"Hey Hun," Rick sat down and kissed Alex on the cheek. It was funny how Rick was so cool in the way he spoke. He would always refer to Alex as 'Hun' but not in a smoochie honey sort of way. He was too cool for that. "How are you feeling today? I'm sorry about the speeding ticket yesterday. I'll pay for the driving school class you'll have to take. When are you going?" Rick asked.

"I don't know. I have to call the driving school people today and arrange a date. I'm hoping I can do it before Thanksgiving. I'm going to have to pluck up the courage to tell my folks." "Relax Hun, your folks will never know. This is only your first speeding ticket so all you have to do is take the class and it won't be put on your record. It's a first-time offence." "Are you sure? How do you know that?" Alex was excited at the possibility that she might not have to tell her parents after all.

"Trust me, I know from previous experience. I've had my fair share of speeding tickets," Rick announced proudly. "Just call them now and see for yourself. I promise, just show up, put the time in at driving class and you're done." "If only it was that simple," Alex thought.

Later that evening, Alex called and made her appointment. Luckily, she got a cancellation for the next evening so she didn't have much time to wait. Just as she hung up the phone, it rang again. It was Tom. "Hi Alex, my little speed demon, how are you doing?" Tom joked. "You're the talk of the campus. I heard all sorts of stories about how the officer had handcuffed you to the car and interrogated you and made you say the alphabet backwards!" "What, are you kidding me? I swear this place is full of Chinese whispers! One tiny incident and they blow it up out of all proportion! Did the bitch from hell, Carla, tell your girlfriend that?" Alex was trying to keep the incident under wraps but it turned out the entire school found out. "Don't worry, Alex, if anything, I think you handled the interrogation well." Tom could tell she was upset. In fact, he was beginning to know Alex just as well as me.

"Sorry Tom, can you hold on for a second, I have another call coming through," Alex explained. "Okay speedy, you can put me on hold." Alex's other call turned out to be Rick who was also concerned for her.

After 20 minutes or so of talking with Rick, there was a knock on the door. It was Tom and Alex realised that she still had him on hold on the other line. She said goodbye to Rick and smiled a big sunshine smile at Tom.

"Why did you hang up on me?" Tom seemed quite hurt. "I didn't hang up on you, I just left you on hold for an extended amount of time, that's all," Alex replied with a 'butter wouldn't melt' look in her eyes. "Yeah, you left me on hold for over 30 minutes!" "Oh Tom, stop exaggerating, it was only like 20 minutes," Alex joked. I couldn't help but laugh. "Anyway, you're here now. Do you want me to treat you to a hot chocolate at the Coffee House? Cat and I are on our way there. You can even have chocolate sprinkles on it!" Tom began to break a smile and relented. "Okay, but only if I can have marshmallows too."

As we walked across campus, Tom asked, "Who were you yacking to on the phone anyway? Cat is with you." "It was lover boy, Rick," I joked. "So Alex, things are going well with the pool boy then?" Tom asked with a concerned father tone again. "Yes, thank you, but I'm not going to go into all the details of my love life just like I don't want to know anything about you and Stacey. I still don't know what you are doing with her, Tom, she is a bit of a clone." Tom laughed, "Yes, I know how much you like her, Alex, but you should get to know her. You guys might get along." "I think Carla would have something to say about that. I'm sorry Tom but all those clones are so far up Carla's ass, they can't see anyone else. But hey, whatever makes them happy, right Cat?" "That's right, bird," I smiled as I knew Alex was being her sarcastic self.

After our coffee fix, Alex excused herself as she had a date with Rick. I, on the other hand, had a date with the microwave popcorn again.

The next day was D-Day for Alex as she had her driving school class to go to. I was working at the pool that afternoon. It was a beautiful day and the sun was beating down on my trusty umbrella. As Alex sat with me, all the scenarios of what driving school would be like went through her head. "Cat, what if I get stuck beside a piss-ass drunk driver or a psycho driver and I get car chased on the way home?"

"Don't worry, you'll be fine. Just go in and sit beside the nice old lady who was stopped for driving too slowly." I was trying to make her feel relaxed as I could tell she was anticipating the worst.

"Cat, would you go with me please? I don't think I can do this on my own."

"Are you serious? I can't go. For a start, I didn't get a speeding ticket! Alex you'll be fine, I'm sure you will. Besides, I'm not finished working here at the pool until 6:30 pm and you have to be at your class by 6:00 pm, right?" "I tell you what, if I ask Rick to work your next few hours, then will you go with me? Please?" I think Alex just wanted the support. "Don't you want Rick to go with you?"

"No, I need my best friend with me. Go on, bird, it'll be fun!"

"Oh, so now it'll be fun? Yeah, about as much fun as stabbing myself in the foot with a fork!" I exclaimed. "Okay, I'll go with you but you have to get someone to cover my shift!"

Rick was happy to cover for me. He said he needed to top up his tan anyway. He was very vain in a macho kind of way. So Alex and I headed off to her driving school class in the city. "Okay speedy, watch your limit!" I joked on the way. "Hey fucker, you'd better not say a word. It was you pointing out my speeding the other day that got me into this mess," Alex warned jokingly.

We were still laughing as we arrived at the driving school. "Okay bird, we have to be serious now," Alex warned. It was hard not to be quite giddy as we knew how serious this was going to be and the more we tried not to smile the more we couldn't help but laugh.

A large State Trooper was standing at the doorway shouting out, "Fines! Can you please have your fines in your hand please?" Once he got to me, I had nothing to show him so I casually told him that I was just there to support my friend. "I'm sorry ma'am, this is not a movie theatre. This is a serious driving violation class. You can't come in without your ticket." What was this? I was being punished for actually not having a speeding ticket!

“I’m sorry, you will have to wait outside.” Alex looked at me as she was ushered away with the rest of the criminals and I stood out in the lobby.

After a few hours, or what felt like forever for me, Alex came out of the class looking relieved. “Cat, Rick was right. I’m in the clear. No record at all and I even got this cute little certificate.” Alex was so proud of herself. I had to wake myself up as I was practically sleeping for the past few hours. “Cat, I’m sorry you had to stay out here. You’re a true friend and I really appreciate the support.” “Anytime you get a speeding ticket, I’ll be there for you!” “This will be the first and last I promise you. I couldn’t sit through that class again. I swear stabbing myself in the foot with that fork of yours would have been a lot more exciting.”

As we drove home, Alex had a sudden urge to shop. After her driving school experience, she needed some retail therapy and I was happy to oblige. The mall was packed with people rushing to buy things for Thanksgiving. “I don’t know why people are buying things now. They’ll get all this shit at half price in the Thanksgiving Day sales,” Alex said. “So why are we shopping, missy?” “Well, it’s always good to look. It’s just like guys, if you already have one, it’s not against the law to look at what else is out there. Although, I don't think I'll be looking anymore. I really do feel so blessed to have found Rick," Alex gushed. "Cat, I'm just worried about the next few days. We head to my folks for Thanksgiving and Rick is going back home for the long weekend. What if he sees any old girlfriends and decides to dump me for someone else?" I could tell Alex was upset but it was more to do with the fact that she didn't want to be hurt again. Jake had really broken her confidence in relationships to the point where every guy was tarred with the same brush and it was going to take a special guy to get Alex to believe again. I only hoped it would be Rick.

"Hey girl, what's with all this negative thinking? Rick is totally in love with you. I can tell, even through that tough guy exterior. I can see the way he looks at you. I really don't think you have anything to worry about. Just enjoy and if it's meant to be and all that bullshit, ya know? Besides, you can't have a relationship if you're constantly thinking that something bad is going to happen. You gotta have faith." I tried to reassure her and I think that's just what she needed, a reassuring word of support from a friend.

At that very instant, Alex's cell phone rang, "Ah speak of the Devil!" Alex smiled broadly as she chatted with Rick. I was so glad that she was happy and hoped the negative thinking would disappear.

"Okay, we gotta hit the road. Rick wants to see me in a bit. He said he has a surprise for me!" Alex was very excited and couldn't wait to see what Rick had in store for her. We raced home, or as fast as the speed limit would allow, as we were constantly wary of Alex getting another speeding ticket.

Rick was sitting outside our dorms waiting for Alex as we drove up to the car park. He was carrying a bunch of beautiful red roses which, of course, I assumed were for Alex.

I decided to say my goodbyes and head over to see Mike so that Alex and Rick could have time together.

Mike and I sat watching another Tom Cruise classic DVD and had two bags of popcorn and a couple of beers. Popcorn and beer – my favourite meal! The best thing about hanging out with Mike was watching all my favourite chick flick movies as he was a fan of the classics also.

A few hours later, Alex called, "Hey girl, what you doin'?" "We're just watching a DVD," I replied. "Now, I know that is all you're doing," Alex joked. "So Cat, are you going to crash at Mike's tonight?" Thinking that was a sign for "Can Rick stay at ours?", I checked with Mike to make sure he was fine with it and decided to stay. Besides, I was just about to watch the special features on Cocktail and check out Tom's moves.

That night, Mike and I sat up talking about relationships and how we both found it difficult to be in one but for completely different reasons. "Cat, you are wonderful, you have a fantastic sense of humour and your pretty Irish complexion makes you just adorable. How come some guy hasn't swept you off of your feet already, or have they and you're just not telling me? Any special lads over there in Ireland?" Mike wanted to know all about my relationships as he was struggling to come to terms with his own sexuality. I think he wanted to hear about my experiences with the other sex or rather his sex.

I started to tell Mike all about James and how I had been too scared to say how I felt to him for fear of rejection. It was strange. I hadn't told anyone in Ireland about James but, in the space of only a few weeks, I had shared my thoughts and feelings with Alex and Mike.

"You really should tell him how you feel," Mike advised. "I know Mike, Alex said the same thing but you don't understand. I've so much to lose. For one, our friendship as James and I have been together forever and two, my family would be torn apart if I was to confess my feelings for James and he didn't feel the same way. I'd just die and would never be able to show my face at our family get-togethers again!"

"So, Mike, there have been a few lads but no one that has been able to sweep me off my feet so to speak," I confessed. "I guess the guys that I would be into are just not into me. They only see me as a friend or one of the guys and then they are asking, 'Cat, who's your friend? Can you hook me up with them?' It's like they can't see me as anything other than a buddy."

"Mike, I just want someone to approach my friends and ask, who's your friend? Ya know? I see Alex and Rick together and I want that. I want someone to call me 'Hun' and give me roses and do anything for me." I was beginning to spill my guts out to Mike who was such a great listener and knew exactly what to say to make me feel better about myself. "Mike, I have to confess, when it came to Rick, I really liked him a lot when I first met him. I thought he was a guy who could sweep me off my feet but it turned out he wanted to sweep my best friend off her feet instead. But it's all good. Alex is so happy with him that I couldn't imagine them not being together. I think they were so meant to be." I smiled at Mike and knew it was right but feeling so lonely, longing for the right guy to come along made me sad inside.

"Oh sweetie. I didn't know you felt that way. Is it not hard to see Alex and Rick together if you really liked him so much?" Mike asked. "No. it's fine, to be honest Mike. That's the story of my so-called love life," I joked. "Anyway, I just want Alex to be happy. She is my best friend and she deserves someone who will treat her right." "Cat, you're a good friend to Alex and she's a lucky girl." "You're a lucky guy, my friend, you also have me in your life! Now spill, what's going on with you? Have you had any boy action you can tell me about? Or how do you feel about coming out? Do you think you could do it?"

As Mike started to spill his guts out to me too, I could tell he had a lot of emotions that had built up for so long. He was slowly coming to terms with his sexuality and also dealing with his parents' demands. Coming from a strong Italian family, they had high expectations of their children which was a daunting prospect for Mike. "I think that's why I've not come out. My family would be in complete shock, especially my father. He would probably have flashbacks to me playing with my sister's dolls and blame my mother for being too soft with me as a kid. He's a very controlling man." Mike was upset and shaking at the thought of his father.

"You have to live your own life. Your father should love you for who you are and if that means telling him you're gay, Mike, you might feel a whole lot better for it." I tried to give Mike the support he needed. "Or it might make things a whole lot worse for my mom." Mike was in a terrible dilemma but I think he knew he had to say something. "I'm going back home tomorrow for Thanksgiving and I'll gauge what type of mood my father is in. Maybe talking to my mom might help? If I say anything I'm just scared that it won't only be the turkey that gets a roasting, if you know what I mean." "Oh Mike, look ya see you made a joke. It won't be so bad and, remember, Thanksgiving is a time for family. If your dad eats too much turkey, he might not be able to move too fast to catch you, haha!" I only hoped that while Mike was plucking the turkey feathers, he could pluck up the courage to say something.

Having talked into the wee small hours of the morning, Mike and I crashed out but were awoken early by the phone ringing. I knew it was for me. "Hey Irish girl, are you coming over? We gotta get packed for our road trip to see my folks!" It was Alex sounding very chirpy for such an early hour in the morning. I got up and sneaked out of the guys' dorms. The stayovers with Mike were doing his reputation good but not mine.

When I got to the dorm, Alex was so glad to see me and was screaming with delight. "Cat, I had the most amazing night last night," Alex gushed. "What another one? Rick really is a stud muffin or what!" I joked. "Cat, he gave me this beautiful bouquet of red roses and told me that he wanted to tell me something before we leave each other for Thanksgiving break. Cat, he told me he loves me!" Alex screamed. "Cat, can you believe it? He really loves me and I told him I love him too." Alex was on such a high. The Rick cocaine was filling her up to the point where she was going to explode!

"Ya see, I told you! No more negative thinking. Everything is going to be fine." I could tell she was so happy and was ready to go see her folks safe in the knowledge that she had the perfect boyfriend who she loved but more importantly, who was in love with her.

Chapter 10

Dancing Queens

The Thanksgiving break was a well-earned rest for Alex and me as we were truly spoilt by her parents. As Thanksgiving Day arrived, we helped Jean and Pete in the preparation of the traditional Thanksgiving dinner. "Now Cat, I do hope you're hungry," Pete joked. "I think we have enough food to fill those hollow legs of yours." As I looked around the table laden with the huge stuffed turkey, vegetables, creamed potatoes and sweet potatoes with actual marshmallows on top, I knew I was in for a treat. We said grace and then tucked into the feast that was before us.

"Oh my goodness, this is amazing! My first ever Thanksgiving dinner and I have to say I am so thankful that you have taken me into your home. I really feel like part of your family." I was so grateful to Alex and her parents. The cafeteria food was not a patch on this.

"Cat, you are so welcome and I want to thank you for helping and supporting Alex through her first semester at Deacon College," Jean said as she squeezed my hand and smiled.

After dinner, as I was feeling like I didn't have room to breathe, Jean came out with dessert, pumpkin pie and whipped cream! "Gosh Mom, I really don't think I could eat another mouthful," Alex confessed as she rubbed her stomach.

"Come on sweetie, you know it's your favourite!" Jean had already cut up the pie and was handing it over to Alex who reluctantly accepted. "Cat, this is the thing about Thanksgiving. All the rules about dieting go out the window. We really will need to walk along the beach later!" Alex admitted after polishing off her slice of pie.

"So Cat, we know you haven't had a chance to see much of the local area, so we were planning on taking a few trips while you're here. Alex, have you any suggestions?" Jean asked. "Mom, can we take Cat to San Francisco? I know this amazing mall we can go to!" Alex pleaded. "Alex, this will be Cat's first time visiting San Francisco. Can't you think of other well-known tourist attractions apart from the mall?" Jean rolled her eyes as she knew only too well her daughter's love for shopping.

Alex and her parents wanted me to enjoy all that California had to offer. Over the next few days, we travelled to Yosemite National Park, visited the Redwood National Park and toured San Francisco where we took a ride on the famous trams with a stop off at the Golden Gate Bridge. I felt like a total tourist and was enjoying every minute of it, taking in all the sights and capturing as many memories as I could on my camera. To Alex and her parents, I was part of the family and I loved being with them.

Pretty soon, it was time to head back to college and Alex and I were back on the road with all our groceries from Jean and laundry bags full of clean, pressed clothes. As we drove down the now-familiar highway, my mind drifted to Mike. I wondered how his Thanksgiving weekend went and if he had the conversation with his parents that I know he so desperately wanted.

"Hey bird, what ya thinkin' about?" Alex nudged me back from my daydreaming. "Oh nothing Alex, just thinking of getting back to the fun of Deacon College. I know you have missed it alright or missed Rick!" I knew that Alex was just bursting to see him.

"Cat, you have no idea. I seriously missed his tight ass so much. I'm glad I had you with me this weekend to take my mind off things. I think my mom and dad want to officially adopt you as soon as possible. They were so glad to have you stay with us." "Alex, thank you so much for everything. You and your mum and dad have been so generous to me. When I first came to College, I was dreading it. I just didn't know how I was going to survive without my family but now I have you guys and, after eating that Thanksgiving Day dinner, I think I've eaten my entire body weight again. I have actually put on weight!" I joked. "Oh please, girl, you could never put on weight. What, did you do, grow your nails over the weekend? I, on the other hand, will need to start working on getting that over-indulgence off my waistline!" "Well Alex, that's what Rick is for." I gave Alex a wink and a smile. She really was dying to see him but, as she was keeping to the speed limit on the highway this time, she had to wait a little longer.

As we drove through the gates of Deacon College, I knew Alex was so excited to see Rick. She didn't have to wait too long. As we headed into the parking lot, Rick was standing at our dorm building holding a bunch of flowers and waving over to Alex. "Hey Hun, did you miss me?" Rick picked Alex up in his strong arms and twirled her around. "Oh Rick, I missed you so much," Alex gushed. It was official, she truly was head over heels and needed her Rick-fix right away. I wanted to let them have their moment so I casually left the love birds to it. I also wanted an excuse to see Mike. I just hoped and prayed that he was okay and had the courage to come out to his family. I made my way over to his dorm and, to my delight, he was back. When Mike saw me he rushed over and hugged me, almost as tight as Alex gave Rick.

"Hi Mike, how are you? How was your Thanksgiving? How were your parents?" "So many questions, my Irish rose. Let's get inside and I'll fill you in." As we got inside, Mike gave out a huge cheer, "Cat, I did it! I came out to my parents!!" "Holy fuck, Mike, that's amazing! How did they take it?" I was so pleased for him but also I hoped that they were understanding. "It was a shock to them, my dad especially. I knew I had to let him watch the traditional Thanksgiving football game first before I could say anything. Luckily, his team won so he was in a good mood. And well, after dinner, the whole family was saying around the table what they were thankful for and I knew this was my time to just say it. So, I told everyone that I was thankful for being a gay man and that I hoped I had the love and support of my family." As Mike was telling me his coming out story, I could see he was a different guy. He had been overwhelmed for such a long time with these pent-up emotions and feelings.

"So Mike, then what happened?" I asked, waiting to hear how his parents reacted. "As you can imagine, Cat, the room fell silent for a few seconds but, to me, it felt like hours. I was waiting for someone to say something and then my sister was like, "Well duh, of course you are!" Then my mom started crying. I thought she was upset and ashamed of me but it was the opposite; she was crying because she knew I was finally happy. I actually think my mom already had an idea. She said to me afterward that she secretly knew about the dance studio but she never told me. Apparently, a letter came to the house after I had registered but she said nothing. My dad actually took it well, or as well as could be expected, but I think it might take a while for him to adjust. His first question was "Do you still like sports?" Mike laughed.

"Cat, now that I've actually come out to my family, I am so relieved. I don't know what I was worried about. We talked a lot this weekend and I told them about how I felt and they gave me a huge hug. I was building this up to be a disaster for my parents and not giving them enough credit. My parents still love me, no matter what." Mike was so happy.

"Mike, that's great! I'm really pleased for you. So are you officially out and about now? Can I actually tell Alex? You know she's still harbouring thoughts of us getting married so that I'll stay in

America and we'll live next door to her and Rick," I joked.

"Yes, go for it Cat!" Mike was ready to tell the world and I was so delighted for him. "Mike, we gotta do something fun to celebrate. Let's go out dancing tonight! You can show me your killer moves and we can take Alex and Rick. I remember when we were sitting on the sidewalk at my birthday, you said you didn't like those types of clubs. Too straight were they?" I joked. "Exactly Cat, not my kinda club."

"Well then fuck it! Let's hit the gay clubs! I'll call Alex and see if she wants to go although I may wait a while. She is catching up on lost time with Rick! Mike, we can have some fun with this? Do you have a plain white T-shirt and a large marker? Let's make a statement!"

As Mike and I headed to the Coffee House, we were both in high spirits. We sat and chatted about how he was going to come out to his friends. I was looking forward to finally telling Alex that Mike and I really were just good friends. I called Alex to let her know about us hitting the clubs. She was totally up for dancing as Rick had to catch up with his macho college buddies which usually entailed a night of drinking at the local dive bar.

As Mike drove Alex and me to the city, we were so excited to be out for the night and back enjoying College life. Alex brought the road trip tunes to educate Mike on our musical tastes and we were getting the party started.

As we walked along the row of clubs, Mike stopped suddenly and turned to Alex. “Alex, we have something to tell you. Actually, I have something to tell you.” “So Mike, are you and Cat getting married and you want me to be your maid of honour?!” Alex said excitedly.

Mike and I looked at each other as Mike proceeded to take his shirt off to reveal his T-shirt with the letters ‘I’M GAY’ on the front. I had added it with his marker earlier. “What?! You’re gay?!” Alex exclaimed. “Yep, I’m gay!” Mike replied, shouting as loud as he could. Alex looked at me and laughed as everything started to make sense. “Oh my goodness Mike, did you just come out to me? It does explain a lot of things though, like why you were just good friends with my girl here.” Alex threw her arms around Mike and me as she realised that all her matchmaking and hoping we’d marry was in vain but she knew this was huge for Mike.

“Now, this is definitely something to celebrate. Let’s go dancing!” Alex announced. We hit the largest gay club on the strip and had so much fun that night. Mike was having the time of his life. The "I'M GAY" T-shirt was basically a man magnet for Mike that night. He got chatted up by so many guys and Alex and I enjoyed the tunes and danced the night away.

When we finally got back to college, our feet were sore and our heads were dizzy with all the cocktails that we had enjoyed. Mike was the perfect gentleman and walked or rather held us up until we got into our dorm room where we immediately crashed onto our beds.

"Cat, I'm so drunkededed!!" Alex joked, as she sat up in her bed and turned to me. "Cat, are you okay? I know you really liked Mike and I had such high hopes for you guys. I honestly thought you were having this wild passionate affair and the whole 'we're just good friends' talk was just a front."

"Oh no, Alex, he is totally gay! Now you see why there could be nothing between Mike and me. I promised him that I wouldn't say anything to anyone. He made me swear. I couldn't tell you until he was ready. It wasn't my story to tell."

"Man that sucks. He's so cute too. I was getting such great vibes." "Yeah Alex, those were gay vibes!" Alex began to laugh she was trying to get her head around it. "Yeah, I know all the cute ones are either gay or wanna be my friend, just my luck!" "Ah bird, you'll find your soulmate just as I have found mine in Rick. If not bird, I'll be your soulmate." Alex smiled and hugged me as she could tell everything made sense now. She would never say anything about Mike and me again.

Chapter 11

Murder on the Dance Floor

After the Thanksgiving holiday, it was all about Christmas which was fast approaching. The festive season was to be a happy time for everyone. For me, I was excited to be going back to see my family and friends in Ireland but I was actually feeling so sad to be leaving this family that I had made in California. What was I going to do without my friend? Alex and I had become inseparable. We had been in each other's pockets for the past four months and she had come to mean more to me in those months than I could put into words.

The week before I left for Ireland was pretty crazy as the Moonlight Winter dance was coming up and Alex and I were frantically looking forward to it. It was our last hurrah before the Christmas break. Alex was just beside herself with excitement to be able to go with the love of her life, Rick, as he too was leaving to go back to his parents.

So, first things first, we had to buy our prom dresses which meant a trip to the mall. Apart from the local bar, this was our favourite place to be. I could tell Alex was fit to burst with excitement to be able to share this special night with Rick. "So bird, what type of dress are you looking for? Hoochie mama short or traditional long gown?" I joked. "Cat, now that I've lost about 300 lbs since my last prom, I want to make sure I get a dress that shows that I actually have a figure." "Oh please girl, you would look amazing in any dress. Let's get this fashion show on the road!" After spending the best part of an afternoon trying on dozens of dresses, we finally picked our favourites and we looked just beautiful.

As we drove back to college, Alex was being unusually quiet. I knew she was thinking about something. "What's up, bird? You're too quiet for my liking. You didn't even curse at that prick in the car in front when he cut in on you a second ago!" I asked concerned.

"I don't know Cat. I guess I'm just scared. I'm actually so unbelievably happy for the first time in my life. I'm really head over heels for Rick and I'm just thinking 'Why me'? Things like this just don't happen to me. You know what Cat, I'm also trying very hard not to think about you heading back home to Ireland. What am I going to do without you?" Suddenly Alex started to cry. She stopped the car at the side of the road and we threw our arms around each other so tightly as if we didn't want to let each other go. I was leaving for a month but, to us, it felt as if part of each other was going to be missing and that was something that we both had to come to terms with.

I tried not to let the thought of me leaving dampen her spirits, even though it was crushing me inside. "You know what? I think after all the dress shopping, we need a well-deserved beer run! What do ya say?" Alex gave me a smile that would light up a room and we headed back to the local.

Usually, when we had a beer run, we would take our College backpacks to hide the evidence from Carla and her posse but, on this occasion, we improvised and had beer bottles in our coats, down our trousers and down our fronts which was great! I finally looked like I had a cleavage!! "Okay Alex, are you ready to make a run for it?" I was ready to make a move. "Are you kidding Cat? Don't run! These bottles are seriously going to go flying down my leg at any minute!" We were in fits of laughter as we walked slowly to the dorm looking like we had both shit our pants! "Just don't bump into Carla," we kept saying, "Just keep going." It was as if we were getting to the end of a marathon. We could see the finish line, our dorm room, in sight but then, as if by magic, Carla came out of her room. "Oh fuck!!" we both said at the same time.

“Hi Catherine and Alexandra. Been doing a bit of shopping have you? I see you’re all set for the dance this Saturday?” We didn’t want to move for fear of half the contents of the local bar falling out of our trousers so we simultaneously greeted her. “Hi Carla.” We really wanted to say, “Fuck off, Carla!” Thankfully, she was on her way to the gym so we were in the clear.

As soon as we got into our dorm room, we carefully removed the bottles from our clothes. It was crazy how many bottles one person could hide! As usual, Alex’s first port of call was the phone to check her messages. “Fuck Cat, how long were we away for? We have like ten messages!” Alex exclaimed. I knew when Alex said ‘we’ have messages, she was actually referring to herself as I never received any calls apart from my parents. “Who are they from?” I asked but I sort of guessed they would be from one person, Rick.

“Oh my goodness, he’s crazy!” Alex laughed. “Let me guess, Rick, right?” “No Cat, it’s that Tom. He’s fucking crazy! He has called ten times leaving stupid ass messages wanting us to get over to the Coffee House for a card night.” Since Alex had become obsessed with Rick, we hadn’t been going to the Coffee House. Playing cards was not what Alex had on her agenda for a good night out. A royal hot flush with Rick was more her thing these days.

Suddenly, there was a knock on the door and Alex opened it up to find Rick standing with a bunch of a dozen red roses once again! “Hey beautiful. I’ve missed you. Where have you been?” Alex’s face lit up and she threw her arms around him. “Thank you babe, the roses are just beautiful. Did you miss me for all of ten hours?” Alex joked. “We have been to the mall to get our prom dresses. You don’t want me to rock up on your arm in a garbage bag right?” Rick laughed, “Babe, you could rock up wearing anything. As long as I have you on my arm this Saturday, I’ll be the luckiest guy on campus.” I could tell that it was time for me to make a quick exit before the love birds got it on right there and then.

“Okay guys, gotta go now.” I quietly slipped out and I don’t think they realised I had left. That’s love for ya! I was just so happy that Alex was happy and that was going to be the belle of the ball. At least she would have someone on her arm. I, on the other hand, was without a date. That was me all over - great friends with the guys but no love in my life.

I suddenly thought of James back home. For a while, I had been able to put him out of my mind. I was having so much fun over the past few months with Alex and, even though looking for love here hadn't turned out the way I had hoped, I had done my best to shake off James. The only thing was that I was going back to Ireland and the thought of seeing him again was scaring me to death. Would I ever really be able to move on from him?

Tom and the guys were in the Coffee House when I arrived and Tom lit up when he saw me. He was a great friend and he was ready for a cards night. "So, where's your partner in crime?" Tom knew that Alex and I came as a pair. "She's otherwise engaged with Rick, I'm afraid Tom!" I gave Tom a wink to say that they were getting their groove on and we both laughed.

The next few days went by in the blink of an eye and suddenly it was Saturday, the day of the dance. Alex woke up and bounced out of bed. "Cat, Cat, are you awake?" she whispered. "No, I'm not awake. I'm totally asleep!" I murmured sarcastically. "Come on Cat, up you get. We need to get ready for our big night!" "Alex, it's 7 am! Do you not think that we could have a lie-in like we always do on a lazy Saturday morning?" Alex was way too excited. "Are you kidding me!? Cat, we have so much to do. Come on, let's get up. Alex had a full day of pampering arranged for us which was fantastic and very unusual for me. Getting a manicure and pedicure was totally alien to me. The pedicure tickled and I laughed the whole way through it. After the manicure and pedicure, we had lunch and then went to our hair and make-up appointments. I was so far out of my comfort zone. It was crazy! Alex was used to getting all this shit done with her buddy, Kim when she was back home.

The time seemed to fly in and, before we knew it, we were having a few celebratory drinks in the dorm, dressed up to the nines. "Cat, we look so elegant but we are downing beers, very classy!" "Sure Alex, class is our middle name, right?" I joked. We looked at each other, knowing that tonight was going to be the last night before I headed back to Ireland for the Christmas holidays. We had become inseparable and we felt that we had a soulmate in each other. Alex started "Okay, so I'm just going to say it, Cat. I'm going to miss you so, so much when you go to Ireland tomorrow. This past week has really flown by so fast with getting ready to go to the prom that I haven't stopped to think about it. And Rick is going back to his folks in Chicago. I'm going to be so alone. You have meant so much to me these past few months. Is it bad that I'm going to miss you more than my boyfriend?" We started to laugh but I felt the same about Alex. She was just my everything here in California. We laughed together, cried together and got into trouble together. The trust that we had in each other was different from any other friendship that I'd ever had before. We were soulmates and had developed a bond that was so precious. I started to fill up a little and tears began to well in my eyes.

"Now Alex, I'm so going to ruin the make-up that I paid $70 for! I'm going to miss you too, my friend. These past few months have been such fun and, even though I'm going back home to see my family, I truly feel like I have made a home here. It's been the best time of my life, Alex. You're my soul sister, I know you are." We gave each other the tightest of hugs to the point where I was unable to breathe in my dress but I didn't care.

"So Cat, when you get back home to Ireland, what are you going to do about the James situation?" Alex brought me back to the reality of James. The one thing about having a soulmate was that they could tell when the other was worried about something. "Oh Alex, I just don't know. I've been able to put him out of my mind over the past few months. To him, I will always be like a sister and he just thinks of me as a friend. I need to move on." "You wanna know what I think bird? I think you should just tell him how you feel. You've had feelings for him for years. You need to be the tough girl that I know and love and just do it!" Alex advised.

"I wish it was that simple. I just don't want to ruin everything. Our families are so tight and what if I fuck everything up?" I was afraid. "You won't fuck everything up, Cat. You will be honest. As much as I want you to marry one of Rick's friends, you need to do what makes you happy. If James makes you happy, tell him." Alex was always that voice in my head, telling me what I needed to hear. "Well, what will be will be, I guess. But for tonight, it's our night to party and enjoy the dance. We look too good to just sit and wonder what might be. Maybe I'll meet a tall dark stranger at the dance and we'll still have our babies together." Alex and I gave each other another huge hug and reminded ourselves that we still had tonight to look forward to. Tomorrow was another day.

Just then, we heard a loud bang on the door and, with that, Alex was back to her excited self as her eyes lit up knowing that it was Rick. She opened the door to a wall of flowers which fell away to show Rick wearing a very sexy black tux and his hair was swept back. He looked amazing. "Oh my fucking

God!" Rick exclaimed. "Alex, you look out of this world! I'm the luckiest guy on campus to be dancing tonight with such a stunner!" "Why thank you, kind sir. You don't look too bad yourself," Alex replied. "Shall we get this party started, babe?" Rick was very handsome and, with Alex on his arm, they were the perfect couple. I, on the other hand, felt like a spare part. I walked alone, behind the happy couple, to the College gym where the dance was being held. I didn't want to invade their space. As I walked up the steps, I was thinking how lucky Alex was to have a relationship with a guy who worshipped her and also made her feel as if she was floating on air. As I was contemplating actually ditching the prom altogether, I felt a tap on my right shoulder. I looked around to find Mike smiling at me. He was dressed in a fabulous white tuxedo and looked amazing. "Hi there, my Irish rose. You're not thinking of bailing on me, are you? I was banking on you being here," Mike smiled.

"I thought you were going to the prom with someone else? Did you not have a hot date last week?" Now that Mike was out and proud, he really was enjoying his new-found freedom. "Yeah I did but, you know what, there is nothing wrong with playing it cool and, besides, I don't think College is ready for a guy-on-guy date or rather I'm not ready, to be honest. I'm still finding my way with all of this." Although Mike had come out, he was still struggling with how people at College were going to react. He was taking small but significant steps.

"Mike, you have come such a long way from that guy I first met at the beginning of the semester. You're just starting this amazing new life so take all the time you need. And, in the meantime, I will be right here on your arm and can't wait to dance with you. Your moves are amazing!"

We headed into the prom together and it felt so good to have Mike with me. He was my male Alex. He really was a great friend and always made me feel good about myself. The gym looked absolutely amazing. A large glitter ball in the centre glistened from wall to wall with soft mood lighting casting a romantic glow throughout the room. The usual athletic look and feel of the large gym had been transformed into an elegant wonderland with draped fabric on the walls and fairy lights providing a captivating backdrop. Many of the kids were already getting down on the dancefloor. To me, this was everything a typical all-American prom would look like.

Mike was fantastic on the dance floor and we danced the night away. This was the perfect way to spend my last night at College before heading home to Ireland but I was trying not to think about that. A mixture of excitement and fear came over me. In just five months, I had changed so much and I wondered what my friends at home would think of my new-found confidence.

We were having the time of our lives with great friends and dancing our asses off to the funky music. Rick excused himself to go act macho with the guys. They decided to go outside to have the cigars that they had saved for a special occasion. Alex and I headed over to the bar for some drinks. Since the dance was being held within the College campus, it was soft drinks only, to our disappointment. Just then, Alex got a tap on the shoulder, she turned round to see Tom and Stacey "Hi there, ladies. My, don't you scrub up well," Tom joked. "Hi Tom, ya know you could have made an effort yourself," Alex laughed back. Tom looked fantastic. He was the perfect athletic guy. It was such a shame that Stacey was his girlfriend. She looked like she was bored to tears and, as pretty as she was, the look on her face would have turned milk sour in two seconds flat. Tom, on the other hand, was his usual friendly self.

"Well Tom my friend, enjoy the dance and maybe, if you're lucky, I'll have a dance with you later," Alex joked. "Now girl, you know I will be very lucky to be in your presence." Much to the annoyance of Stacey, Tom couldn't resist flirting back. Stacey suddenly grabbed Tom's arm and turned on her stilettos. "You're terrible, Alex!" I laughed. "You're such a flirt with Tom and you know it gets Stacey's back up every time." "I know Cat. It's either me or that stick up her ass that gets her back up. I can't decide which."

After a few dances, Alex went to look for Rick who was busy with the guys outside enjoying a few drinks and smoking cigars while fist-pumping each other and celebrating their macho manhood. "Rick, do you want to come in for a dance with me?" Alex asked, a little annoyed by Rick's actions. Her love seemed to be more engrossed in a cloud of cigar smoke and male bonding than he was in her.

"Hey hun. I'm just hanging out with the guys here for a while. I'll be back inside in a minute." I could tell Rick was starting to get a little drunk and a little obnoxious. Alex looked at me and shrugged her shoulders. "Cat is it just me or am I being pushed aside by the guys tonight?"

As we returned to the gym, Tom came over to cash in that promise of a dance with Alex. She was more than happy to take to the dance floor with Tom although she wished it was with Rick but he was too busy with his boys. Tom and Alex danced for a while and then the slow songs started to play and all the lovers took to the dancefloor. Alex and Tom appeared to feel a bit awkward as I don't think they were expecting to slow dance with each other, especially given that their other loves were close by.

As they began to dance slowly together, Tom and Alex were startled by an energised Rick knocking Tom to the floor. "What the fuck are you doing dancing with my girlfriend, ass hole?!" Rick came hurtling through the air and landed right on top of Tom. Alex looked shocked. She wasn't expecting this reaction from Rick and she rushed to help Tom off the floor. As Tom got to his feet, his eyes narrowed and he glared at Rick radiating a simmering sense of fury.

"What the hell man?!" Tom yelled back. "You're dancing with my girl, bro! No one dances with my girl!" Rick had turned into this incredible green-eyed monster that Alex had never seen before. He was also drunk off his ass and it looked like cigars were not the only thing he had been smoking. Rick was wasted.

"Rick, what the fuck are you doing?" Alex exclaimed. She was so taken aback as Rick tried to take another swing at Tom. Rick had totally overreacted seeing Alex with another guy and along with the alcohol that he had consumed, it was the perfect mix for a complete Rick explosion. Having heard the commotion, Stacey came running over to see what was going on. "What's happening, Tom?" Stacey asked, looking confused.

"Stacey, you need to keep a leash on your guy. He was all up on my woman." Rick was talking like he owned Alex and she didn't like it one bit. She shouted back, "Rick, why are you acting like an egotistical jerk? We were just dancing and you don't own me!" Alex was furious and also a little embarrassed as the music had stopped and everyone was watching.

She ran out of the gym in tears and, to my surprise, Rick didn't go after her. I was so mad at him for the way he had acted and I shouted, "Rick, what the hell are you still here for? Go and make sure Alex is okay. She loves you and only you. Tom and Alex are just friends, that's all. Besides, you basically spent the entire evening drinking and getting high with your buddies. Alex was just having fun." Rick stood in the hallway, looking as though his pride had been dented and I sensed his ego had been wounded. "Cat. I know what I saw. They were all over each other. I'm not the one who should apologise!" Rick shouted as he stormed out of the gym.

My initial thought was Alex. I had to find her and make sure she was okay. What was meant to be the most amazing night of her life had ended so abruptly in a total shit storm that she had not anticipated. I ran back to the dorm as fast as my dress and stiletto heels would allow. Alex was lying on her bed with tears covering her pillow.

"Cat, what just happened? Have I lost Rick? I just started dancing and then all hell broke loose. I just don't know how this happened. Did you see Rick?" "Yes, I saw him and I told him to follow you. You guys have to work this out. It was just a misunderstanding. I know you love him." "I do but I've never seen this side of him before. He was a completely different person." "Alex, the green-eyed monster came out tonight, fuelled by the gallon of alcohol he consumed."

"What should I do Cat? Should I go talk to Rick or what?" Given Alex's emotional distress about the whole situation, I wasn't sure if talking to Rick was the most appropriate course of action given his current behaviour. "Alex, just leave him to it. He has a few things to sort out himself and, if anything, he's the one that owes you an apology. You did nothing wrong and if you go chasing him, he will think that his behaviour was okay and it wasn't. Let him cool off and he will come looking for you. I know he will." I just hoped what I was telling Alex was the truth after Rick left in such a temper. As I held Alex close, and her tears ran down my back along with her mascara, I felt so sorry for her. What was to be the best night of her life ended in disaster with Rick acting like a male chauvinistic psycho.

Alex jumped up. "Cat, hand me the phone. I'm going to call him. I need to explain everything. He's totally overreacting right?" "Okay bird, call him if it will make you feel better but he needs to apologise to you." Alex called but it went straight to answer machine. Calling a few more times, I could tell Alex was holding her breath in the hope that Rick would pick up the phone but nothing.

Eventually, I had to tell Alex to give up. "Come on bird, just leave it for tonight. He's probably drowning his sorrows and won't be in the mood to talk." I tried to convince Alex that it would be okay and she could sort it out in the morning. We eventually went to bed but I knew that Alex wouldn't sleep a wink thinking of what she was going to say to Rick. How could what was supposed to be an amazing night turn into such a disaster?

Chapter 12

Leaving on a Jet Plane

I woke up early to find Alex's bed empty and I knew she had gone to search for Rick. It was like her mission to talk to him. This was our last day of College before heading home for the Christmas holidays and she wasn't going to let things end like this.

At that moment, the phone began to ring. It was Tom. "Hi Cat, I just wanted to call to make sure Alex was okay. Is she there?" "That's nice of you Tom, it's more than her boyfriend has done. Sorry Tom, Alex isn't here. I think she's talking with Rick." Or rather I hoped she was. This had to be resolved today.

"Cat, can you ask Alex to call me? I really am sorry if I caused any problems between Alex and Rick. I don't understand. We were just dancing as friends. There was nothing to it. I love my girlfriend and Stacey and I have been together for three years. Rick knows this." Tom seemed so sad that all of this had happened but that was him all over - a true gent. "Tom, I'll tell Alex that you called and hopefully we'll see you before we leave later. I can't believe that I'm travelling back to Ireland with this crazy shit going on. I know Alex will need a friend right now. I just hope they sort it out." "That's right, Cat, you have a flight to catch tonight. Take care and it will get sorted. This morning, in the light of day, it will all blow over." "Thanks Tom, I'll call you later before I leave." I was just hoping that Tom's words would be true.

Just then, the phone rang again. It was Alex. "Hey bird, are you okay? Where are you?" I was concerned as I could hear that Alex was upset. "I'm down by the lake. Can you meet me there?" I could tell that things were serious and I immediately ran out of the dorm and past Carla and her posse who I'm certain were gossiping about last night's events.

Running as fast as I could to get to my friend, I spotted Alex sitting by the picnic benches with her head in her hands. I sat down beside her and gave her a huge hug. It was just what she needed as she sobbed uncontrollably onto my shoulder. I gave her time to cry it out before asking what had happened with Rick. "Cat, it's over! He said that I disrespected him, that I want to fuck Tom and that he has seen the way I flirt with him and other guys. He said he's had enough of it and he's had enough of me!" Alex was inconsolable. "Cat, it is my fault. I should never have danced with Tom. Tom and I are friends and I told Rick that. I told him I loved him and that he needed to understand that."

"Alex, it's not your fault. It sounds like Rick is being an overbearing asshole and he evidently doesn't think much of you if this is what gets him in a crazy fit of jealousy. Alex, Rick was a total prick last night. He spent most of it getting drunk with his buddies and I think he really showed his true colours."

"Just leave it for a while and call him back later. You'll see him before we leave later." "Cat, I can't believe this is happening to me. What a difference a day makes. We were getting our makeup done for the dance yesterday and never in a million years would I have thought that I'd be feeling like this today. I'm just so lost and confused right now." "I know you are, bird, but let's get back to our dorm. You know we have to pack before we go on Christmas break." "Cat, what am I going to do without you too? Just when I need you most. I'm going to be so lost." We knew we were leaving soon and we gave each other another heartfelt hug.

After lunch, Alex and I set about packing. I had a few more things to bring home after my shopping excursions at the mall. I loved my new wardrobe and I was all set to bring it back to Ireland. Alex took a lot longer to pack as she had pretty much brought her entire wardrobe with her. We were both too numb to think about what the next few weeks would be like without having each other to talk to.

I was torn. To be going back home to see my family was going to be great but I was going to miss Alex terribly. College friends sure do make you feel like a family and Alex and I were total soul sisters. “Okay Cat, I’ve packed my shit up so let’s get the car packed up. We have the drive to the airport and I’m going to drive home straight after. Cat, I’ll have to listen to my tunes in the car without your lovely accent to keep me company.”

I could tell Alex was trying not to think about Rick but the urge was too great. “Cat, come on. Let’s go over to Rick’s room. I need to see him again before we leave. I just don’t understand why he’s being like this.” “Okay Alex, if you need to get over and sort things out, I’ll wait for you at the Coffee House.” “Cat, please come with me. I need you for moral support.” So, we walked out of our room and straight into the Carla posse who gave Alex and me, but mainly Alex, the fiercest look I had ever seen.

“Oh, look who it is! So Alexandra, how are you and Rick doing? I take it he’s dumped your ass after what you did last night? You do know that Tom is completely in love with Stacey. He would never be interested in you. I mean look at her and then look at you. No comparison." Carla's tongue was as sharp as a razor blade and Alex didn't need to hear it at that moment in time. "For the love of Christ, Carla, would you ever go and fuck yourself because there is no one else who would want to!" "At least I don't go dancing with another woman's man!" Carla retorted. "No man would want you, Carla, so I think you're good." Carla definitely chose the wrong time to pick on Alex, all she wanted to do was see Rick.

As we walked across campus, I knew that Alex wanted to kiss and make up with Rick before we left for the Christmas break. She was ready to take full responsibility for what had happened. She wanted to see him but I was hoping that she could see what an asshole he had been. His drunken macho man behaviour was not acceptable.

Just as we got to the guys' dorm, a familiar face was sitting outside but I don't think it was the one Alex wanted to see. It was Tom. As he walked towards us, it was clear that Alex was not in the mood to talk to him. "Alex, can we talk? I'm really sorry about the way things turned out last night. I didn't mean to cause you any trouble with Rick. We are just friends and I would never want to jeopardise our friendship." I could tell that Tom was being sincere. "Tom, I really don't have time to talk to you right now. I have to speak to Rick and, no, we are not okay. He thinks I'm not serious about him and I have to make him see that you mean nothing to me, Tom." On hearing Alex's sharp words, Tom held his hands up and stood to the side while she walked towards the dorms.

As we got to Rick's dorm, I gave Alex a reassuring smile. "Okay bird, go get him. I'll stay outside so that you can talk privately. Remember, he was being a jerk about this so don't take all the blame." I was trying to make sure that Alex stood her ground. Rick's behaviour was still pissing me off but, for now, all Alex wanted was to have his strong arms wrapped around her again. As I waited outside, I heard Alex cry out from inside the building. I rushed to Rick's room to find Alex standing in front of Rick's empty wardrobe. His books had gone and the posters on his walls had gone. Rick had left!

Alex was hysterical and I knew it was going to take some time to calm her down. Rick had left without even saying goodbye to her. Perhaps this was it. The love story was over and Alex had no way of getting it back, before the holidays at least. She was devastated. I was so angry with Rick. How could he be such a jerk about everything? His love for Alex didn't compare to his love for his ego. Alex had one dance with a friend and he exploded and caused all this hurt and destruction. As I tried to comfort Alex, I didn't want to leave her but I knew that, in a few hours, I'd be flying home and all I wanted to do was to stay and make sure my best friend was okay.

"Alex you're strong and you'll get through this. Rick is a dick for not trying to work this out with you. Fuck him, Alex! He's not the guy you thought he was if this is the way he behaves. Come on bird, we have a few hours left before my flight. Let's go to the mall. I might just need one more purchase before I leave." I was hoping that shopping would take her mind off Rick.

As we sat having a coffee at the mall, Alex seemed to be feeling a little better. "So Cat, let's talk about your love life, please, to take my mind off Rick! What are you going to do about James when you get home?" Alex asked the big question that, to be honest, I didn't have the answer for. "Oh Alex, I just don't know. We are like family and always will be. He sees me as a sister. Nothing will ever happen." "Nothing will happen if you don't make it happen, bird." Alex always said how she felt and went for things and I loved that about her. I, on the other hand, just wished I had the courage to say something. I was a total chicken shit.

"Cat, just talk to the guy. Tell him how you feel. If you don't, you'll only regret it. Take it from me. I'm now lost in limbo with Rick until I see him after the holidays. Maybe James feels the same way about you and he just couldn't tell you for the same reasons you don't want to tell him." "I doubt it. How many times has James asked me to hook him up with my friends? He clearly has his eye elsewhere." I was thinking back to all my friends that James had dated and I felt sad that it would never be me but at least I knew that we were and would always be friends.

The next few hours seemed to fly by and pretty soon Alex and I were on the road to the airport. As Alex drove, it was the quietest either one of us had ever been since we met. Alex had Rick on her mind and I had James on mine. I had to say something just to break the silence. "Hey clucker," I said with a little smile and, just like that, the mood was lifted. "Cat, I'm going to miss you so, so much. You have no idea. You have been there for me these past few months like no one else in my life has. I feel as though you're more than a friend, you're the sister I never had." "Alex, I feel exactly the same. You are everything to me and I wish I could stay." Just as I said it, Alex shouted out, "Stay! Do you need to go back to Ireland? It's cold and rainy there and look at all the lovely palm trees we have here. Do you want me to drive past the airport?" For a second, I actually thought about it but, of course, I had to get back to see my family. It was Christmas and I needed to go home. "I wish I could but you know I can't. It's just going to be for a few weeks and then I'll be back for the next semester. Time will fly in, I promise." I wasn't sure if I was trying to convince Alex or myself.

Arriving at the Departure Gate, my heart felt so heavy and hurt like hell. Alex and I gave each other the biggest hug as tears streamed down our faces. Alex squeezed me so tightly. "I thought I had cried all my tears today over Rick but, Cat, these tears are for you. I'm going to miss you, girl. Have a great time back home and remember your American home." "I will and I'll miss you too, bird. Birds of a feather flock together, right?" And with that, I made my way to the security check. I was going home.

As I boarded the flight, I could tell people were staring at me as tears were streaming down my face. I was a mess. Thank goodness it was an overnight flight. I just closed my eyes and tried to sleep but all I could think about was how I was going to miss my best friend for the next three weeks. I began to cry again. I was excited to see my family again but part of me was missing.

Chapter 13

You've Got Mail

Touching down at Dublin Airport, I woke up to see a rain-soaked runway and I knew I was back in Ireland. No more palm trees or blazing sunshine for a few weeks. Gathering my belongings together, I began to feel better as if setting foot on home soil made me content to be home at last. As I approached the Arrivals Gate, I could see my parents and a huge smile came over my face. I ran as fast as I could and gave them both the biggest hug. All the emotion of the past twenty-four hours and now seeing my parents was too much and I started to sob. I was pretty much an emotional wreck.

"Welcome home, Kitty Cat. We've missed you so much." My dad always knew just what to say to make me feel safe. Mum was so overjoyed to see me, she was crying too. "Catherine, my darlin', you look so well and you have a bit of a tan!" I started laughing, "Mum, I can't believe you think I have a tan. I'm the whitest person on campus." "Come on, let's get you home. You'll be freezing. Sure, you're only wearing a light shirt! Cat, remember it's Irish weather. No more Californian sunshine for a few weeks. We have your snow jacket right here. Put this on." It was so great to see my parents again. I didn't realise how much I had missed them. College life in America was non-stop and I rarely had a chance to think about home.

As my mum and dad drove me home, I looked at all the familiar sights of Dublin; the sights and sounds that I had known and loved for years but which felt so distant to me now. In only a few months, I had found a new home back in California and I now had to get used to being back in Dublin.

When we arrived home, I found my bedroom exactly the way I had left it, apart from mum giving it a good clean and tidy. The first thing I wanted to do was get into the computer room and check my emails. I wanted to send a message to Alex as I had promised her I would let her know that I had arrived safely. I was delighted to see an email already waiting for me.

To: Cat

From: Alex

Subject: Hey Fucker

Hey there hoochie. It's only me, the funny-looking blonde in America. I already miss your smelly ass. I kept hoping that you would come off of that plane but you never did. I kept trying to think of a way to say goodbye to you at the airport but it seemed so inappropriate as goodbye is long-term and this is temporary. I miss you like crazy, Cat, and I wish you were here. You had me at hello (even if I couldn't understand your accent at the time).

After Rick left and you left, I think I'm now dehydrated I've cried so friggin' much. Now that you have gone, I have even more time to think. How scary is that?! I haven't heard from Rick at all. I don't even know if he's in Chicago. I still can't believe this happened, Cat. How can something so wonderful and full-on just stop? How can he cut off all communication with me? Cat, maybe you could try to email him? He might answer you, his Irish buddy. He sure as hell is not talking to me. Life is so confusing and you have only been gone a few hours.

Well, I will let you go. Welcome home, to your home that is, don't forget about your American home. Love you, miss you like crazy.

Your friend always, Alex. x

To: Alex

From: Cat

Subject: Hey American girl

Hi bird,! It's so lovely to hear from you, well, virtually at least. I miss that American accent and your bad language. Another thing we need to thank your dad for!! I got home safely and it was lovely to see my parents at the airport. I was freezing my Irish arse off though. There's no sunshine, just the rain which has been pissin' out of the heavens since I arrived back! I'm glad to be back home but I do miss my American home, Alex. I miss you too, bird. I was the same leaving you yesterday. I think we didn't need words to tell each other. It's not goodbye at all. I'll see you in a few weeks. So, you have time to think now. Oh, heaven help us!!

I'm so sorry that you're going through this uncertainty with Rick. He seriously needs medication or help. He is acting like a totally different guy and, Alex, maybe you have dodged a bullet here. Maybe I should send him a message just to see what the fuck is going on but, as you know, Alex, birds of a feather flock together so I'd probably not get anything back.

Okay Bird, I gotta go. My parents have barely seen me. I've been catching up with my online chat. I wish you could be here.

Love and miss you.

Always

Cat x

I closed my computer and went downstairs to see my parents. The joy on their faces was so heart-warming. Even though I was missing Alex, I was happy to see them.

"Come on Kitty Cat, sit down beside your old man and tell me all about College in sunny California. From your emails, you sound like you're having a ball with your roommate and new friends. I hope you are concentrating on studying and not so much on getting a tan," my dad joked.

"Oh Dad, I love the College life over there and, yes, I'm getting used to the weather after a few mishaps with the sunscreen. I've made great friends and Alex is the best. We do everything together and have so much fun." As I filled my mum and dad in on my College adventures over the past few months, leaving out a few details of course, I realised that I had come so far in only a short while.

"Catherine, I'm so proud of you!" my mum gushed. "Going away by yourself and getting into College in America is going to be life-changing for you. I wish I had the chance to do that when I was young." "Helen, your life-changing experience happened when you met me, right?" My dad teased. Mum was not impressed.

"Darlin', we must get ourselves ready for the Flanagan's. They've invited us over for drinks this evening to welcome you back. I know James has really missed you. He's been asking when you're coming back home. Maybe absence makes the heart grow fonder," Mum smiled in such a way that suggested she was going to be picking out her mother-of-the-bride outfit for our wedding. I, on the other hand, knew only too well that James wasn't interested in walking up the aisle, not with me anyway.

As we drove over to the Flanagan family home, I was thinking about what Alex had said to me before I left. 'Just tell him how you feel' but I knew it was a risk that I couldn't take. Kate and Jim were waiting to welcome us with a Welcome Home banner for me. Kate was so kind and, as she was my Godmother, she thought of me as her own daughter.

"Welcome home, Catherine!" Kate screamed as she threw her arms around me. "My, you have changed, look at that lovely tan and your hair is blonde. Are those highlights from the sun?" I laughed at the thought of everyone thinking that I had a tan. To anyone in wet and rainy Dublin, I guess I had. "James, James! Catherine is here! Come on down and see our California girl!" Kate shouted upstairs to James and my heart began to pound as it had been four months since I had seen him and so much had changed, for me that was.

James ran downstairs and lifted me up in his arms as if he were a soldier coming back from a war. He whirled me around and hugged me so tightly that I thought I was going to break. "Cat, you're back! I've missed you so much!" James exclaimed. "James, put her down, let the rest of us get a hug," Kate joked. "No mum, she's mine tonight. It's been way too long and I need a catch-up with my sis,"

James declared. He quickly took me by the hand and marched me up to his room. James' bedroom was so familiar to me. I'd had many sleepovers and had hung out with him in his room over the years. I felt like I was truly home but, again, I was back in familiar territory with James and our "friendship."

"So Cat, tell me everything about California," James demanded. I retold my adventures to James, as I had before to my mum and dad, only this time I included in all the juicy details of our drunken escapades, the Lake House parties, the clubs and also the cute guys. James was mesmerised or at least I think he was. He looked at me with a weird smile that I hadn't seen before or maybe I hadn't seen in a while. We talked all night and it was as if we were back to our familiar friendship. As much as that was comforting, I was trying to find a way to tell James how I felt but tonight was not the right time. Maybe never was the right time.

My parents called from downstairs to say that we were leaving. James looked disappointed to see me go so soon. "Cat, won't you stay over? We can have one of our all-night ice cream binges. There's plenty in the fridge," James asked, hoping to have more time to catch up. "James, I can't and, besides, we aren't kids anymore. I'll see you again soon. I promise." I needed to be strong and not get caught up in the friendship-safe zone again.

As we drove back home from the Flanagan's house, I felt very different. James was so much a part of my life but I realised that sleepovers and staying up late were not what I needed. Alex was right. James wanted me as a friend but, from his reaction when I mentioned the guys at College, I was now certain he didn't want anyone else to have me either.

I got up early the following morning to check my emails. I had to fill Alex in on my meeting with James and, again, I had an email waiting in my inbox.

To: Cat

From Alex

Subject: It's Over

Hey there hoochie. It's official. Rick and I are over. I got the Dear John email late last night. Cat, what do you say in your Irish language...What a fucking wanker!! He is unbelievable saying that I didn't take our relationship seriously and that, if I had, then I wouldn't have been running around with Tom behind his back.

Apparently, you will never guess, Carla had been filling his head with all sorts of shit about me. He said he didn't believe it but when he saw Tom and I dancing together, he knew it was true. Can you believe that shit?! Fucking Carla had it in for me from the beginning. I can't believe Rick believed her over me. I guess he just was not the guy I thought he was. He really showed his true colours and, besides, every time he drank he turned into a jerk. Remember the way he was talking to Mike after a few drinks? He loved the liquor probably more than me. I was just way too loved up to see it.

He told me that he wasn't coming back to Deacon College, that he was staying in Chicago and that I broke his heart because I was pretending to love him. That couldn't be farther from the truth. Cat, I had totally fallen for him and I don't know why he won't come back. I have cried so many tears this past week over him but I'm not giving him anymore.

Cat, I miss you, I am so totally depressed. I come home late at night from work, I got my old part-time job back which is keeping me sane, but I'm stuck with my dad. Mom still works 90 hours a week. I wish you were here. I miss our late-night chats and our once-in-a-while beer runs. I miss your laugh and your sarcasm. I miss everything and I feel like a piece of me is gone. I will stop now. I've been thinking way too much. I guess Rick has made me realise how precious a good friend, especially my best friend, is. I took you for granted a lot, I AM SORRY!! I am gonna go now. I miss you and love you loads.

Hugs and farts. Alex x

To: Alex

From: Cat

Subject: Rick is a Prick

Hey bird, well where do I start?

Firstly, I have to say forget about Rick. He is a prize Prick!! I've just realised - Prick and Dick rhyme with Rick, I see a theme. He is definitely not the guy either of us thought he was. You're right, he had a mean streak when he drank. I can't believe Carla had something to do with this. Oh wait, I can. Asking Carla to be nice is like asking a turkey to vote for Thanksgiving, it will never happen! She has absolutely no life so now she is trying to ruin yours. Alex, fuck them both. Just concentrate on enjoying your Christmas holiday. It will be Christmas soon and not long until we get back to College. I have to level with you, Alex. Thank you for being so honest with me. You haven't taken me for granted. You were just in love with Rick and, at the time, he was your world. I'm always here for you, you know that.

Alex, guess what? I saw James last night and it was so weird. I felt different around him. I think my time away from him has made me realise that there is life after James. He was still in friend-mode and even wanted me to stay over. I've had enough of the slumber parties and I think I need to move on from James. Maybe find an American guy when I get back to College? Like you said, we could live near each other and have babies at the same time.

I have to go now as I'm meeting my friends later for drinks and I need to decide what to wear from my new American wardrobe! Something that shows off my arms. By the way, everyone here thinks I actually have a tan. Miss you, wish you were here with me.

Lots of love and pints of beer. Cat x

To: Cat

From: Alex

Subject: Friends with Benefits

So Cat, you have been hanging out with James? Well, you know what I think about this situation. I think you should fuck his brains out and get it over with J. Go on Cat, you know you want to! Seriously though, I really think you need to tell him how you feel. It's eating you up inside, I know that and I just want to see you happy. You're my best friend in the whole world and you have been there for me through this whole Rick disaster. Your emails have been keeping me going. Now, I want to hear all about your Dublin adventures as there is dipshit going on here in my world. The weather has been great at least so I can top up my tan. I can't believe your family thinks you have a tan, that's hilarious!! Take care, my little white Irish girl.

Lots of love and sunscreen. Alex x

To: Alex

From: Cat

Subject: Santa's Coming!

Hi bird, it's only me your Irish girl checking in to see if you're okay and if you had any word from Rick the prick. I'm thinking of you. Now more than ever. Fuck, I really miss you, Alex. I went to the pub with my friends last night and I actually never felt so alone in my whole life. They all think I have become too Americanised and teased me for wearing my College campus sweater, white socks and blue jeans. My friends are all into black right now so I looked like an outsider. I just wished that you were here to say "Hey clucker." It's so strange. I was surrounded by friends that I've known for over a decade and yet I felt as though I had nothing in common with them. I don't know if that makes sense?

They have been telling me that James has missed his 'buddy', as they call me. He had been calling them to hang out but none of them were interested in him anymore. I think he burned too many bridges while he was playing the field. I've to meet James tomorrow to go into town. He needs to buy his mum's Christmas present and we always go to Grafton Street to buy something nice. If it wasn't for me, Kate would be getting World's Best Mum mugs each year. Okay bird, I gotta go.

Lots of love and Christmas Cheer.

Cat x

Chapter 14

Party like it's 1999!

As I began to get ready to meet James, I started thinking about what my friends had said about him; never one to stay committed, playing the field all the time. Maybe it was a good thing that we were just friends. He clearly had commitment issues and I didn't want to be another one of those girls.

Standing at the train platform, I was startled by James who had come up from behind me to give me another one of his bear hugs. "Thank you for coming into town with me, Cat." "Of course, it's our annual tradition and, besides, Kate deserves a decent present, not the shitty things you pick up for her. I saw last year's birthday present remember?" I jokingly gave James a nudge.

The train into Dublin was very busy, packed with commuters and shoppers all heading in to do their last-minute Christmas shopping. All the Christmas lights and festive shop windows shone brightly and I realised that I loved being back in Dublin again with James. We chatted and laughed, just like old times, and it felt safe and comfortable. That's what I wanted. No more thinking of James - the romance. I just couldn't risk losing him. He meant too much to me.

After hours of shopping and having fun, James and I went to our favourite pub that we always went to after our Christmas day out. The owner knew us well, welcomed us in and sat us at our usual table. I was telling James about all the restaurants that Alex and I had frequented to escape the cafeteria food that we had to eat. "My Cat, you and Alex have become quite a pair," James joked. "Yes, James. Alex is fearless and, in a way, she has taught me so much about courage and saying how I feel. She always says I should be honest about my feelings, although honesty may not be the best policy sometimes," I said.

"Cat, I want to be honest with you," James said, taking my hand and looking into my eyes. "Cat, I've missed you so much, you have no idea. I guess you have been too busy with your life in California to even give me a second thought." "James, you know I will always have time for you. You're my brother from another mother, right?" I needed him to know that he would always be important in my life and, even though my life had moved on and I had developed new friendships, I wasn't going to forget him.

"Cat, I just want to let you know how much you mean to me and I'm sorry if I've never said it to you before. I guess I thought you would always be here and, when you left for America, the thought of losing you was too much." James was so sincere and was becoming a little emotional. I guess absence does make friendships grow fonder. "Okay, my friend, we should be getting back now. It's Christmas Eve and the trains are going to be crazy busy. Besides, these presents aren't going to wrap themselves." I tried to make a joke to lighten the mood.

It was Christmas morning and I woke up to a blanket of snow on the ground and a wintry chill. Since coming home, I had been wearing five layers of clothes to keep warm. I went downstairs to be greeted by my mum and dad who were sitting by the tree with Christmas breakfast already laid out on the table.

"Merry Christmas, darlin'." My mum hugged me and handed me their present to me. I ripped open the wrapping paper to see a bright, shiny new laptop which was just what I wanted. "We thought you needed an upgrade to your computer and, with all those emails you have been sending lately, you've probably worn out the PC!" Dad laughed, as he knew how often I was emailing Alex.

"Oh Mum and Dad, this is perfect, my own laptop! I love it!! Look at me, I can take this anywhere, well anywhere that has a modem," I laughed. The only thing about getting onto the internet was the long phone cable that had to be attached to the computer to get access, then the ten-minute dial-up connection to get online.

I quickly set up my new laptop and hooked it up to the modem. I waited for dial-up connection and finally, I was online. After the busy Christmas Eve with James, I needed to check my emails and see how Alex was. An email was sitting waiting for me.

To: Cat

From Alex

Subject: Merry Christmas Mother Clucker

Hey there, my lovely Irish bird, Merry Christmas!! I'm so excited that Christmas is finally here. That means only another week and a half before we go back to College and you get your ass back over here! I hope you have some lovely things planned for the festivities today.

Mom has to work the morning shift today so Dad and I are getting the food ready for our Christmas feast. It's going to be as big as Thanksgiving! I'd better not gain back all that weight I lost last year but these stuffing balls are looking way too good!

So I have some CRAZY news to tell you. So, you know me, when I get depressed and all else fails, I go shopping. Well, yesterday I did just that. I put a 500 dollar music system in my car. Yes, I'm very serious, Cat, my car is the shit and this system is amazing. We are going to have so much fun on our road trips when you get back with plenty of cool tunes to keep us going. Needless to say, I felt better temporarily, but then I had the reality check of the huge bill I'll be getting, but it's worth it. Get ready for our monster road trips.

I'm sorry you're feeling so alone over there but I know exactly what you mean. I've been hanging out with Kim and, as much as I love her, we really are in two different places right now. I totally get how old friends and new friends can be so different. You just get me, Cat, It's like we were separated at birth! Merry Christmas, my sis from another miss!!

Lots of love and Christmas turkey!!

Alex x

P.S. Have you and James had sex yet? J

To: Alex

From: Cat

Subject: Merry Christmas Bird!

Hi bird, Merry Christmas!! I hope you're enjoying the tunes on your new sound system! I can't wait for our road trips! I'm sitting here with my brand new laptop and it's even got internet access! How cool is that! I guess 1998 is getting up to speed with the latest technology, here's to 1999!

I didn't get a chance to email yesterday. I was out with James and, no, we have not had sex yet, you dirty bird!! We were taking in the streets and pubs of Dublin.! Alex, I think something is really off with James. I'm worried about him. He just seemed so down yesterday. Not the happy-go-lucky, cheeky chappy I know. I think he's having problems and I just hope he is okay. Maybe it's girlfriend problems? My friends did say he was out and about a lot while I was away. That's really why I'm glad we are just friends. I just don't want to be another girl that he dumps after a while. I guess being friends is good, but with no benefits!

I hope that you and Jean and Pete have a wonderful Christmas and eat some turkey for me. I'm going to have some Christmas dinner and enjoy the snow. Can you believe it's snowing over here and you're sitting in the sunshine?

Lots of love and Christmas pudding

Cat x

PS Any word from Rick?

Christmas came and went, and the following week went by so slowly. I was housebound because of the heavy snow. There was nothing to do outside so sitting in and catching up on the TV soaps while eating the contents of the Christmas cupboard, was just bliss. I knew I had to recharge my batteries after the past few months. A week of rest, drink, eat and repeat was just what the doctor ordered. I spent most of my time on my new laptop which I loved and it was so good to be able to take it anywhere in the house.

Mum and Dad were busy with work. Mum was inundated with patients with winter colds and flu and my dad was as busy as ever with many surgeries planned for the week. I was so proud of both of them. They had dedicated their lives to medicine and also to me. Every evening, we had our traditional sit-down meal and talked about the events of the day. I always loved to hear about the amazing work they were doing.

Pretty soon, it was New Year's Eve and another year was to be celebrated at the Flanagan house. The annual New Year's Eve Flanagan's party was always the highlight of the festive season. I also wanted to see James again just to make sure he was okay. His mood the last time we met was not the James I knew and loved. Before the party, I had one quick email to send to Alex.

To: Alex

From: Cat

Subject: Let's party like it's 1999!

Hey Girl, It's New Year's Eve!! Another year is ahead of us and I can't wait to see what's in store!! The good thing about New Year's is that we can start over. A New Year and a new you, Alex. Leave all the bullshit behind you and just get back to College life. I can't wait to see what Carla has to say for herself! From now on, we will have nothing to do with her or the clones. I'm going to James' family New Year's Eve party but it won't be the same without you. Remember our first party at the Lake House with the guys? You got so drunkededeeded!! We have had such great times these past few months. I can't wait to get back to have plenty more! I miss the sun shine, the pool and how I can go out and not freeze my arse off like here in Dublin.

Alex, it would seriously freeze the balls off of a brass monkey over here. I never thought I'd get used to sunshine!! My tan looks more like a tea stain right now! It's not just the sunshine I miss - I miss you so, so much, bird. I know you're feeling depressed with everything but just stay strong - you can get through this. I'll be back soon and time will fly by now that it's New Year's. I always think the week between Christmas and New Year's is the longest week of the year! There are no rules when it comes to eating or drinking either. I have seriously eaten my entire body weight this past week, it's like Thanksgiving all over again!

Alex, take care of yourself and I hope you're okay. Just think of the fun we are going to have.

Lots of love and New Year's resolutions.

Cat x

As our taxi pulled up to the Flanagan's house, I became quite excited to welcome in the New Year. It was finally going to be 1999, the last year of the twentieth century, and I was ready to enjoy every second of it. The Flanagan's house was always packed with friends and family for New Year's and it was lovely to see people that I hadn't seen in such a long time. As I made my way around the house, getting hugs and kisses from James' aunts who were practically my aunts, I felt so warm inside. Friends and family were so important and it was wonderful to be able to celebrate with those that I loved. Suddenly two hands covered my eyes and I knew it was James.

"Where have you been, stranger?" I joked. "Aunt Emily is already doing shots of sherry and it's not even midnight!" James looked at me as he had on Christmas Eve. "My Cat is here! I've been dying for you to get here. If I get one more pinch of a cheek from an old aunt, I'm going to explode! Come on, let's go upstairs to put on some music."

As James led me upstairs, it felt all too familiar. We would always stay in his room and pig out on chocolate and beer while the revellers partied downstairs. I knew it was time to make sure that James was okay, he just wasn't himself.

"Okay bro, now tell me what's going on? You're not a happy chappy these days. Is it girl problems again? You know you can tell me anything." I wanted to get James to open up. "Cat, you know me too well and it is girl problems. I'm in love!" James declared. "Fuck me, James, that's huge! Who's the lucky girl?" I asked. "Cat, you do know her but she doesn't feel the same way about me. I just don't know what to do." I was familiar with the problem so I gave James the advice I had given to myself but ignored, "James, have you told this girl how you feel? Maybe she does feel the same way about you." Now, I was offering James up to someone else. It was as if I was talking to Rick again!

"Cat, I just can't take it anymore, my heart is in knots and I'm all over the place. Cat, it's you! I'm in love with YOU! Please don't hate me but I have to tell you the truth. Since you've been gone, I've finally realised that I love you. You are my other half, my missing piece. I've been lost without you these past few months. I love you, Cat," James confessed. He looked at me for some sort of a sign but I was frozen. Were those the words coming out of James' mouth, the words I had longed to hear practically my entire life?

"James, wait what? You love me? But we've always just been friends. You've always tried to date all my friends. We've always just been buddies," I said, feeling so confused.

"I know Cat. I was dating your friends, trying to find someone like you but no one could compare to you. I want you. Maybe it's taken me this long to realise and not having you here has made me even more sure that it's you I want to be with. Cat, you don't have to say anything. I know I'm asking a lot. We've been friends for forever but if I don't say anything to you now before you go back to America, I feel like I will have missed my chance. Then you'll fall for one of those hot Californian guys and forget all about me. I just had to say the words. I love you, Cat." I was floored. Those were the words I wanted to hear for so long.

"I think I've said too much," James said as he moved towards the door but I touched his arm and moved in to kiss him. We had the most magical kiss

I have ever had in my entire life. I felt like I was floating or maybe I'd had too many beers! "Does this mean what I think it means?" James asked hopefully. "James Flanagan, you complete eejit! I've loved you for as long as I can remember, silly. I just thought you would never be interested in me. I'm practically your sister remember?" "Now Cat, no more brother and sister talk. That's just weird," James cringed as we both started to laugh.

Just then, my mum called up the stairs to us. "Kids, it's almost midnight! Come downstairs and celebrate with the family and turn that music off!" Mum's voice brought us back to reality and we smiled at each other, knowing that everything was out in the open and we could finally be honest with each other. We arrived downstairs just in time to welcome in the New Year and we were all finally able to party like was 1999 - Prince style!

As my mum and dad were about to leave for home, I told them I was going to stay over with James. They knew it was our usual slumber party, staying up all night talking and antics. But this time, there was no talking involved. We had the most wonderful night together and made up for lost time.

The next morning, I woke up to James pinching me. "What are you doing?" "I'm just pinching you to make sure you're really here. Cat, I have wanted to be with you all these months and now you're here. I can't believe it." James put his strong arms around me and held me tight. "Yes, I'm here but you know it's only for one more day. I go back to California tomorrow." Suddenly, the thought of going back to America was bittersweet. I couldn't wait to see Alex but now it was going to be so hard to leave James. "That's right, you're leaving me again!" James looked sadly at me. "Now don't go chasing any more American guys, Cat. You're taken. I don't want to lose you to one of those American football players!" "Oh James, you won't. I am 100% in love with you silly." I promised that I would be back home in no time.

Everything was happening so fast. I wanted to be with James for one more night before I left for America. Why did it take him so long to tell me his feelings? We could have had the past few weeks together. Although, I really couldn't criticise, after all, it only took me ten years of silence to tell him how I felt.

I got dressed and did the walk of shame down the stairs with James behind me. Kate was in the kitchen and had no idea that we had just had an unforgettable night. As far as she knew, we had our usual sleepover. "Hi there sleepy heads, did you both stay up half the night talking?" Kate smiled and hugged me. "Something like that mum," James replied, winking at me with a cheeky grin on his face.

After eating a delicious full Irish breakfast that Kate had made, James drove me back home. I had to start getting my bags packed again.

On returning home, I went straight to my laptop. I couldn't wait to tell Alex all about my night of passion with James. I had already received an email from Alex.

To: Cat

From Alex

Subject: Counting the days!!

Hi there bird! Okay, we only have one day to go and you will be back on these shores! Have you packed?? Just kidding, I'm just hoping these days will fly and I get to see you again. Is it Saturday yet??

Cat, I have to tell you that Tom has been in touch over the past few days. I told him about Rick and he felt so bad. He told me that Carla and Rick had dated during freshman year but only for a short while. Maybe Carla thought if she couldn't have him, she wasn't going to let me have him. More fool Rick, the dumb fuck, for believing her.

I've been so depressed lately. I miss your shitty ass so I just started crying on the phone to Tom. I told him everything, about Rick and how I felt, but you know, I finally realised why Rick had such a strong hold on me, you. It's like I cannot connect with anyone here like I do to you and he was so much like you (when the fun side of him was there), so I hold on to it so I do not have to think about you not being here. Make sense? Probably not to you, but it did to Tom. I just miss you soooo much, Cat. What I wouldn't give to have you here right now. Miss you loads, lots of love. Alex x

To: Alex

From: Cat

Subject: Not long Now

Hey sunshine!

Are you ready for the Irish girl to come back??? I've only one more day to go but who's counting?!

I know you're sad at the moment and it's breaking my heart that you're so depressed. I'm glad to hear that Tom has been in touch with you too. He is a good friend and, before all this bullshit, he was like one of us. Alex, I totally get it! Since we met I've known that we have something special. The way we talk and just know each other is different from anyone else. I feel complete with you, bird. I want to feel complete again.

Can't wait to see you. I'm going to miss my family and Dublin again, I know I am but I've actually spent more time in my room emailing you than doing anything else. How weird is that!! Okay bird, get ready for some beer runs and all-night chats. Are you ready to get drunkededed!! See you at Arrivals tomorrow.

Lots of love and duty-free booze!!

Cat x

PS James and I had sex!!

To: Cat

From: Alex

Subject: One more day!!

WHAT!! You had sex with James?! You have to hurry up and get your ass over here and tell me everything!! I knew you guys would do it! Did you finally grow a pair and tell him how you feel? I'm all packed and ready to collect you from the airport. Now remember to make plenty of time to get through security and also to stop off at the Duty-Free!! Can I have some rum please? Oh, and some of that fabulous Irish chocolate!!

I'll be there early for you so that I don't miss you! Cat, I'm so excited to see you. These past few weeks have felt like forever. I'm finally getting out of my Rick illness and you're the medicine I need. Safe travels and make sure you leave some beer for everyone else on the airline trolley!

See you soon. Lots of love and tequila shots! Alex x

Chapter 15

Happy New Year

With less than twenty-four hours to go before I was due to fly back to California, I tried to process the events of the night before. Did that just happen? Did James just say he loved me? Did I just have the most amazing night of my life with him? It really was as James had described - a pinch-me moment. Then the realisation that I'd soon be 5,000 miles away kicked in.

There was a knock at the door. It was James. "Hello James, come on in," my mum welcomed him in. "Are you trying to get as much Cat time as you can before she goes tomorrow?" my mum joked, although I wanted as much James time as I could get too. "Absolutely Helen, do you mind if I take her out for a while?" James asked with a smile on his face and a twinkle in his eye. I knew what sort of Cat time James was thinking of. "Okay, James but remember, Catherine, you need to be back early. You have a flight to catch tomorrow morning," my mum warned.

As we got into James' car, he looked at me like he had never looked at me before; like he wanted to take a picture of this moment and keep it. Then he leaned over to kiss me. "Where are we going?" I asked. "You'll see." As James drove us out of town, we were surrounded by snow-covered trees and white glistening hedges but I knew that tomorrow I'd be looking out at the palm trees of California. Pretty soon, James stopped the car and, to my delight, it was at his old family holiday home in the country. I hadn't been there in such a long time but the place was full of happy memories for me. Memories of time spent with James and our families. I wanted to be able to make more memories that I could take back to America with me.

"I got the keys to our special place, Cat." James knew only too well how much fun we had here and he wanted to make each minute count. After lighting the fire and putting down the rugs to keep warm, James held me in his arms. "Cat, last night was just amazing. I can't believe I waited until now to pluck up the courage to tell you how I feel. Now we only have today and you'll be off to America again." James was so sincere.

"I know, you dummy, you should have told me two weeks ago! But James, I guess I should have told you like ten years ago so we're even." I couldn't believe that James had felt the same way about me. We had wasted so much time. I should have taken a leaf out of Alex's book and just gone for it. "Cat, we have today to catch up on lost time and I want to spend every minute of it with you. Your absence over these past few months has made me realise that I love you so much and I just had to tell you!" James said excitedly and, as he leaned in to kiss me and took me in his arms, we laid down on the rugs by the fire. We were in a passionate embrace and started to undress. It was the most romantic moment of my life, making love by the blazing fire, our bodies cold from the winter freeze but making enough body heat to melt an iceberg. At that moment, I was in heaven. All the fantasising and wondering were worth the wait.

As we lay in each other's arms, James suddenly jumped up. "Wait, I have a surprise!" James tied a rug around his naked body and ran outside to the car. "What are you doing? It's freezing out there!" I laughed at the sight of James running out with no clothes or shoes on his feet. He came back from the car with a food hamper.

"I thought we might get hungry so I made us a picnic from all of the New Year's party leftovers." "I'm building up quite an appetite here," I laughed. James had brought candles and two flute glasses with the last of the New Year's wine. He really had thought this out. I was impressed and actually surprised. From my memories of James with previous girlfriends, he wasn't much of a romantic. I guess when it's the right girl, everything falls into place.

I felt like I could lie there with James forever. I still couldn't quite believe it was happening. Was this a dream and I was going to wake up soon? For now, I didn't want the dream to end. James looked at the clock. It was past 6 pm. We had spent the entire day together.

"Cat, I know I have to get you home. It's going to take a while to get back and, as much as I want to stay, Helen and George will be sending out a search party for you." James gave me a loving look. "I know James, we have to go. This has been the most amazing day. Thank you." Neither of us wanted it to end.

As James drove us back, we gave each other a loving smile and knew at that moment that we would be together, always. Back in Dublin, James stopped a few houses away from my parents' house. Although we had declared our undying love for each other, our parents had no idea and we wanted to keep it that way. We were just starting on our journey from friends to lovers and we didn't need the added pressure of our parents picking out the wedding date just yet.

We sat in the car and looked longingly at each other. “Cat, being with you today and just knowing that you love me the way I love you, makes it a little easier to say goodbye. Although now I’ve finally got you, you’re leaving and this is the end of our time together – for now. I can’t believe I’m losing you again to America. Now, make sure you don’t fall for one of these American guys.” James looked worried as if he was going to lose me forever.

“James, this isn’t the end of our time together, it’s only just the beginning. I’ll be back by the summer and we have the rest of our lives to be together. I’m yours, I’ve always been yours. I just never had the courage to tell you. I know I have to leave tomorrow but it’s only going to be for a few months, just another semester and I’ll be back. Just make sure you don’t hook up with another one of my friends,” I joked and gave James a playful nudge. “I won’t, I promise and besides, none of them compares to you, Cat. You’re the one for me.” James leaned over to give me a final kiss. As I got out of the car and stood at the side of the road to watch his car drive off, tears started to well up in my eyes. I was leaving James just at the time when we were finally honest with each other and wanted to be together. One thing was for sure, I knew that I was able to go back to America safe in the knowledge that James loved me.

After enjoying the best sleep of my life, I was suddenly awoken by my alarm which I had to set for 4:30 am. I knew I had an early morning start to get to the airport. My mum and dad were already up and had arranged a beautiful breakfast for me. I knew my parents had loved me being there over the past few weeks and it was hard for them to see me go. As we enjoyed my last supper, or rather last breakfast, and set off for the airport, I had such mixed emotions. As much as I wanted to return to my life in America and to all my friends who had become like family to me, I also wanted to stay in Ireland with my mum and dad and, most of all, with James. I felt as if I was living two lives and each one brought me happiness and sadness at the same time as I left one behind for the other.

As I had an early flight, the roads were pretty quiet and we arrived at the airport on time. I checked in and headed to the Departure Gate. My mum and dad looked so sad. "Catherine my darlin', are you ready to continue your adventure in America? I can't believe we're here again, leaving you at the airport." My mum hugged me and held me tight. "Go and enjoy yourself, Kitty Cat. It'll be no time until you're back home again. Make sure you send us plenty of emails now you have this new laptop," my dad joked as he gave me a huge hug.

As I stood at Departures, I was sad to leave but it was a different sadness than before. The first time I flew off in August, I had no clue what to expect in another country. This time, I knew I had my friends waiting for me back there. I said my tearful goodbyes to my parents and then boarded the flight.

As the plane touched down on the runway in San Francisco, I couldn't contain my excitement about being back in California and seeing that sunshine. One of the few things I wasn't going to miss was the rainy days in Dublin.

I couldn't wait to see my other ray of sunshine, Alex, and tell her everything about my time back home, especially all about James. I collected my luggage and ran to Immigration only to be met by the longest line I had ever seen. I think everyone had decided to fly into San Francisco that day. "Hurry the fuck up!" I thought. It was like they were punishing me for all my excitement. Eventually, I made my way to Baggage Collection and, again, another wait. "Come on people, give me a break!!"

Eventually, after what felt like forever and a day, I emerged into the Arrivals area and was greeted by the loudest almighty scream that I'd ever heard. It could only be one person! Alex!!

“I’ve missed your stank ass so much, bird!” Alex screamed as she threw her arms around me. We stood for a good five minutes just hugging, neither one of us wanting to let go. It was just so good to see my friend again.

After loading up the car with my suitcase and trusty Duty-Free drinks collection, Alex and I hit the road back to College. “So, my little Irish slut, tell me all about James!” We were barely outside the airport parking lot before Alex wanted to know all the details. As I filled Alex in on James’ declaration of love, she was so excited to hear everything. “Holy Fuck, Cat! When he said I love you, what did you say?” Alex shouted. She couldn’t wait to hear it all.

“Alex I seriously froze! These were the words I had longed to hear from him but I kept thinking, WWAD,” I joked. “WWAD? What’s that? Some sort of code for sex in Ireland?” Alex laughed. “No, it means What Would Alex Do! I kept thinking ‘What would Alex do?’ so I grew a pair and kissed him.”

“Well about fucking time! Cat, I’m so pleased for you. You deserve this happiness. Now, there goes my plan to hook you up with an American guy.” Alex was so excited to hear my tales of passion and about the trip to the holiday home the next day. She was hooked on my every word as though I was reading from a steamy romance novel.

Alex and I were back into our old routine but this time listening to Alex's amazing new music system in her car. "Cat, isn't this amazing? You can pick whatever you want and it will just play it. After the bill arrived, my dad decided to treat me for Christmas." We sang our hearts out on the drive back and laughed and chatted about our holidays, even though we had been emailing practically 24/7.

"Alex, how are you feeling about going back to College without Rick?" I asked. "Particularly now that you know that he is never to return and also that Carla had something to do with it." "Cat, I'm fine. These past few weeks have made me realise what's important. I partied hard with Rick. He was a fun guy but, oh my God, he did love himself, right?" "Alex if he was chocolate, he would eat himself," I joked.

"Oh, and do you know what else? Tom found out something really interesting about Rick the Dick. He didn't leave College to stay in Chicago because I supposedly broke his heart. He actually got kicked out of school!" Alex announced. "What?! Shut the front door!!" I exclaimed. "Yes, I'm serious, Cat. The dumb fuck was on academic probation at the beginning of the semester and thought he could still party hard and do fuck all work but the Probation Board thought differently and he was out. I guess he found out a few days before the dance. I don't know, maybe he blamed me for spending too much time with him or something," Alex thought.

"Get that out of your head right now, Alex. It's not your fault. It takes two to tango and he knew what he was doing. If he didn't put the work in, well, tough shit. You snooze you lose!" I wanted to make sure that Alex was not blaming herself for that selfish prick's actions.

As we arrived back to campus, Alex and I looked at each other and took a deep breath. We knew that we would have to run the wrath of Carla and the clones. Luckily for us, we were among the first to arrive back at the dorms, so we were able to get in quickly and undeterred.

"Cat, this is going to be a fun semester living with the bitch troll from hell on our floor. I'm going to keep my distance as I need to get on with my studies this year. I let Rick take over and I really need to study." "Alex, I know, she's not worth it. I've seen her type before, just out for destruction and trying to justify her own boring life, so she interferes in other people's lives." We made a pact to lie low and get on with our studies.

"So Cat, I see you've managed to bring back a few beverages!" Alex had spotted my bag of Duty-Free. "Why yes, I did, as ordered!" I laughed. Our fridge last semester looked like a hotel minibar as we managed to get through plenty with Rick as the mastermind. "I'll get things chilling for later. It's strange, I probably would have been calling Rick to see if he wanted to party later," Alex smiled. "Ah well, more for us! Hey let's call Tom! Maybe he wants to hang out at the Coffee House later. Cat, he really is a good friend. We talked a lot over the holidays and he really helped me. I missed you so much and Tom was like my mini-you. I'm looking forward to seeing him again. Let's call over and see if he is free for a card game with the guys. Do you know what? All that time spent with Rick, I actually missed hanging out at the Coffee House," Alex confessed.

As we walked out of our room, the moment that we were dreading arrived. Carla and her posse were standing in the corridor. "Hello Alexandra and Catherine," Carla muttered. "I do hope you will keep yourselves out of trouble this semester." Alex couldn't let it go, she had to say her piece as Carla spouted her lies. "Carla, what have I ever done to you? You told Rick that I was a total slut when, all the time, you were just a jealous bitch!" "Oh come on Alexandra, you and Catherine were out with guys practically every night and, as floor leader, I am duty-bound to report any antisocial behaviour to anyone who asks." Carla acted as if she was judge and jury but Alex had just about had enough of her and her bullshit. "Carla, you can judge me all you want. I really don't care what you think anymore." Looking at Stacey, Alex asked, "Stacey, can we talk?" Alex walked Stacey over to the bench and sat down. "Stacey, you know I'm not the person Carla is claiming. I really thought Rick was the one for me. Tom is absolutely head over heels in love with you. I can tell when he talks about you and when he looks at you. He's smitten. Trust me Stacey, Tom and I are friends and I could do with friends right now." Alex's olive branch seemed to work.

"Thanks Alex. I really don't want to fight with you. Tom told me it was all a big misunderstanding and I believe him. He said he would never be interested in you or anyone else." Alex looked at Stacey and realised that, in Stacey's own way, that was not a put-down. She was absolutely stunning so who wouldn't want to be with her? "So, can we be friends?" Alex asked and Stacey agreed.

Chapter 16

Good Girls Gone Bad

As the first week of College began, we managed to evade the clones as much as possible and made sure that we were nowhere near them when we set out. We hunkered down and kept to ourselves. I had a great catch-up with Mike who was still working on his newfound freedom and being the person he wanted to be. He was getting there, day by day, and I was so proud of him. Everything was going really well. Classes were as easy as ever and I was flying through the work which meant I had plenty of time to email James.

Soon, it was the weekend and that meant it was time to go to the city to party!! Alex and I had been longing to get out to the clubs for a chance to get our groove on. So, following our trusty ritual of calling the guys, Tom and Stacey were going and Mike was going to be our designated driver, so we could have a few cocktails. Girls drink free on Saturdays!!

As we were getting ready, I was busy curling Alex's hair with the hot curlers, remembering the cold beer for cooling down my fingers. We were so excited.

"Cat, I'm sooooo ready to have a great night!" Alex said. "I was just bored silly over the holidays at home. There was fuck all to do in my dead-end town. I bet you hit the Irish pubs hard though, right?" "To be honest Alex, I didn't. I went to the pub with a few friends but I wasn't in the mood to go clubbing." "That's right, you were too busy clubbing hard with James," Alex joked.

As we got to the clubs, the downtown strip was buzzing. The music was pumping and we were all having a great time. Tom was dancing with Stacey and we were enjoying the dance floor with all the guys. I think Alex enjoyed the fact that she was single again and had a chance to mingle. I was enjoying my dance partner, Mike.

Tom came over to dance and he joked, "Watch out Alex, I don't want to start dancing too close. I got knocked out the last time that happened!" "Yeah Tom, it's my killer moves. They'll get you every time!" Alex was always up for a bit of banter with Tom.

"Where's Stacey, is she having a good time?" Alex and Stacey were now friends which made things a lot easier. "She's in the bathroom," Tom said. That gave Tom a chance to let loose on the dance floor. We danced for what felt like hours and, as the club started to close, we walked our drunken asses down the strip.

The city had nightclub after nightclub and gift stores and tattoo parlours for all those who, after a few drinks, would get a fat Elvis inked on their arm and then regret it the next morning. Alex and I walked, or rather stumbled, down the sidewalk singing at the top of our voices. Mike was there to make sure we were going in the right direction. "Okay ladies, I think you are officially what do you call it? Drunkededed!" Mike laughed at our antics.

Alex stopped us in our tracks and shouted "Okay, let's go crazy. I have an idea! Let's pierce something!" She had stopped outside one of the tattoo-piercing places and was all set to jump onto the chair.

"What? Are you crazy?" I exclaimed. "You're not going to pierce anything. You have your ears pierced already." "Cat, I wanna get my tongue pierced!" Alex said with an excited look on her face. The guys agreed and were all for it. "Alex, go for it, girl!!" Tom shouted out. "Come on Cat, I wanna do this! Birds of a feather, right?" I realised Alex was serious and so I followed her into the store as she was already chatting to the guy who had about a million tattoos on his body.

As Alex sat in the chair and tentatively stuck her tongue out, the tat man said, "Sweetie, you're going to have to stick your tongue out a bit more than that." Then with a big cheer from all of us, Alex stuck it out, a clamp came down and it was done. Her tongue was pierced!

"Okay hoochie, it's your turn now!" Alex looked at me and I started to step back. "Eh, I'll do it next time," I joked. "Catherine, get your ass on that chair, come on, do it, do it!!" I could feel the pressure mounting and, with that and the alcohol still kicking in, I agreed. "Okay, but no tongue!! I'll do my belly button. What the hell, you only live once right?" So, as the tat man stabbed my belly, everyone let out a huge cheer! It was done, we were stamped. It was as if Alex and I had cemented our friendship but I wasn't sure how we would feel in the cold light of day!

The next morning Alex and I woke up to two things, thumping hangovers and two large holes. The drink had worn off and the reality of having our piercings had kicked in.

"Aaaaawwweeee!" Alex shouted out. "Cat, my tongue feels enormous!" As Alex opened her mouth, I could see her swollen tongue. I looked down at my belly but I seemed to be okay. In better shape than Alex anyway. "Ohhhh bird, what did we do? It was a good idea at the time!" I exclaimed. "Cat, it was a crazy idea. Never listen to me when I'm drunk! My mouth hurts like hell!" "Okay, I think you need a lot of ice. I'll go and get some at the store." "Cat, don't leave me! What if I pass out or something or worse, get sepsis or something." I could tell Alex was getting into a bit of a panic. "Okay, I'll call Tom." So, after about an hour, or what felt like five hours, Tom arrived at the door with a bag of ice. "So, where's the tough girl who wanted her piercing?" Tom was kidding.

As Alex pushed out her tongue, Tom and I couldn't help laughing. "Hey, you two are supposed to be my friends. It's no laughing matter." Alex tried to talk but the words just came out as jumbled sounds as her swollen tongue made it hard for her to speak. "Alex, you need to rest that mouth of yours. I know it's going to be hard as you always have a smart-ass response for me but just chow down on this ice." Tom was like my dad going into surgery as he rolled up his sleeves and washed his hands to go in for the incision or rather ice. "This is what the guy at the store said might happen last night, do you remember?" "Tom, I don't think we remember much of last night, we were too wasted," I joked. Tom laughed "That's true. He said it might swell a bit for a few days but you will be fine. You're just going through your swelling process but, after that, I think you'll be very popular with the guys, Alex. A girl with a tongue ring is every guy's dream. I should ask Stacey if she wants one too." Tom was trying to keep Alex amused and, as she couldn't say anything, I found it amusing too.

The next few days went by very quickly and Alex and I kept studying in the dorm as she didn't want to have to talk to anyone, given her swollen tongue. "Cat, I feel like you when you had your God-awful sunburn. Everyone has been asking me what's wrong with my mouth. I swear I am going to sock it to the next person who asks me. At least one good thing has come from it, I've lost weight from not being able to eat anything." Alex's mouth was finally getting back to normal and she was finding the new-found piercing to be a bit of a plaything.

"Cat, I'm actually getting used to my tongue stud. How are you liking the belly button?" "Alex, I still can't believe we did this. If my mum found out, I'd be shipped to a convent in Alaska," I joked. "So, are you ready to take a trip to the cafeteria for lunch today?" I asked hesitantly as we had only managed food off campus and then straight back to the dorm. "Yeah sure, why not. I'm ready to face the outside world now." So Alex and I ventured to the cafeteria to get our trusty bagel sandwiches.

Spotting the guys, we sat down beside Tom, Stacey, of course, and Mike who were glad to see us. “Look who it is, the body piercers!” Mike joked. “How’s the mouth, Alex?” Tom asked. As Alex stuck out her tongue to show her prized metal bar, all the guys were in sync “Damn!” I think they were all fascinated by it.

As Alex was finally able to open her mouth and take a bite out of the bagel, she exhaled, “Oh my goodness, I forgot how much I missed food. It’s really strange to have to navigate my sandwich with a metal bar in my mouth.” “Alex, try a bit of sausage. How does it feel?” Tom was always one for innuendos. “Tom, you’re such a pervert!” Alex and I laughed.

“So, what are you all doing for the long weekend, getting tattoos?” Tom joked. “No, we’re going home to see my folks which I’m absolutely dreading. If you guys think the tongue is cool, I’m not sure my parents are going to see the funny side. At that exact moment, a sense of nervousness came over Alex. What would her parents think of her drunken decision to get pierced? She was afraid to find out.

Pretty soon, we were on the road to Jean and Pete’s house and enjoying our road trip tunes. Alex’s tongue had returned to a normal size but still looked raw. She knew she had to refrain from opening her mouth too much.

"So Alex, what's the plan with the parents? Are you going to just stick out your tongue and shout 'What's Up!' in a Gene Simmons out of Kiss style?" "Oh hell no, Cat. I need to just come up with a plan to say I have a sore mouth or something. Yes, toothache, that sounds good. I can do this. The last thing I need is a lecture about going out and partying." As we approached Alex's parents' house, I could feel the sense of dread coming over her. "Okay bird, you can do this. Toothache. We'll go with that," I agreed.

As soon as Alex's car entered the driveway, Jean and Pete came running out to meet us. They were always so excited to see us like they had stayed on their front porch just waiting for us to return from our last visit. "Oh my girls, you're back!" Jean was overjoyed and I was so pleased to see her too. She had become my American mum and treated me like another daughter.

"You girls must be tired from your journey. Come on inside. We have dinner all rcady for you." Pete had been busy all day on the slow wood burner baking his brisket which was heavenly.

“Hi Jean and Pete, it’s so good to see you again. Now, Alex might not be able to talk too much as she has a really bad toothache.” “Yeah Mom, it’s very painful. I can barely open my mouth,” Alex mumbled. “Oh my goodness, my darling dear, let me see.” Jean looked up at her daughter concerned. Alex hadn’t anticipated the looking down the throat request and she backed away. “No Mom, I can’t even open my mouth. It’s too painful.” “That’s terrible. You know what you need, some salt water to rinse your mouth. It’s supposed to do the trick. Let me get the saltshaker.” Jean ran to the kitchen. Alex didn’t know what to do and I had no idea. We had to play the game and do our best to keep Alex’s mouth firmly shut.

After we had dinner, Alex had to rinse her mother out with a gallon of salt water at Jean’s request. She made an excuse to go upstairs to her room as she was in too much pain. It was painful to watch her mumbling through dinner and trying her best to act normal. “How long is she going to be able to keep this up?” I thought.

The next morning, we woke up early and went for a long walk on the beach. That was one thing I missed when I was in Ireland, the warm sandy beach and the feel of the water splashing up on my legs.

"Do you want any more salt water?" I joked. "Oh my God Cat, that was awful last night with my parents. I tried so hard to shut up, you know how hard that is for me." Alex started to laugh, "I can't believe I have another day of this and salt water!" As we power walked along the beach, Alex talked and joked as if she wanted to get as much talking in as possible before we went back to her parents' house.

We tried to stay away from Jean and Pete, going to the mall and meeting Kim for dinner and, eventually, we returned to the house later that evening to the smell of warm freshly baked pancakes. "Come on in girls!" Jean shouted.

As Alex and I went into the kitchen we were greeted by a huge pile of homemade pancakes which looked delicious. "Alex, I know these are your favourite and pancakes are soft on the mouth. They are the perfect food for toothache," Jean smiled. She didn't want to see her daughter hurting and wanted to do whatever she could to make her happy. That was just Jean. "Oh Mom, thank you so much, you know how much I love your pancakes." Alex gave Jean a big hug and we both delved into the pile of fluffy golden-brown pancakes with lashings of maple syrup. "Well my love, I know you're still hurting and if I could take that pain away I would."

“Thanks Mom,” Alex replied, feeling guilty about the metal bar in her tongue. She knew she couldn’t reveal it as the lie of the toothache had gone on too long. One more night and we were back on the road to College. She had to keep going.

“Mom, do you mind if Cat and I just go upstairs to bed? We have an early start in the morning.” “I know, don’t remind me. You girls will be off so soon. Yes, of course, go on up and get some rest. Oh and make sure you...” Jean had almost finished her sentence when Alex replied, “I know, wash my mouth with salt water.” Jean smiled at us both and blew a kiss as we walked up the stairs.

As we got to the sanctuary of Alex’s room, she fell on the bed and let out a loud sigh. “Cat, am I a terrible daughter? My mom is the best, bless her heart. Like making pancakes for me. I must be the worst daughter in the world.” Alex lay with her face in her pillow. “Alex, you’re not the worst daughter, you just don’t want your mom to see that skanky ass tongue of yours,” I laughed. Alex started to see the funny side. “I just feel awful. I hate keeping anything from her. We’re so close but there are some things I just can’t reveal, not yet anyway, maybe when I’m thirty-five years old or something.”

"What's the worst that can happen, Alex? You can't mumble your way through conversations with your parents until you're thirty-five." I brought Alex back to reality. "Look, why don't you just show them your mouth tomorrow before we leave and do it like a Band-aid - just rip it off," I advised. "Yeah, I can just show them and we make a quick getaway in the car." As we laughed so much about the situation, we knew our crazy night at the body piercing shop would have a ripple effect.

The next morning, as we got our bags packed and Pete and Jean gave us the contents of the fridge to take with us on the road trip, I looked at Alex. She was sitting on her bed feeling sad. "What's up buttercup? Are you okay?" I asked concerned. I knew that look on Alex's face. She was thinking about something. "Cat, I feel awful. This entire weekend has been one big lie to my parents. I guess I'm always going to worry about what they think of me. Maybe hiding the tongue ring wasn't such a great idea. You're right. I can't hide it forever." And with that, Alex got up and marched downstairs to see her parents.

"Mom, Dad, I've something to show you." As Alex opened up her mouth wide to show the metal bar protruding from her mouth in all its glory, her mom and dad opened their mouths just as wide in shock. “Alexandra, what on God’s great earth is that in your mouth?” Jean cried out. “So, that was your toothache that you were trying to hide from me? What have you done getting a piercing like that?” Jean cried out.

“Mom, it’s not that bad really,” Alex explained. “What were you thinking? You know what those piercings bring!” Jean said alarmed. “Metal detectors,” Pete said in a joking kind of way which Jean did not find funny. “Are you not angry about this Pete?” Jean was furious. “No, I’m not happy. I’d rather she got a tattoo across her forehead but it’s done now.” Surprisingly, Pete was calm. “Those things bring infections and God knows what else.” “Mom, actually the saliva in my mouth keeps it clean,” Alex replied but I don’t think that Jean was listening. “I know what else those things bring, boys!” Jean was going off on a long list of hazards but Alex didn’t need a piercing to attract the boys, she was doing pretty well all on her own before the tongue ring intervention.

“Mom, I’m sorry. I’m young and I just wanted to have some fun. Is that so hard for you to understand?” Alex wanted her mom and dad to also see that she was growing up and making her own decisions even though, sometimes, those decisions may not be the right ones. After a while, Jean seemed to calm down. They didn't want us to leave with a piercing argument hanging over everyone and eventually, we all had to agree to disagree. We had to hit the road soon to get back to College.

As we said our goodbyes, I knew that Jean and Pete were sad, not only because their little girl was leaving again but also because their little girl was growing up and a piercing was all part of the process.

Chapter 17

The Fight

The next morning, we woke up bright and early, back in our dorm room and back to College life. Alex and I headed straight for the cafeteria for breakfast to get away from the clones who would be crawling out from under their rocks soon.

"So, are you going to call your parents today?" I asked Alex, wondering if they were going to be able to mend the piercing rift that had developed. "Yeah, I have to talk to my mom again. I love my parents so much but they have to understand that I'm not a little girl anymore and if that means getting a piercing, well then they need to be supportive of my decisions." "At least you didn't get that tattoo across your forehead that Pete wanted," I laughed. "Cat, let's save that for the next time we get drunk and I decide to do something crazy." We both started to laugh at the thought of it.

As Alex got up to get her second helping of bagels and coffee, Mike came over to join me as he was just back from his long break and we had lots of catching up to do. " Hi Mike, how did you enjoy the weekend? Did you do anything exciting?" I asked. "I had a fabulous weekend and guess what, I actually bumped into an old friend, Matty." Mike was excited. "What? You did? Oh my goodness! What did you say to him? What did you guys talk about? Is he still hot?" I had so many questions.

"He's definitely still hot, yes! I met him on the street. I was walking along and I saw him coming in my direction. He saw me too and we both just stopped and started talking. He asked me for my phone number and we caught up later for a coffee. He asked me how I was and I told him about coming out. Cat, guess what? He came out too!" Mike shouted. "I guess he knew he was gay too and he had feelings for me but, just like me, he didn't know what was going on. He was going through all these changes and struggling with his feelings. We sat and talked for hours and had a really great time together."

"Mike, that's wonderful, so how did you leave things? Did you ask him out? Oh, please don't tell me he already has a boyfriend?" I was asking a million questions again. "The good news is, he doesn't have a boyfriend and, get this, he asked me out! Cat, this is amazing, this never happens to me!" Mike was so excited to be able to finally have a glimpse of happiness with someone that he had loved for so long, just as I had with James.

As Alex came back from the bagel stand, still enjoying the fact that she could now eat and actually open her mouth instead of taking the itty-bitty bites that she had to endure at her parents' house, Mike and I were smiling and thinking that we were both getting our happy ending.

Just then, I spotted a poster on the wall that caught my attention. The College was planning a trip to see the Golden State Warriors vs. LA Lakers game that evening. I was so excited. One of the things I watched back home with my dad was NBA basketball. It was our thing and I always wanted to go and see a live game. Now was my chance!

"Oh my goodness, the College has tickets for the Golden State Warriors game. My lifetime wish is to see an NBA game! Alex, let's go! I've always wanted to see a live NBA basketball game so it would be a dream come true!" I exclaimed. I couldn't hold back my excitement. "Cat, you know I don't like sports that much. Ask Mike." Alex was definitely not as enthusiastic as me. "Sorry, my Irish rose, but I have a student council meeting to go to tonight and I can't miss it." "Alex, come on, please go with me. I don't want to go on my own. I need my bird to come too!" I pleaded. "I'll see Cat. I'm not really a fan of basketball." I could tell Alex was coming around. "Okay Alex, can you get the tickets? I'm working at the pool later and they are starting to sell them after lunch. Here's the money for two tickets. I'll pay for yours, so you're not out of pocket." I rushed off to start my classes and then headed to the pool.

I couldn't wait for my shift to be over and get ready for the game. Of course, Alex would probably want her hair curled so that she would look her best, even at a basketball game. I had to make sure to take plenty of pictures to show my dad. He would have loved to be going too. I hadn't thought of home for a while with so much going on in College but sometimes a little memory or even just something that I used to do with my folks would remind me that I was a long way from home. I also missed James. It was like, just when I was finally with him, I was leaving him. For now though, I had to enjoy my American experience and that meant getting to see a basketball game.

After work, I met Alex back at the dorm. She was lying on her bed watching a movie. "Hey girl, here's your ticket for the game tonight." Alex handed me one ticket. Ticket. Singular. She hadn't bought one for herself. "What about your ticket? Did you not get one? Aren't you coming too?" I asked, becoming a little upset. "No, I told you Cat, I don't like basketball." I couldn't believe it. Alex had just left me to go to the game on my own. "I just can't believe that you won't go with me! You don't like basketball? So what? I'm your best friend! Could you not do this one thing for me? That's what friends do. Do ya think I wanted to go to frikkin' driving school with you? But I did that for you! Why are you being a fucking bitch?" I was getting so mad at Alex. I had never let her down and she wouldn't do this one thing I wanted to do. It was just too much for her. "What do you want me to say, Cat, that I'm a bitch? Well, obviously I am if I don't want to go to some dumb-ass basketball game. Did you not know that? Deal with it! Shit, I'm outta here!" Alex took her car keys and left the dorm, slamming the door behind her.

As I heard the bang of the door, I broke down and cried. It was our first fight! I couldn't understand why Alex was being like this. She had never acted like this before and I had never seen her so mad. I needed to get myself together. I had a game to go to and needed to shower and get myself ready to go. While I was drying my hair, the phone rang. It's Alex calling, I thought. She's calmed down and is ready to apologise. Maybe it was all just a big joke and she was going to call me to say that she was just kidding, she had her ticket in her pocket and was just messing with me. I answered the phone and it was Mike.

"Hi Cat, are you and Alex all set for the big game tonight? I just wanted to call to say enjoy your first big NBA game. I wish I was going too." Mike was so nice and I couldn't hold back the tears. "I wish you were going too. I'm going on my own," I confessed. "What? Why? What about Alex, is she not going with you?" Mike exclaimed. "I know she wasn't that keen but you guys do everything together." Even Mike knew that Alex's behaviour was strange.

"You would think so, Mike, but no, she only bought one ticket for me and then we had a huge fight and Alex took her keys, slammed the door and ran out on me. I don't know where she is. She could be anywhere in the car." "Cat, I wish I could go with you but I have this meeting. Go to the game and enjoy it. I know how much you want to see this. Don't worry about Alex, she'll be fine. She just needs to remember how much you do for her and not take you for granted so much." I knew Mike was right so I decided to wipe the tears away and put on my game face.

I got on the bus but didn't know any of the other students very well. I had spotted a few from my classes but none that I could hang out with. Going to an NBA game had been an ambition for me and my dad and now I was actually going but would have no one to share the experience with. I sat at the back of the bus on my own and tears started to come down my face again.

As I got to the large Arena, the game night build-up looked amazing. Then the lights went down and the excitement of the crowd was just electric. The razzmatazz was everything I had expected. The two teams came out to rapturous cheers from the crowd. It was an amazing experience. I should have been in my element but instead I was thinking about Alex the entire time. I just couldn't enjoy myself. Was I being unreasonable by asking her to go with me? Where did Alex drive off to in the car? I just hoped she was okay. I knew she had a temper and that, coupled with her driving, was not a good combination.

We had never fought over anything before. Was Alex going to talk to me again? A huge lump welled in my throat. I felt terrible. So what if she didn't go to the game with me? She was my best friend and her friendship meant more to me than a game of basketball. I couldn't wait for the game to be over so that I could get back to sort things out.

The bus journey back to campus felt like forever as it took us out of the streets of San Francisco and onto the highway. The whole way back to college, I was hoping that Alex was okay.

Back at the campus, I was just about to open our door when Carla came around the corner like a snake lurking in the shadows and ready to strike. "Hello, Catherine, are you on your own? Where's Alexandra, is she not with you?" Carla asked. It was true Alex and I had always been together. It was very unusual to see either of us alone. Not wanting to go into any detail with Carla, I muttered back, "Don't know Carla, maybe she is up your ass like the rest of the fuckin' dorm!" "Sorry Catherine, what did you just say? I didn't hear you properly." I quickly had to backtrack as I didn't want Carla to know that we were fighting. This would have been the best news ever for her. "I said Carla, I don't know she is probably in study class with others in the dorm." "Well, I heard you guys had words. You know what Cat, if you ever want someone to talk to I, as your floor leader, am always here to listen," Carla smiled back at me.

How on earth did she know? I was convinced she had our dorm room tapped or something. Carla seemed to know everything about everyone. I bet she was here to listen and then report back to the rest of the clone bitches. Talking to her was the last thing on my mind. The only person I wanted to talk to was Alex. I felt as if part of me was missing because she wasn't with me. She would probably never talk to me again!

I got into our dorm room as fast as I could but Alex wasn't there. Her car keys were still missing. I started to panic. Where was she? The only other place she could be was the Coffee House which was our usual evening hangout. As I walked across campus and got to the Coffee House, I saw Alex sitting inside with Tom. As I went over to their table, Alex got up and rushed over to me. We just gave each other a great big hug which probably lasted for about five minutes.

"Alex, I don't want to fight with you. I just thought you would go because you knew how important it was to me. But you didn't and I just don't understand. I kept thinking of everything I have done for you and I wasn't getting anything back. Alex, I feel like you take me so much for granted. I thought you would go with me just because you are my friend and it meant so much to me." I let it all out as I needed to clear the air or it would build up inside.

"Cat, I'm sorry that I wasn't there for you. When it came to basketball, well, I just had flashbacks of Jake. Cat, he was the captain of the basketball team and I went to all his games, cheering him on from the sidelines for all those years we were together. After we broke up, I swore I'd never go to a game again. When you asked me to go to the game, I just felt all that hurt come back. I'm sorry, I should have told you about Jake but that, coupled with my parents' disappointment this weekend, Cat, I just took it all out on you. I went for a drive to clear my head and then Tom and I talked all evening. He has made me see that I was being an asshole. Cat, I never really had many friends. It was always Jake and me, but you, you have been there for me through so much these past few months and you have taught me how to trust someone completely. For the first time in my life, I've found a friend in you that just accepts me and you have no idea how much you mean to me. You're a sister to me and a part of me. I am sorry, I sometimes do take you for granted. I guess tonight made me realise just how important you are to me and how much I'm going to miss you when you go back to Ireland. Cat, what am I going to do without you?"

It seemed the ghost of this past boyfriend kept coming back to haunt Alex. Just when she thought she was moving on, a memory would creep in and remind her of Jake and the sadness he brought her. At that very moment, Alex burst into tears and I followed right after. We knew that we had such a special friendship, the kind that would last a lifetime.

I felt so humble that Alex had let her walls down and let me into her heart. We both felt the same; so glad to have each other but realised that we would be parted at the end of the semester. No matter what, we would always have our friendship and never take it for granted!

"Alex, thank you for telling me your feelings. Sorry, I called you a fucking bitch," I smiled at Alex, "Cat, no I'm sorry I was being a fucking bitch! But I know you love me the way I am," Alex smiled back at me. "Yeah well, you're my fucking bitch and I wouldn't change you for the world… maybe that foul temper of yours! Is that another thing you got from your dad?" I joked. "Alex, you know you mean the world to me, you have given me the strength and courage to face my fears, to go for things in life that I never thought I could. If it wasn't for you, I'd still be wondering 'what if' about James. I would never have had the courage to tell James the truth. You're fearless and I love you for taking chances and putting your heart out there. Before I met you, I would never have gone with my heart, I was always too chicken shit."

"Yeah Cat, but where has that got me? A bad breakup with Jake and Rick just using me for fun and games. But you're right, Cat, I'll keep looking for that knight in shining armour. I believe in love," Alex said determined to have the happiness she craved and deserved.

"How was the game anyway? Did you enjoy it?" Alex asked. "I did but I cried the whole way there. Then someone in the crowd shouted, "You fucker!" and you weren't there!"

"You know what, it's hump day! Let's drink a toast to Rick the Dick prick!" I jumped up, remembering it was Wednesday. "Well, it would be rude not to celebrate hump day right?" We headed back to our dorm room ready to enjoy a few drinks to celebrate hump day and also to celebrate our friendship which was the most precious thing in the world to both of us.

The next morning, we woke up to what sounded like a cat screeching at the top of its voice. It was Carla calling on everyone to meet her in the recreation room for another one of her, 'Everyone aren't I wonderful' speeches. As I lifted my head from the pillow, the room started to spin out of control. I had to lay my head back down. "Alex, are you awake?" I called. "Aaagggg fuckkkkkk!" Alex moaned back. "Are you feeling as shitty as I am? I totally feel like a freight train has just ploughed into my head!" She was as hungover as I was! "Alex, I feel like the whole room is spinning! What the fuck did we drink last night? I feel as sick as a dog!" Just then, I had to get up and run for the rubbish bin and emptied the contents of my stomach into it.

"Cat, are you okay? I think I'm going to be sick!" Alex shot up and came over to the bin also. We were both sick to our stomachs! We were so sick we had to take turns to hold each other's hair back while the other used the bin! "Holy Fuck, I'm dying!" exclaimed Alex as we both lay on the dorm room floor looking at the empty tequila bottles that lay beside us. "Cat, let's never fight again! I feel like shit!" We tried to laugh but we were just way too hungover to move.

After an hour or two of throwing up, we decided it was best to get back into bed and see if we could sleep it off. With a few Advil and gallons of water, we crashed out. When I woke up, it was dark outside. We slept the whole day! What a hangover from hell! "Alex, are you alive?" I called out to see if she was still feeling as rough as I was. "Cat, I'm seriously dying!" Alex confessed.

"Alex, you know it's nighttime and we have slept the whole day!" I couldn't believe that we had been like zombies. Our night of celebrating our friendship had almost killed us! "Alex, you know we really do need to get some food. I feel as if the lining of my stomach has been ripped out." "Hey, fancy another tequila?" Alex joked. "Oh no thanks, even the thought of it and the word tequila is making me nauseous! I don't think we can move out of this room though. Man, we really got shit-faced!"

We laughed at our situation as neither one of us was able to move out of our beds. The room was still swaying too much for any form of activity. "Okay, I have an idea. I'll call Mike and see if he can get us some takeout. I think we need some fried-up yellow food. French fries should do it!"

I called Mike hoping that he would answer and, thank goodness, I heard his voice on the other end. "Hi Mike, it's Cat. What are you doing?" "Hey Irish rose, what are you doing? I haven't seen you or Alex for the past two days!" "What? Two days?" I exclaimed. I hadn't realised that we had passed out for two days instead of one. Oh my goodness, we had seriously died a slow death but we were getting back to the land of the living.

I explained to Mike that Alex and I had drunk ourselves into oblivion and basically were fit for nothing over the past few days. We really needed to get some form of food and drinks (preferably not alcohol) to get us back to normality. "Fuck, do you guys go all out or what?! Okay, let me get to the store and get provisions for you. I'm guessing soup and crackers to soak up the alcohol and Gatorade to give you some hydration. That should do the trick." Mike was always looking out for us and making sure we were okay. He truly had a very caring nature.

After an hour or so, there was a knock at the dorm door. "I'll get it," Alex said as she dragged her ass off of the bed to answer the door. Mike stood there with his mouth open at the sight of our hungover lifeless bodies and a really strange look on his face as if he was our mother telling us off.

"My, you two know how to party!" Mike smiled. Alex and I seriously looked like death warmed up but thank goodness we could rely on Mike as we weren't our usual hot selves and wouldn't want any other guy to see us. We were not Mike's type and that was handy right now.

"Mike, thank you so much for coming! I could kiss you right now but my breath still stinks of tequila," I joked. As Alex and I dove into the bag of French fries, we felt like we had never seen food before. Our appetite was coming back and, for the first time, we were able to hold something down without running for the rubbish bin.

"So you guys have seriously been in here these past two days?" Mike laughed. "Yeah, we got up to vomit and I held Cat's hair back and she held my hair back while we upchucked. It was actually quite cute if our drunkededed asses weren't so hungover. We celebrated hump day alright and, shit, now it's the weekend!" Alex always knew how to make a joke about things. Mike stayed with us for a while just in case we needed anything. I loved that he was so kind and, in a way, he was the perfect guy - just not for me!

As the weekend flew by, Alex and I stayed in our room so that we didn't have to move too far. We watched movies and chatted about life. We were enjoying just chilling out and not having to rush anywhere. There was something to be said for hangover recovery. We had now spent four days in the dorm and, with the help of Mike's food deliveries, we were fully recovered and ready to face the world again. Just not ready to ever face another bottle of tequila!

Chapter 18

The Cold War

After the last few days of self-inflicted post-hangover recovery, Monday came soon enough and it was back to classes for us. That meant back to face the world again.

"Cat, I've to go to study hall this morning so I'll see you back here for lunch," Alex said as we headed to our respective classes. It was the first time that we had been apart in four days. What I found so comforting about our friendship was the fact that we never ran out of things to say, we were always able to make something funny out of nothing and were always there for each other. Even when it meant holding each other's hair back while the other one spewed into a rubbish bin!

After class, I headed for the library and opened up my laptop to email James who was wondering where I had been for the past few days. It was funny, when I was back in Ireland my daily ritual was to email Alex and now that I was in California, I was emailing James every day. I had really missed him ever since our time together. I couldn't wait to hear from him. Soon, I was ready for lunch. Luckily for me, the hangover had not affected my appetite. I was ready to eat a cow to make up for losing so much weight. As Alex and I sat in the cafeteria, Tom came bounding over.

"Where were you two? There is a conspiracy theory going around campus that you two bumped each other off after the big fight the other day and you haven't been seen since! I hope you guys have made up. I can't handle any more break-ups!" We laughed as if it was true. We hadn't seen a soul apart from Mike. "Don't worry Tom, we totally made up," Alex reassured him. "We made up too much to the point where we emptied a whole bottle of tequila and I can't remember what else we drank that night! Oh fuck, even saying the word tequila makes me want to barf! Tom, we have been recovering from an almighty hangover the past three days!"

"What, you guys had a tequila party and didn't invite me?" Tom joked as if he was offended. "Oh please, when are you able to hang out with us without having to ask your girlfriend these days?" Alex teased as she stuck out her tongue piercing at him.

"Girl, you better put that tongue away, you're killing me!" Tom loved the fact that Alex was adventurous and had a great personality. Pity the same couldn't be said for Stacey who had the model looks but had nothing on Alex who just shone through and was able for Tom's sarcasm.

“Sorry ladies, I have to go now!” and, in a flash, Tom jumped up and raced over to the other side of the cafeteria. “What the fuck just ate Tom? He ran off so fast he left a trail of smoke behind!” I asked. Just then, Alex and I spotted Stacey coming in through the door. “Figures,” we said together and laughed. “I’m telling you, Cat, Tom is going to have to watch out or he will become like a bitch slapped husband who can’t even choose what to wear without asking Stacey,” Alex laughed but she was concerned about her friend too. “Do you feel that way, Cat? Like every time Tom is around us, he is constantly looking over his shoulder?” “You’re right Alex, he can’t live like this. It’s not right.”

Later that evening, Alex called Tom but there was no answer so she decided to leave him a message. Nothing –She called him back again. Still no answer from Tom. “Cat, I do hope Tom is okay. It’s just strange that he hasn’t called back.” Alex seemed concerned.

“Alex, I wouldn’t worry. He’s probably just catching up with Stacey, if you know what I mean.” “Yeah, you’re right Cat. He talked a lot about her and I think that, without Carla beside her poisoning her mind, we could be good friends.” Alex had come back to college with a new way of thinking and I was really proud of her. Only one thing wasn't right. Alex and I had barely heard from Tom. It was really starting to bother us.

"Cat, there is definitely something up with Tom. I don't know what it is but he has been acting very strange this past week. I even saw him in class. He arrived late, so I couldn't talk to him. Then, when I caught up with him after class, I asked if his fingers were all bandaged up since he couldn't call a girl back. He told me he was sorry, that he had a lot on and we would catch up later. That was two days ago. Something's not right at all," Alex said, concerned.

"I know what you mean, it's not just you. I saw Tom in the library and he told me he couldn't stop as he was late for class and he ran out of there like he was possessed. I don't know, Alex, maybe he's going through something. I do hope we get to hang out soon. I miss our card games with him and the guys."

It wasn't Alex's imagination. Tom was keeping a very low profile and Alex needed to know what was going on. She was worried about him and she missed her friend. "Cat, okay, let's go see what's crawled up Tom's ass and died. We can call over to the guys' dorm." Alex and I set out to get to the bottom of Tom's mysterious disappearance.

As we got to the dorms, we didn't have to go too far to find Tom. He was sitting outside, lost in his own thoughts. Alex and I walked up from behind him and we both grabbed his waist to give him a jolt. "Hey stranger, where the hell have you been hiding?" Alex quizzed. "Hi girls, I didn't realise I was in demand," Tom joked but he clearly was not himself. He was usually a happy-go-lucky, smiley guy but he looked sad. "Tom, what's wrong? Has something happened? You have been really distant and I can tell something's up."

Tom looked at the ground and started to talk. "Look guys, we can't hang out anymore. I need to spend time with Stacey and work on our relationship. She's not happy at all with us hanging out together so much. She thinks I've been neglecting her." "What? But that's crazy, Tom! We've all been hanging out together, including Stacey. We've made a really big effort to get to know her and include her even though her best buddy is that fucking bitch face, Carla. Tom, come on, grow some balls, we are all friends, this is ridiculous!" Alex was fuming and so was I for that matter.

"Stacey is my girlfriend and I love her. We've been together for three years and I need to give her my full attention. It's not right for me to be hanging out with other girls. I'm disrespecting her," Tom muttered.

"Who the fuck are you trying to convince us or yourself, Tom? This is bullshit. What are we going to do to you? We get it, you're with Stacey. We're friends. What's the problem? Well, if that's the way you feel, fine Tom. I hope that you and Stacey are happy together and have a nice life." Alex was fuming. Tom was acting just like all the other asshole jerks in College. We couldn't believe it. He actually didn't want to hang out with us anymore because his girlfriend said so! What was going on?

So we left Tom where we found him and returned to our dorm. As we were walking across campus, I could see the obvious rage building up in Alex. "This is fucking bullshit, Cat! I'm ready to have it out with Stacey right now. She can't tell Tom who he can and can't hang out with. What is this, the dark ages?!" "Okay bird, just calm down. You have that look on your face where you might say something that you might regret!" I tried to diffuse the situation but I knew it was no use. Alex's fiery temper had been ignited and I couldn't dampen the flames.

Getting to the girls' dorm, Stacey was hanging out with the Carla clan clones and Alex confronted her. “So, are you happy now bitch?” Alex shouted. Stacey looked shocked as if she had no clue. “What are you talking about, Alex? And excuse me, I am no bitch, bitch!”

“So, you won’t let Tom hang out with us? What’s that all about? Stacey, do you know how fucked up that is?” Alex shouted. “Oh no, Tom can talk to Cat, that’s fine. It’s you, Alex, you are the one I have a problem with. I see you flirting with him. You want to take my man and I am not going to let you. Tom and I have been together for three years and I’m not ready to let him go - not to someone like you!”

Alex was so mad, “Stacey, I am not interested in Tom and he is not interested in me. We’re friends. Why can’t you accept that? I thought that you and I had sorted all this out after Rick. Tom loves you. This is crazy! Stacey, I thought you and I were friends.”

“Friends?” Stacey laughed “Oh please girl, we were never friends! They say to keep your friends close and your enemies closer. Ever since the dance, I’ve been watching you and making sure you’re not getting your claws into my man. Tom agrees with me that you’re just not worth it. He loves me too much to upset me so you can just leave him alone!” “Fine, I’m done with this. I’m sure that you and Tom will be very happy together. Why don't you tell him what to eat and what to say!" This had been building up all year and now it was war!

As we got back to our dorm room, Alex was still mad. "Cat, I just can't believe this is happening! Sure Tom and I have a friendly relationship but that's it, we're friends, why can't Stacey see that?" "Alex, she's controlling him and he's letting her do it. Their relationship won't last the way it's going. Tom must see what she's doing." I had to agree with Alex, it just wasn't fair. "Cat, at least you're okay. You can still hang out with Tom. It's only me that she has the problem with, remember?" Alex shrugged her shoulders.

"I'm not sure about that. Birds of a feather flock together remember?" I joked and we smiled together and laughed, "Mother Cluckers!" We knew that, with all the shit that was happening, at least one thing was true and that was that we had each other. I hugged Alex to reassure her that it wasn't her fault. Tom just had a crazy controlling girlfriend and there was nothing she could do about it.

The next few days were hard for Alex. She was trying to get on with her College life but, every time she turned around, Tom was close by and turned the other way. It was sad to see how such a great friendship had suddenly been smashed to pieces. Alex knew she just had to get on without Tom and his friendship which meant a lot to her.

In the weeks that followed, Alex wouldn't look at Tom but flirted wildly with other guys. She even got back into the dating scene and was enjoying getting back out there.

"Cat, do you know what I think? The whole Tom being a pussy situation has helped me. We were spending so much time hanging out and having fun with Tom as friends that I didn't see anyone else. Well, after Rick I just didn't want to but I'm going out on a date tonight!" Alex was so excited as she picked up her heated rollers, which was a cue for me to ice my fingers and curl her hair before her big date. "Alex, I didn't know you were interested in anyone. This is the first I've heard of it." I was a bit shocked as usually I would have been the first-person Alex would have told. "Alex, tell me all, who is he?"

Alex began to tell me all about her encounter with this new man. "Cat, it was really strange. I've seen this guy, Harry, in my classes but I never really spoke to him. He's a bit shy and quiet, not the usual type I'd go for but he's incredibly sweet. We were put together in class today. We got talking and one thing led to another and, well, I asked him out!" "You asked him out?" I said curiously as it was rather forward of Alex to do that. "Yeah, I don't know Cat, I just felt like I needed to take the bull by the horns, if you know what I mean. Harry wasn't going to do it, he's too shy, I could tell. I'm becoming a new modern woman and going for it. Cat, I've been so mixed up and chasing the guys who treat me like shit, maybe I just want a good, quiet guy with no drama."

As I started to curl Alex's hair, cursing the heated rollers every time I touched one, Alex began to tell me more about Harry, or as much as she could know after their brief encounter in class. Harry loved computers and was incredibly smart. His major was computer software engineering so he seemed to breeze through Alex's algebra class and kindly helped her with a few equations. We had a few beers to give Alex some Dutch courage before she set off on her date. Harry called at the dorm door and, as I opened it, I was surprised to see a short, incredibly skinny, shy-looking guy standing in front of me. My first impression was that he was the total opposite of Alex. Harry barely lifted his head to say 'hi'. There was definitely no drama but there appeared to be no personality there either!

I walked out with Alex and Harry to go over to Mike's dorm as we were going to watch a movie while Alex was on her hot date. As I left the love birds, I saw Tom standing at the guys' dorm door and he was watching Alex and Harry leave. "Cat, where the fuck is Alex going in the car with Harry?" Tom asked but I wasn't in the mood to speak. I was too mad at him but I just had to say something about how he was behaving. "So Tom, you're talking to me now that Alex isn't here? What the fuck do you care? You can't hang out with Alex, remember? For your information, they are going on a date," I said.

"A date? They are going on a date?" Tom was acting like this was the worst thing in the world. "Cat, Harry's not right for Alex. He's, He's…" Tom couldn't get the words out he was so flustered. "He's what, Tom?" I asked, becoming annoyed with him. "Cat, he's just weird and he's not right for Alex." "What are you now, her dad? So who is right for Alex, Tom, tell me that?" I knew Tom was right. Harry was definitely not Alex's type. But why was Tom getting so upset? After all, he wanted nothing to do with her.

"Cat, I still care about Alex. I just don't want to see her get hurt," Tom confessed "Well Tom, you have a funny way of showing it. If you care for Alex, be her friend like before and don't have some bitch ass girlfriend dictate what you can and can't do.

Tom, you can't have it both ways. What do you want? You have to do what YOU want to do." I suddenly realised that Tom was torn between his loyalty to Stacey and also his friendship with Alex.

"I don't know, Cat, I just don't know what I want," Tom replied and walked away with his head down. I got to Mike's door and completely flaked on his bed. Having told Mike what was going on, he agreed with me. "Cat, it sounds like Tom is jealous as hell. He needs to stand up to Stacey and tell her that he can be friends with whoever he wants. I spent way too long pretending to be someone I wasn't and I'm a totally different person now that my secret is out in the open. Being true to yourself is what matters." I was in total agreement. I loved to hang out with Mike. He was so good to talk to and I was proud of what he had accomplished, coming out and being who he wanted to be.

A while later, I got a call from Alex, "Hey bitch, where are you? I'm back, are you coming over?" Mike smiled at me and said, "So I guess you're going to have to leave me now to check out all the hot gossip from the date?" "Sorry Mike, do you mind? I know the movie isn't over but you know us girls, we need to talk." "Yeah, yeah, you're birds of a feather, right?" Mike joked but he was right again. I had been worried about Alex all evening. Who was this Harry character and what did Alex think of him given Tom's and Mike's assessment of him? I even had my doubts about him but it was up to Alex to decide if he was the man for her.

When I got back to the dorm, Alex had already laid out our drinks. "Are we drinking tonight?" I laughed as Alex downed a shot. "That had better not be tequila. It isn't, is it?" "Oh hell no, I am never drinking tequila again! Cat, I need a drink, the date was awful!"

"Okay, tell me all, what went wrong?" I sort of knew this was coming and, in a way, I was glad that Alex found out for herself.

"Well, to start off with we went for food. He's a vegetarian so we had to go to some fucking vegan place. I was so ready for a burger and fries by the end of my dinner. I was still hungry as hell. He barely talked to me either. Dinner was like the longest ever time and I was really struggling to get any conversation out of him. Thank fuck for the movies so I could sit and listen instead of having to come up with conversation." As I listened to Alex, I laughed so hard because it literally sounded like the date from hell. "It's not funny, Cat, it was a nightmare! I was running out of things to say at dinner that I resorted to the 'So why did you become a vegetarian?' question!" "Why did you become a vegetarian? Riveting conversation, Alex!" as I laughed even harder.

"And another thing, he doesn't drink either and he doesn't go to clubs. What the hell do we have in common, Cat? I'm going to put this one down to experience. I asked him if he wanted to put his arm around me at the movies and he said no thanks! Best of all, we had to have separate popcorn buckets as he only eats out of his own bucket. Like I'm going to give him a disease!"

"I don't know Cat, after my disasters with Jake back in High School and Rick at College, I was all set to find The One, ya know? I convinced myself that I could be with a guy who was the total opposite of me because opposites attract right? But everything about Harry was just, I don't know…" "BORING!!" I screamed! As we downed another shot and laughed, we both knew that Harry was not going to be The One!

"So, what were you up to tonight, anything exciting?" Alex asked. I wasn't going to say anything to Alex about my talk with Tom but I felt she had the right to know. "I did have an interesting conversation with Tom this evening, to be honest. Tom saw you and Harry go out together and asked why you were hanging out with him. I told him you guys were on a date and, well, he was really upset. He told me that Harry wasn't right for you and that you deserved better."

Alex was shocked to hear that Tom was even interested in anything that she was doing, considering she hadn't been talking to him for weeks. "So Cat, let me get this right. Tom was upset that I was hanging out with Harry and yet I can't hang out with him? What the fuck, is he my dad?! Cat, I'm so annoyed with him. He needs to keep his opinions to himself!"

"He is really hurting Alex and, the way the situation is with you guys, I know he misses your friendship." I explained what Tom had said and, in a way, I felt sorry for him. He couldn't get past how Stacey was behaving and be his own man. "To be honest Alex, Tom is right. Harry is definitely not the guy for you." It was true. They were total opposites.

"Fuck him! He's not my friend and doesn't have the right to say who I can and can't date. Coming from Tom who is dating the biggest bitch on campus, apart from Carla of course, he can hurt all he wants. That's what happens when you lose a friendship. But Cat, me dating Harry might not be all that bad after all.” Alex said with a glint in her eye. I knew she was planning something but wasn’t quite sure what.

“You’re not seriously going to go on another date with Harry, are you? I’m so confused. Did the past few hours of awkwardness not just make you want to run for the hills?” I didn’t understand why Alex wanted to have a second date with him.

“Cat, hear me out,” Alex started to explain the method to her madness. “So what if I go on a few more dates with Harry, casually walk past Tom when we’re together and show Tom that he can’t just tell me who to date and that I make my own decisions? Even if it’s with Harry.” Alex smiled as she could see her plan coming together.

“Alex, Tom will go crazy. He knows you guys aren’t right for each other.” “Ahh, but Cat, he doesn’t know that I know that too, ya know?” “Oh I know, you badass mother clucker!” I smiled.

Let the games begin!

Chapter 19

It's All Fun and Games Until Someone Gets Hurt

For the next few weeks, Alex hung out as much as possible with Harry. In class, in the cafeteria, outside the guys' dorms, basically anywhere that Alex knew Tom and Stacey would be. Conveniently, Tom was always within eyeshot. Alex tried her best not to look at him but, of course, she wanted to make sure he saw her.

The game of hanging out with Harry was hard work for Alex. Trying to have fun and be happy with someone who was so antisocial was like having to go off beer for a week for Alex - it was excruciating!

I did have to play my part in the fun and games and, as soon as Tom and Stacey were out of eyeshot, I was there to rescue Alex from the boredom of hanging out with Harry.

Alex knew it was a wicked game but she was determined to make sure that Tom and Stacey didn't get the better of her. We decided to go to the mall. Everything always seemed better after some retail therapy. We always had our go-to shops, purchases at Bath & Body Works then time for a well-deserved Starbucks. I could tell that there was something up with Alex as she was unusually quiet. As we sat in Starbucks surrounded by our purchases that we probably didn't need, I asked Alex what was wrong. "So bird, what's up? You're too quiet for my liking this evening and you're starting to become just as antisocial as Harry! How long are we going to play the 'hang out with Harry' game by the way?" I tried to make a joke about it as I could see it was taking its toll on Alex. "I know Cat, I don't know what I'm doing. This is not me. I'm never like this. I gotta stop with the games. Harry is actually a nice guy. I think he is starting to really like me and I just don't want to give him the wrong impression. He's so not my type and I have no feelings for him but I'm worried that he has feelings for me and I don't want to lead him on. He told me how much he likes me today and it's freaking me out. I never wanted to play with his feelings and, in all the fun and games, I haven't thought about that."

"Well bird, as my mum used to say, it's all fun and games until someone gets hurt!" I could have seen this coming a mile off. Alex had a way of making guys want to be with her and even Harry, who wasn't her type or anyone's type for that matter, was falling for her. "Alex, I have to say this was bound to happen. You guys were spending time together and Harry is only human. You may not have meant for this to happen but you need to decide what to do and stop playing games. Forget about Tom and

Stacey. You need to concentrate on yourself and let Harry down gently." I needed to bring Alex back to reality. She had allowed her anger towards Tom to consume her.

"Cat, I know, you're right. At least we have our spring break coming up next week. I meant to say to you that Mom and Dad want us to come home for the week. I think I need to be away from College for a while. I feel like I'm living a lie right now and I just need a break." Alex was exhausted and she knew what she had to do. It was just a matter of time before she had to have the chat with Harry.

The week flew in and, soon enough, Alex and I were on our road trip heading to her parents' house. Luckily, Jean and Pete had calmed down and had accepted the piercing which Alex had now firmly established. Pete and Jean had become my surrogate parents while I was in America. They would always send Alex packages of food and include some treats for me. They were the best and I always looked forward to visiting my American home as they always said to me. The Spring Break was just what we needed, time to get away from the drama of College life and just chill out, go to the beach and enjoy the Californian sunshine. Many of the college kids used Spring Break to party but Alex and I had felt the effects of partying all too often. It was time to rest, recharge the batteries and enjoy some home-cooked meals for a change.

Most evenings, Alex and I had our daily walk, trying to keep fit and, because Jean had been feeding us up with so much food, we needed the exercise. During one walk, Alex received a message on her phone which made her uneasy.

"Oh fucking hell, Cat, it's a message from Tom!" Alex looked like she had been knocked down by a bus. This past week had been bliss for Alex without the distractions of College and the ping on her phone just reminded her that, although she was away from the drama, sometimes drama follows you. "Are you kidding me? What the fuck has he got to say? You were right. Stacey is a bitch and we broke up?" I joked in the hope that it was true. "I wish Cat. This is what he has to say. Hey Alex. I hope you're well and enjoying your Spring Break. I was just wondering how you are. Thinking of you." As Alex finished reading the text, I could tell that she was pissed.

"Now, I'm fucked off!" Alex fumed. "What are you going to do, Alex? Sounds like Tom wants to get back in touch." I didn't know what to say to her. The message came completely out of the blue and was a surprise to me too. "I've really enjoyed a week off from this bullshit and now Tom wants to chat? Has he forgotten we are no longer friends? He doesn't have Stacey breathing down his neck or checking his messages, I bet!" Alex exclaimed.

"Ya know what, Cat, I'm going to do exactly what he has been doing to me. Nothing! Ghost him and let him get on with his life with Stacey. That ship has sailed, Tom. Nice knowing ya!" As much as it was hard for Alex to give up on her friendship, she was right. "Alex you're right. Tom has the safety of chatting on a text message but doesn't have the balls to chat with you in person. That is just total bollocks. The best thing you can do is to do nothing. Come on, Mother Clucker, let's get our steps in and get back home. Your dad might have a few beers in the fridge for us."

We picked up the pace on our walk as the thought of the ice-cold beers in the fridge was way too inviting and, within moments, we were racing each other and sprinting back to the house, laughing so hard that we collapsed on the lawn.

We looked at each other with a knowing gaze. Even though drama was drama, friendship was the most important thing in the world and what we had was so rare that we knew it would last forever.

Over the following days, Alex received more 'Hi how are you?' messages from Tom but she just ignored them. It was the best thing to do. Messages also came from Harry, which Alex didn't want either but she knew that she had started this so-called relationship with him and she had to keep going until she could see him back at College again. The breakup was inevitable as Alex was done with playing games.

Soon, it was time to head back to College after a relaxing Spring Break, feeling fresh, relaxed and ready to get back to study. With so much going on in College life, it was hard to remember that we needed to study. Finals were coming up, as Alex's mum and dad reminded us before we hit the road.

Alex and I always loved our road trips. We were used to our ritual of getting the music playlist on and our snacks at the ready. We chatted about everything and anything and enjoyed a few truck driver honks along the way. I didn't want to bring up the subject but I knew we couldn't avoid it forever. As much as we were looking forward to going back to College, it was going to bring on some reality checks, especially Alex's unfinished business with Harry. "So bird, there is one person you have to speak to when you get back. You know that." I was preparing Alex for the inevitable.

"Cat, I told you I'm not going near Tom. He can go and fuck himself." "No Alex, Harry, you need to talk to Harry!" I reminded her. "Oh yes, Harry. I know I've been avoiding the subject of Harry." "Okay, Calamity Jane!" I joked. "You need to let him down gently. The games must stop and let's get back to normal." "I know Cat, he is a really nice guy. I don't want to lead him on. I gotta do this and besides, I just can't go to any more vegetarian restaurants! I miss my meat!" "No more 'so why did you become a vegetarian' conversations then." We both laughed. As much as Harry was nice, he was boring as fuck!

As we drove up to the College gates, we looked at each other and knew – we've got this. It was going to be our last semester and, as much as we didn't want the year to end, we knew that we were going to get back to our College life and embrace it as much as possible. No more drama!

Once we got settled back in and unpacked our clean clothes and food supplies that Jean and Pete had given us, Alex knew what she had to do. She had to have the conversation with Harry. She knew she had to do it quickly before things went too far.

As we walked across campus, saying hi to all the familiar faces, we came across some not-so-friendly faces. Carla, Stacey and the clones were sitting outside soaking up the sun and topping up their tans. As we walked past, Carla couldn't help but comment, "Hello Catherine and Alexandra. Did you manage to keep yourselves sober over the break?" As Stacey and the clones laughed, I could see Alex was ready to say something about Tom messaging her but then thought better of it. They weren't worth it and a drama-free life was where we were at right now.

"Well done bird, I know that was hard." I could tell Alex was over them now and she wanted to get on with her study. "No more of them getting the better of me, Cat. This is a new Alex you see before you!" she declared. "I'm proud of you. You had every right to lay into her and give her one of your comebacks." And I hugged her as we got to the cafeteria, ready to get back to bagel sandwiches.

Later that evening, Mike called round to see us. "Hey birds of a feather, how's it going? Have you ruffled any feathers lately?" Mike knew us only too well but not the new us. "No Mike, we're staying away from craziness this semester and keeping a low profile," Alex explained. "What you two? Keeping it low? That's no fun. Where are my dancing partners? I wanted to go to the clubs this weekend. I've been at home with my two sisters for a week and they have been driving me crazy. I missed my two College sisters." And with a snap of the fingers and hands on the hips, Mike made us both laugh out loud. Gay Mike wanted to party. "You can't go quiet on me. It's like when Danny Zuko turned jock. The T-Birds were devastated." Mike did love his musicals. "Well, maybe we could make an exception for weekends," I joked.

As we hung out at the Coffee House with Mike, Alex was anxiously waiting for Harry to arrive after arranging to meet him. Mike and I were there for moral support. Alex looked nervous. "Just remember, it's like ripping off a Band-Aid," I reminded her.

Just then, Alex's expression changed as Tom and Stacey arrived at the Coffee House. Tom stopped in his tracks and then, realising what he had done, continued to walk in, not looking in our direction at all. Stacey being Stacey couldn't resist commenting for our benefit, "Babe, I missed you so much over Spring Break," giving Tom a long and lingering kiss which was an over-the-top, for the benefit of those in the audience, type of kiss. If Stacey only knew that Tom was texting Alex, she would be singing a different tune. As they got their coffees and walked out, the atmosphere was almost as frosty as my ice-cold Frappuccino!

"That kiss was a bit dramatic, don't ya think?" Mike, being Mike, pointed out the obvious. "Shoot, I think Stacey practically ate Tom's face off there! Is Tom still being a pussy and not talking to you guys?" We didn't want to let Mike know that Tom wasn't talking but it was okay for him to text. "I guess so, Mike. We're over Tom and his girlfriend. Friends come and go but only those that are true friends remain," Alex declared.

A few coffees later, Harry arrived at the Coffee House much to Alex's relief. Her anxious wait was over. Harry always had his head down and shoulders hunched as if he was carrying the weight of the world on them. Alex gave Harry a nervous smile and left Mike and me to chat. As she walked over to Harry, I could see his face light up seeing her there. I could tell he was hooked and, unfortunately, Alex was about to give him the old, 'It's not you, it's me' speech.

As Mike and I sat patiently waiting for Alex to return, I explained what was happening. "I could see that coming. Alex has nothing in common with Harry at all. They're like night and day. I know Harry from some of my classes and he wouldn't say boo to a goose. Nice guy but not for Alex." Mike's assessment of the situation was spot on. He had no idea that Alex didn't have any intention of being with Harry for more than one or two dates. The game had run on for too long and it needed to end.

"So, my Irish rose, are you looking forward to going back home? We only have this semester left. I'm going to miss you when you go back to Ireland, ya know. You've always been there and listened to me. I want to thank you for that."

"Mike, thank you so much for your friendship. I'm so grateful to have you in my life. You've been my College husband for sure." We laughed together, remembering our long conversations and movie nights together.

Mike was so genuine and gave me a big hug. His realisation that my time at Deacon College and America was coming to an end felt all too real for me too. With only weeks to go before heading home, how was I going to leave my home here in America? As much as the anticipation of seeing James and my parents was exciting me, how was I going to leave my best friend? Alex was a part of me. Being in each other's pockets every day was just as normal as waking up every morning. I was going to miss her so much. I didn't want to think about it for now. We had plenty of time to make more memories so I had to make every moment count.

After what felt like forever, Alex finally came back to the table with a somewhat relieved look on her face. Mike, as always, knew when it was his cue to leave. "Okay birds, I'm going to go back to the dorm. I'm sure you have plenty to chat about." And with that, he and his take-out coffee left us to talk.

"The Band-Aid is well and truly ripped off! That was harder than I thought!" she exclaimed flopping down on the sofa and puffing out her cheeks. "How did he take it?" I asked. "He cried, Cat! I made the guy cry! He said that he had never felt these feelings for anyone before and that I made him feel special and noticed. He said that these past few weeks had been the best of his life! Oh, I'm the worst person in the world! Cat, I just feel terrible. I never wanted to mess with his feelings I just wanted to…" Alex stopped as she knew her game had gone too far and she never wanted Harry to get caught in the crossfire. "I know Alex, I know." I gave her a reassuring hug, relieved that everything was out in the open.

"Cat, thank you," Alex said in a sad voice. "Thank you for what?" I asked. "Thank you for not judging me. I know what I did was wrong and I hope Harry can forgive me. I know I have such a hot head and I do things to get a reaction. I need to stop, think about things and consider the consequences." I could tell Alex was trying to learn from this. "Alex, I would never judge you. You did what you did as a reaction to a situation and we all do that sometimes. I know you didn't mean to hurt Harry." As I tried to comfort Alex, I could tell she felt guilty.

"What am I going to do without you, Cat?" The realisation that this was our final semester had hit Alex too. We had the most incredible bond that was so strong we knew that we were always going to be there for each other. The concept of leaving America and Alex was becoming a reality that I didn't want to face just yet. Our time was precious and we were going to make the most of it.

"Okay hoochie! Let's get back to the dorm. We have beers in the fridge remember?" I smiled at Alex and we agreed it was time to drink!

Over the next few weeks, Alex tried to avoid Harry as much as possible. It was difficult, given the fact that they were in class together. She suggested that they stay friends but Harry was too angry and upset to go there. He even went so far as to have a cheeseburger with fries at lunch! Alex felt terrible. Playing with Harry's feelings was not what she wanted to do.

Just as Alex was getting to grips with being the bad guy, we were walking to the Coffee House one evening when we heard a familiar voice call out to us. It was Tom - another bad guy! As Tom caught up with us, he looked sad. “Hey guys, how are you doing? I haven’t seen you since Spring break. Alex, can we talk? I feel bad about this situation we have created.” Alex looked at Tom, still angry and said, “The situation WE have created? Tom, this was all you. You don’t want anything to do with us for fear that your girlfriend will freak out. Is she not going to freak out right now?”

“Stacey is at the mall with the girls tonight. I’m here on my own and I’m asking you to listen to me. I need to talk to you, it’s important. Cat, can you leave Alex and me alone to talk please?” Tom looked serious and very upset. I looked at Alex to see what she wanted me to do. “It’s okay Cat, go on and get our seat in the Coffee House. This won’t take long.” I left them to it and walked across the campus. The evening was warm and clear and, as the Californian sun was setting, I walked the long way to the Coffee House, past the lake. I wasn’t sure if the conversation between Alex and Tom was going to take some time.

Tom looked at Alex and said, “Alex, I miss you. I can’t bear us not talking and I want it to be like it was.” “You can’t have it both ways, Tom.” Alex was not in the mood for having to justify her friendship.

"No Alex, I don't want it both ways, I want you! You don't know what you do to me. When I'm near you, it's as if you've cast a spell over me and I need to be with you. I want you. Alex, I'm falling in love with you." Tom poured his heart out to Alex but she wasn't as receptive as he had hoped.

"What? You think you love me? Tom, you have a girlfriend and I can never compete with Stacey. She is perfect. You don't want me. You just want what you can't have!" "You're wrong, Alex. Stacey doesn't get me like you do. When I see you, I just want to take you in my arms and kiss you. I have to confess when you got that tongue ring, it drove me crazy! I know you're dating Harry and I know I don't have the right to say these things to you but I just can't help it. Alex. I love you! There I said it!" Tom felt relieved that he had finally been honest with Alex and with himself.

Alex was taken aback by Tom's confession. "Tom, I'm not going to break you and Stacey up. I don't want to do that." "Alex, I've already done that. We broke up earlier this afternoon. I think that's why she is away with the girls tonight. She didn't take it well. I'm single and free to make up my own mind about what I want and Alex, I want you." Alex couldn't believe that Tom and Stacey had split up.

Slowly, Tom came closer to her, with a look of vulnerability in his eyes. He took her in his arms and kissed her passionately. As they kissed, Alex's anger disappeared. She had put aside all her feelings for Tom but now, they came flooding back. Tom stopped kissing Alex and looked at her like he had never looked at her before. "I love you, Alex." At that moment, all the drama and hurt was forgotten and she embraced Tom with a kiss. Facing each other, their eyes locked in this moment of surrender, Alex reached up to cup Tom's face. "Tom, you're an ass hole, you know that? I think I love you too," she confessed. "I know, I'm an ass hole, Alex. I don't know why it took me so long to say this to you and to finally realise that I wasn't being true to myself and to you. I'm so sorry I did that to you."

As Tom held Alex in his arms, she felt happy for the first time in so long. "Let me try that again?" Tom asked Alex and he leaned in for another kiss. "Yes, I definitely like the tongue ring." "Asshole!" Alex smiled and gave him a thump in the arm then gave the kiss another go. "Well, you'd better get used to it." "Oh I think I'll enjoy practising," Tom said smiling a warm and enduring smile at Alex.

I had been sitting in the Coffee House patiently waiting for Alex to come in for her coffee, for a long time and I began to worry. Her initial chat with Tom was taking hours. Had Tom upset her? Had she gone back to the dorm? I decided to go look for her and went to all our usual spots then back to the dorm. Still no sign of Alex. I called and texted but nothing. This was getting weird. Just then, I heard the Clara clones come back to the dorm. It was so hard not to eavesdrop as I heard a loud wailing noise. If they had done something to Alex, I was ready for them. I walked out to see Stacey in tears with her make-up running down her face. Not a pretty picture.

I couldn't help but listen to the conversation. "I don't know how he can do this to me, I mean ME, the most popular girl on campus. We were meant to be together. This can't be happening!" As Carla and the clones tried to comfort Stacey, I put two and two together and realised that Tom had done it. He had finally broken up with Stacey. That's what he wanted to talk to Alex about. It all made sense.

Just then, Carla looked up and saw me walking or rather creeping past. I didn't want them to see me at all. "Hello, Catherine, on your own I see. Where is Alexandra?" Busted! As she always pointed out, Alex and I came as a package. "Carla, Alex has a study session this evening if you must know." I'm not sure if she believed me as Alex and I were not ones to study and Carla knew it. I quickly made my escape and got back to our room.

Just then, a message came from Alex on the answering machine. "I'm okay. Sorry, can't talk right now. Tom is here too." I guess he needed his friend back to talk about the breakup. Alex was always a good friend to Tom and he needed her. I decided to get some sleep. It had been a hectic day and I was ready to hit the hay.

In the middle of the night, Alex returned to our dorm room. She came over and sat on the bed. "Cat, are you awake? Cat, Cat, I need to talk to you!" Alex needed to talk right now so I woke myself up. I knew I wasn't going to get any sleep. I was just glad that Alex was back safe.

"Where the hell have you been, young lady?" I asked as if I were Jean. "Tom and Stacey broke up!" We both said the same words at the same time! It was a total jinx! "How did you know, Cat?" Alex asked and I told her all about the encounter with Stacey, Carla and the clones. "So, did Tom tell you all about it?" I asked intuitively. "If anyone asks, you were at a study session by the way! I had to tell that nosey fucker, Carla, something."

"Cat, he told me more than that. He told me he loved me! He wants to be with me!" Alex told me all about the conversation and the way Tom started to kiss her. They went back to his dorm and made out like crazy. I couldn't believe it but, in a way, I was so happy. Tom finally came to his senses and Alex finally realised that Tom was the guy for her.

"Shut the front door, Alex! What a lot to take in!" "Cat, I love him. I've finally realised why I've been so angry and upset with him. I wanted to be with him too," Alex revealed. "Well duh, of course you did. I had a feeling you might and I just didn't want to say anything. Tom was dating Stacey. I didn't want you to get hurt. I still don't want you to get hurt. So what happens now?" "I don't know but I know I'll get a frosty reception from the dorm bitches. I gotta take this slow."

Chapter 20

All You Need Is Love

The following weeks were some of the best weeks of Alex's life. She had finally found true love with Tom but, as we all know, true love never runs smoothly. The aftermath of Tom and Stacey's breakup was beginning to play out. Tom and Alex didn't want to rub their new relationship in Stacey's face so they were seeing each other discreetly and never showed any public displays of affection. They made up for it in private though.

As Alex came into the dorm room from the night before, she leaned over to wake me up. "Cat, are you awake?" I slowly woke up to the sound of Alex singing 'You are my sunshine' in a high-pitched voice. It always got me up just so that I could stop her singing.

"Well I am now! How's it going, stranger? I haven't seen you in like a day. I missed my partner in crime!" I had to confess that, as much as I loved the fact that Alex and Tom had finally got together, my bird had flown the nest over to Tom's on too many nights.

"Cat, I'm great!! I think Tom is addicted to my tongue ring," Alex laughed. "Oh, I'm sure he is," I smiled back. "Cat, I know I said this about Rick but

I am totally in love with Tom. I can see how much he cares for me by the way he looks at me. He said he always had a thing for me but I was always dating someone else and I was too stupid to see it. I wasted my time with those dumb-ass morons, Rick the dick, Jonny and even Harry although that one was on me. I only hope and pray it works out. We just totally click. He always tried to have his shifts at the Coffee House with me. I didn't realise. He was devastated that I quit my job and that he didn't have a chance to spend time with me. When I was dating Rick, it drove him crazy." I knew this was it for Alex. I knew Tom well enough to know that he was madly in love with her and cared for her so much that he had to end it with Stacey.

"Tom wants us to go public with our relationship but it's just so hard with the Stacey situation at the moment. Cat, I remembered when Jake had completely broken my heart and cheated on me. I just don't want Stacey to feel like the woman scorned. It's the worst feeling." Alex was conscious of not wanting to hurt Stacey even after all the shit Stacey had put her through. "Alex, you guys are going to have to come out in the open some time. It's been weeks now. I agree with Tom and it's not like he was cheating on Stacey. He broke up with her and, to be honest, he should have broken up with her months ago if he had such strong feelings for you. I know he didn't want to hurt her but that's the wrong reason to stay with anyone." I was trying to get Alex to see that she needed to move on with her life with Tom and that meant being a proper couple.

"I know Cat, you're right but it's easier said than done. We'll see how things go but for now, I'm just so happy, Cat." Alex was beaming and I knew she was happy. "If you're happy then I'm happy, my friend. By the way, are you sneaking off with Tom tonight? Mike wants me to go to the movies with him. He's all about this new musical that has come out." "Yeah, Tom's taking me out to dinner somewhere fancy, I think. He said it's a surprise so no idea where we are going." Alex smiled at me as if she was going to ask a huge favour and, of course, I knew what was coming next. "So, you want me to curl your hair?" I laughed. "Cat, you're a star!! You know me too well. I'll make sure we have the ice-cold beer bottles in the fridge to cool down your fingers." "Alex, you are so considerate." "Anything for you, my bestie. I love you. You complete me!" "Okay, okay, I'll do it!" I relented. "Come on, we'd better get to class."

After a busy day of school, it was soon time for Alex's hot date with Tom. We arrived back to our dorm room at exactly the same time and started to get ready. My date with Mike was not as high maintenance so I made sure Alex was looking amazing for hers. After about two hours of getting ready and, as usual, Alex trying on everything in her closet, she was ready. "So, how do I look?" Alex asked. "Bird, you look stunning and your hair is just perfect even if I do say so myself," I said, showing my red fingertips and laughing. "So, what time is Tom picking you up?" "I'm meeting him at the gates in five minutes. We don't want to be seen by you know who." Alex had a worried look on her face. "Okay bird, but you can't keep creeping around the campus all the time and don't worry about you know who. Just go out tonight and have a great time. You deserve to be happy. Okay, let's go. I have to get to my hot date with Mike too, you know!" I gave Alex a hug and a reassuring smile so she knew it was okay to just enjoy being with Tom.

As we walked out of the dorm, we were greeted, as usual, by Carla and her crew giving us the third degree. "Hello, Alexandra and Catherine. My, don't you look all done up like a dog's dinner. Going anywhere special?" Carla was always so nosey. She always needed to know who was doing what and where everyone was going. It was like we were living next to the FBI! "Just going out with Cat for dinner."

Alex knew she might have said the wrong thing. "Oh, well you've gone to a lot of effort to be going out to dinner with Cat," Carla remarked.

"Fuck Cat, can we ever get away from Carla and her questions?" Alex whispered to me. "Carla, didn't you know, I'm practising my hairdressing skills? I'm also practising my skills in minding my own business. You should try it sometime." I wasn't in the mood for Carla's sly remarks. Alex was going to enjoy her night out with Tom and she didn't need Carla to ruin it.

As I left Alex at the College gates, Tom was there waiting. His eyes lit up when he saw her. "You look stunning," Tom said and kissed Alex. She smiled a beaming smile. "Now, you take care of my girl tonight, Tom." "Of course, Cat, she's going to love it." "Love what, where are you taking me?" "You'll see." Tom gave a wink as they sped out of the gates.

I was all set now to go to the movies with Mike. As I walked to the guys' dorm to meet Mike, I was overcome with a haunting feeling, like I had someone following me. I looked round to see Carla, Stacey and the crew there. "Cat, where's your other half now? I thought that you and Alex were going out for dinner." Carla was like a Rottweiler with a bone.

"Jesus, does she ever stop?" I thought. "Goodbye Carla." I left it at that and went on to meet Mike.

Mike and I had a great time at the movies, laughing, chatting and also people-watching which was Mike's favourite pastime. "I swear you're so pass-remarkable Mike," I joked, as he casually made strange eyes at an unusually dressed teenager as they walked by. We took a walk with the last of our popcorn and enjoyed each other's company.

"I can't believe this semester finishes in a few weeks and you'll be back in Ireland." Mike's sentence hit me like a ton of bricks. There were only weeks left of my time in America. For some reason, I felt as though I had lived here all my life.

"I know Mike. I'm trying not to think about it. I've made such great friends here and what are you going to do without your movie buddy?" I gave Mike a friendly nudge and he put his arm around my shoulders. "You're my Irish rose alright." I was going to miss Mike terribly. He was like a brother to me. As we drove into campus, we were met at the parking lot by Alex and Tom. It was as if we had synchronized our watches or something.

"Hey bird!" Alex called over as they walked in our direction. "So, I hope you both had a lovely evening." "It was amazing, Cat. I managed to have pasta and not get a stain on my shirt!" Tom was always joking about the fact that I would spill coffee practically every time. As we walked up to our dorms, Tom gave Alex a kiss goodnight and left us at the door.

As soon as we entered the building, Alex and I heard a wailing sound. We looked around to see Stacey bounding down the hallway towards us. This was not good! She lunged for Alex, screaming out in anger, "I knew it! I knew you were with Tom! I knew you had taken my man!" Stacey was like a woman possessed. Pretty soon, Carla and the posse came running down the hall after. I jumped on Stacey, to prize her off of Alex who was shocked and I could see was hurt. As I pulled her away and handed her over to Carla, Stacey kept screaming, "I saw you from my window, kissing my man! You bitch!" The one moment that Alex and Tom let their guard down with a kiss goodnight and Stacey was ready for war. "Stacey, I'm sorry. I never meant for you to find out like this. Tom and I…" "Tom and I what Alex? You're just friends, right? Like you have been telling me for months. How long has this been going on?" Stacey snarled back. "Stacey, I promise we have just started dating. You and Tom had already broken up. I truly didn't want to hurt you." Alex was sounding so apologetic. "I knew there was something up earlier too. No one gets dressed up to go for dinner with a friend looking like that." Carla couldn't help but get involved and add her two cents in.

"Oh, shut the fuck up, Carla!" I snapped back. "Look Stacey, Alex and Tom were never seeing each other behind your back. You guys had already broken up weeks ago. I can tell you that now." I tried to be the voice of reason in what had become a screaming match with Alex on the losing side. "Well, I don't believe that. Alex, you have had your eye on Tom for months. You took him away from me." "Stacey, I didn't. You did that all by yourself. You suffocated him by telling him what he could and couldn't do. He had enough of being treated like a slave."

Alex started to say everything that she had been thinking over the past few months and she needed to say it. When she was finished, Stacey stood in shock that Alex had finally stood up to her. "Stacey, leave me alone. I've done nothing wrong." As Alex and I rushed into our dorm room, Stacey shouted. "You may watch your back because no one does this to me, no one!"

As I closed the door behind us, Alex was shaking and burst into tears. The whole episode was just too much for her. "Cat, this is all my fault. Why does everything happen to me?" "Bird, you have done nothing wrong. Stacey is just going to have to get over the fact that Tom and she are no longer together. He's not her man. She doesn't have a hold on him anymore and that's what is killing her. Remember, before you were attacked out there, you were happy and you had a great night with Tom, right?" "Cat, it was amazing. Tom and I just talked and laughed about everything. I have such a great connection with him. I think it's because we started off as friends and now we know each other so well. Dinner was beautiful and then we went dancing and enjoyed spending time with each other." Alex had a smile back on her face, she was beaming from ear to ear and pretty soon had forgotten all about the incident with Stacey. She was happy and that was all I wanted to see.

The next day, we got up to what I can only describe as the worst stench imaginable. "Alex, are you awake?" I ran over to wake her up as I could see smoke bellowing into our room. "Shit Cat, what the fuck is the smell? Is there a fire? What's with the smoke?" Alex shouted as she jumped up. We soon realised that a stink bomb had been set off under our door! This could only mean one thing. Stacey had declared war!

We threw on our clothes and ran downstairs but were greeted by another stench. Stacey was sitting with the posse outside on the bench. "Well bird, our room isn't the only thing that stinks to high heaven," I whispered to Alex. "Cat, I don't want to start a fight again. I just don't want to give them the satisfaction of seeing that they've got to me. Let's just walk on and say nothing." Alex sounded exhausted and really didn't want to retaliate to Stacey's act of aggression.

As we walked past the glares, we heard, "Does anyone smell a bitch in the air?" It was Carla giving her what for and, as usual, putting her nose into other people's business. "All I can smell is your bullshit, Carla. Mind your own. Oh, and if you want to smell something, why not check out that stink bomb that has gone off in our room? As floor leader, you really should be aware of these things. Oh wait, you probably already knew!" I was in no mood for Carla and her spitefulness. "Let's just go Cat," Alex said as if she clearly had enough.

Getting to the cafeteria was light relief but we were both now stinking of rotten eggs or some sort of shit. We sat as far away from everyone as possible but, even at that, we could see people sniffing and wondering what the smell was, like they had just walked in the biggest pile of dog shit and couldn't get it off. Tom came over to join us for breakfast and had the same look on his face.

"What's that…" Tom didn't get the words out before Alex said, "Yes, we know it smells like shit." "I didn't want to say guys but there does seem to be a bit of a waft coming from your direction," Tom joked. Alex filled Tom in on the events of the previous night after we had left him and also the rude awakening we received this morning. "Fuckin' hell, this is bullshit! Sorry, I don't mean you guys smell of bullshit but the way Stacey is treating you is not on. I'm going to talk to her. I never knew she could be so vindictive, she's insane!" Tom was furious and was ready to go right then but Alex held him back. "Tom stop. She's hurting and I get it. You guys were together for a long time." Alex tried to rationalise why Stacey was behaving this way. "That doesn't give her the right to verbally abuse you or wreck your room. Alex, I love you and I am not prepared for you to have to deal with this." Tom wanted to protect her. "Tom, just leave it and let me deal with it," Alex said, trying to calm Tom down as much as possible.

For the rest of the day, Alex and I tried to stay away from the dorm to avoid the drama queens but we were met with another ice-cold reception when we eventually returned from class. As we walked into our room, we looked at each other and sighed. “This place stinks. We can’t stay here. Cat, I need to get out of here tonight. Let’s just stay at that hotel off of the Interstate. Besides the fact that our room is now off limits, I hate this feeling of having to watch my back every second. What are they going to do next? Cat, I’m scared!” “Okay bird, we can go. Let me open up these windows to let the smell out and we can pack a few things for the night.” I quickly grabbed what I needed and we got the hell out of there.

As we drove out of the College gates, with the fresh air blowing through our hair, we were for a short while free from all that was behind us. College life certainly did bring with it plenty of drama. We made a short stop at the local store for the beers and snacks we needed for our night of relaxation. We settled into the hotel room. It was pretty basic as it was what we could afford but what a relief it was to just chill out.

“Cat, thanks for this and for always having my back. I just don’t know what I will do without you. I know we haven’t talked about it but, seriously, what am I going to do? I want you to stay here with me at college. Don’t go back to Ireland. I need you. You had me at hello, remember?”

"Bird, I can't stay. I have to go back home in a few weeks and I know I'm going to miss you terribly. We are soul sisters, you and me. We will always have each other." I knew this was true. The bond that we had was so special that distance or time could not affect it. We sat up most of the night chatting about where we would be in five years, still together with Tom and James visiting each other every summer. It was like we were mapping out our future and we were loving every second of it.

We woke up early the next morning to get back to College in time for class. "Did you sleep okay, Alex? I have to say that was the best sleep I've had in a while. No music blasting or doors slamming in the hallways." I had forgotten what a quiet night's sleep felt like. "Me too, Cat. I was out cold all night. Do we really have to go back to those dorms?" Alex groaned. She felt as if going back to the dorm was like going to the dentist. She knew she had to go but didn't want to handle the pain of having to deal with the drama. "Come on, let's go bird. We gotta get to class. Stay strong. We are badass Mother Cluckers, remember?" And with that, we dragged ourselves back to College, stopping off at our usual Starbucks for a quick breakfast first. After a good twenty-four-hours airing, the dorm room smelled almost normal and no longer like a garbage dump.

In the days that followed, one thing was for sure, we were the plague of the dorm. From shaving foam graffiti on the door to photos of nooses on the walls, the bitches of Daisy Hall were in full swing. Alex was actually getting to the point where she found it quite amusing. Their childish witch hunt was becoming ridiculous. Tom and Alex were able to be a proper couple and be in public together now, which was great. They were finally able to do what they wanted. If Stacey had a problem with it, she wasn't doing herself any favours by acting in such a mean way.

"Fuck me, Cat! Did you see the latest picture on the noticeboard outside? It was of someone who looks exactly like me getting run over by a fucking car! I'm actually surprised that they've gone to so much trouble to make me look bad. Someone spent hours on a computer designing this shit!" Alex was over this high school or even junior school behaviour.

"It's like you dared to touch Stacey's property and now you're going to pay!" We had to see the fun in it. "Cat, you're right. They're acting like a pack of hyenas ready to jump me at any time." "I've got your back, bird." I hugged Alex as I knew that, even though the behaviour was childish, she had been worried as to what they were going to do next or if it was going to escalate.

"Although I feel like a dead man walking, Cat, I know you have my back and will be a witness to any crime scene!" Alex joked. "Fuck, Alex there had better not be any crimes of passion. I don't think Stacey could do that. She might break a nail!" It was good to see the funny side.

Pretty soon, the posse became bored and stopped their vendetta and, over the next few weeks, they realised that the more they tried to make life hard for Alex, the more she laughed and smiled and didn't rise to it. Alex had learned not to play the game. Stacey and the Carla clones could do what they wanted but couldn't take away the fact that she was happy and in love. Love beats hate any day.

Chapter 21

I hope You Had the Time of Your Life

As much as I wanted time to stand still, the following weeks went by in the blink of an eye and I had to face the fact that my time at College and in America was coming to an end. Alex and I did as much as we could to make as many memories as possible and take a thousand photos to remember and enjoy our friendship.

And so, it was the day before I was leaving and it was a day I will never forget. I woke up to Alex singing in my ear. "You are my sunshine, my only sunshine. You make me happy when skies are grey. You'll never know dear, how much I love you. Please don't take my sunshine away! Up and at 'em, lazy bones! This is our last full day and I want to make it a good one. I have lots planned, so let's go!" Alex was surprisingly chirpy and full of energy for so early in the morning. I think, like me, she was in a bit of denial, as though tomorrow was never going to come.

"Okay sunshine, I'm getting up, just stop singing!" I joked. As much as I loved Alex, she was a terrible singer and she was always able to get me moving just by singing one note. Anything to stop the noise!

“So what’s the plan today, bird?” I asked. “You’ll see, now hurry up and get dressed!” Alex demanded. After getting dressed, we hopped in the car and hit the road. Alex had made a playlist of all our favourite road trip songs and we sang our hearts out pretty badly but we didn’t care. No one could hear us and we were making the most of our day.

Alex pulled into our familiar parking spot at the mall. My favourite pastime - shopping! “Come on bird, you have to get some shopping in before you leave me.” Alex gave me a sad face but then quickly turned it around and burst out laughing. Our best times were at the mall and also our best conversations when talked about anything and everything. We shopped until our arms couldn’t carry any more bags. We had lunch in our favourite place at the mall, an all you could eat salad buffet and steak house and we savoured every bite. The steaks were amazing and, with half a cow on my plate, I knew I wasn’t going to see the likes of that in Dublin.

Soon, we were back on the road to somewhere but I had no clue where. Alex had a plan and didn’t tell me what it was, she wanted it to be a surprise. We really were on a road trip. A few hours had gone by but as usual, with our chat and the music, the time went by quickly. Eventually, Alex took the turn-off for San Francisco. I was intrigued. Where were we going?

"Okay bird, where are you taking us now? Are we going to Alcatraz and you're going to lock me up and not let me go back to Ireland?" I laughed. "Don't tempt me! I'm considering locking you up so that you'll miss your flight tomorrow. No, I have a little surprise for you, you'll see. Now put this blindfold on!" Alex demanded. "What are you doing? This is all so cloak and dagger!" As we drove into San Francisco, I could hear the car stop and Alex took the blindfold off.

"Surprise! Wanna go watch a basketball game with me?" Alex handed me a pair of tickets to tonight's game! "Remember our one and only fight when I was an asshole and didn't go with you to the game? Well, I wanted to make up for that." "Now, I'm just checking you're coming with me and that these two tickets aren't for me to take some random stranger on the street," I laughed. "Of course the other one is for me, you fuck nut! I tried to think of a way to show how much I love you and will miss you more than you can ever imagine and, if that means watching a game of basketball, well then, that's what I'll do… As long as we get to buy popcorn." "You're on bird!" I was so excited to see another basketball game and also to have Alex there to share it with me. The game was amazing even though we were up in the top rafters as that was all that Alex could afford but, even so, the atmosphere was electric and the game was so competitive. I was loving it and having my best friend there made it that much more special. Soon, it was half-time and Alex poked me in the ribs and said. "Hey look at that." I couldn't believe it, we had our faces on the giant screen! The text said, 'Birds of a Feather Flock Together!' Then an announcement came over the intercom. "Hi folks, I want to welcome Cat from Dublin, Ireland, who is here tonight with her best friend, Alex. We hope you're enjoying the game, Cat!"

"What are you like? How did you get that on the screen?" I was so excited. "Oh, I had to pull a few strings!" Alex said impressively. "Just a sob story email to the team's media department and they were more than happy to wish you goodbye." Alex and I looked at each other and gave each other a huge hug. The tears started to roll down my face. The last time I was at a game, I was in tears but this time it was for totally different reasons. We sat and watched the game and took it all in, together.

Alex and I had the best night ever and, as we drove back to College, we didn't want the day to end.

Alex had another surprise planned. She got a backpack and blankets out of the back seat of the car, we walked down to the lake and sat on the wooden loungers that had been left by the sun worshippers earlier. “Cat, I don’t want this day to end because I know tomorrow will be too sad for me to bear.” From her backpack, Alex produced a six-pack of beer and my favourite American foods. She even brought the road trip playlist songs so we could listen to them one more time. It was so sweet. “You’ve thought of everything, Alex,” I laughed and then looked at her, taking in her face to remember this moment. “I hope so. I just couldn’t think of a better way to spend our last night together.”

“At least the sun is going down so you don’t need to put on any sunscreen, Cat,” Alex joked, “I will never forget the day we met. You were so white and Dad thought you were a devil worshipper with your pale skin. Remember the guys were so helpful getting my gear unpacked and they also helped us be the Mother Cluckers we are. Birds of a feather! I guess we can thank Josh for something.”

“What about Johnny and his obsession with you and tennis,” I laughed “I think he loved his racket more than he loved being with me.” Alex was right about that.

"Oh, and then there was Rick. When he came to the pool that day, I have to say that was a pleasant distraction." "Yeah, then you met him at my birthday, getting in with that crazy ass ID that looked nothing like you. I ended up outside on the street. That's the night Mike told me he was gay, remember? That was not the way I had thought my twenty-first birthday party would be. Although, you did get a little drunkededed."

"Remember the first night you got drunkededed?" I laughed. "How could I forget, Cat? It was followed by the first time I had a God-awful hangover!" Alex would never forget that feeling. "Oh, the hangovers. We did have a few. I think we hold the College record for our three-day hangover from hell."

"Alex, I have a confession to make. I actually had a crush on Rick when I first met him," I confessed. "What? You never told me that!" Alex was surprised. "Come on Alex, he was gorgeous! Not a great boyfriend, the worst actually, but he did have a killer body." Alex smiled and agreed. "Yeah, he did have the body and the ego and the attitude but he was such a cocky fucker!" As we laughed at the thought of Rick and what an arrogant asshole he was. "Alex, you dodged a bullet right there," I said. "For sure, Cat and look at me now. If you had said to me at the start of school that I'd end up in a relationship with Tom, I would have said you were crazy. I guess you just don't know what's around the corner." "That's true, Alex. You've come a long way this year; from your heartbreak with that high school guy, Jake, to the love you have for Tom. Things surely happen for a reason."

"They surely do my friend and you have your love to go back to in Ireland. Are you looking forward to seeing James again?" Alex asked. "I can't wait to see him. It's been so long since we were together at Christmas and yet, in some ways, time has flown by. His emails over the past few months have been wonderful, like beautiful love letters. I think being friends for such a long time was a good thing. We know each other so well and we finally know how we feel about each other. He really is the love of my life. I can't wait to start our lives together as boyfriend and girlfriend, not just as good friends.

"Alex, you were the one who made me realise that it's okay to go for things and to never be afraid. I want to thank you for that. I'm going to miss this. The long talks, our visits to the mall, our road trips to your parents' house, our beer runs, the piercings and the trips to the beach. I'll miss it all. If one thing is for sure, Factor 50 has been my second best friend here."

"Cat, remember that time you forgot to apply sunscreen to your face and you ended up looking like a red lobster." Alex doubled over with laughter at the thought of my beaming red face. "That's not all I burnt when I tried to curl your hair with those rollers. I think I've lost the feeling in the tips of my fingers! If it wasn't for the cold beer bottles cooling them down, I'd have Band-Aids on each finger by now."

"Cat we surely have been through it all. Remember my worst day ever? Black eye with a baseball ball, getting fired from the Coffee House and, to top it all off, I got a speeding ticket!" "That was too funny! Well not at the time, you seriously had a day of it alright! Remember, there's no crying in baseball!" I laughed.

"I have to say, we are never stuck for conversation, not like poor Harry. Remember the time you had nothing interesting to say to him and the only thing was, 'So why did you become a vegetarian?' What a conversation killer."

"Ya know what Cat, throughout this whole year, you have been the one constant thing in my life. You have supported me and never judged me, even when I've made bad decisions and lost my way, you've kept me on track. You're the sister I never had. I love you, Cat." "I love you too, bird, and I promise we are going to stick together forever. We will have years of stories and 'remember that one time' moments to talk about for years to come. We will be those two old birds in a nursing home sitting there telling everyone about the time you got your tongue pierced and I got my belly button pierced." "For sure, we'll be the old ladies telling the stories and not listening to the stories. Let's promise to be those old ladies and share a lifetime of stories." Alex and I gave each other the tightest hug we could, knowing that this was all going to end tomorrow. It was unimaginable. Alex and I were like one being. I felt as if my right arm was going to be ripped off tomorrow. How was I going to survive without her?

As night fell and Alex and I lay on the loungers, wrapped in blankets to keep us warm from the now chilly Californian dusk, we were exhausted from crying and reminiscing about the unforgettable year we shared together. Neither one of us wanted to fall asleep. We wanted to have as much time as we could together. We chatted through the night until the sun came up. At some point, we both fell asleep, still holding on to each other. We were both too emotional to move.

As I woke up to see the sun rising over the lake, I knew that the day ahead would be so difficult for me and Alex. “Hey bird, are you awake?” I whispered. Alex had fallen into a deep sleep and, as much as I didn’t want to wake her, I knew we had to get moving. Time wasn’t on our side and I still had a lot of packing to do. I started to sing Alex’s favourite song. “You are my sunshine my only sunshine, you make me happy when skies are grey….” I tried to finish when Alex reached over to cover my mouth. “Oh my God Cat, I love you but that was awful!” Alex laughed as she knew I too was a terrible singer, another thing we had in common. “Fancy getting our final bagel sandwich from the cafeteria?” I smiled at Alex and she smiled back, knowing that today was going to bring a lot of ‘finals’ for us. “As long as we can have a final latté at the Coffee House too.” Alex loved her lattés and I had come to appreciate coffee. I’d soon be returning home to my Irish tea.

As we walked across the campus with our arms around each other, Mike and Tom came out of their dorm. They knew that it was time for us to spend our last precious moments together and they waved over but didn’t join us. I wanted to take in as much as I could. The warm sunshine on my back and the fresh crisp grass under my feet. As flip-flops had become my new footwear, going back to winter boots and shoes was going to be tough.

Our last supper, so to speak, consisted of our usual cafeteria toasted bagel and then a trip to the Coffee House. "Oh, the fun we had in here, Cat." Alex smiled as we sat thinking back about our card games with the guys and the crazy times we spent at the Coffee House. "We can't cry. I don't think we'll have any tears left by the end of today." Holding each other's hand across the table, we just didn't want our breakfast to end. As we slowly finished our coffee and got up to leave, so many emotions and thoughts were going around in my head. It was time to get back to the dorm to pack before leaving for the airport.

Arriving back to our dorm before the Carla clones was a blessing. I don't think either Alex or I could handle an encounter with them today. Today was not about them. We had wasted so much time on them lately that we were beyond done. Packing all my clothes and reminders of my time at Deacon College was heartbreaking. Each piece of clothing and each memento had a story behind it that would be an everlasting reminder of my unforgettable time here. I had double the baggage that I had come to California with, thanks to our many visits to the mall and I knew I was going to pay for it at the check-in. I didn't want to leave anything and even one of the cups from the Coffee House went into my luggage.

Alex had a lot more to pack, of course, but at least all her belongings were going to be picked up. Pete and Jean, who I now call my American parents, arrived to collect Alex's possessions. This time, with the help of Tom and Mike, we managed to get all of Alex's stuff into the back of Pete's pick-up pretty quickly. Within an hour, we had packed up an entire year's worth of memories and, as Alex and I stood in the empty dorm room, so many emotions came flooding over me.

"Well bird, I guess that's everything. All our College adventures are packed up and ready to go. What a ride we've had though, right?" As we hugged each other as tight as we could, we knew it was time to go. "I know Cat, what a ride. If I had been told before I came to College that I would find a friend like you, I'd have said no chance. You mean the world to me, Cat. I've never had a friend like you. You make me want to be a better person and make me see that I am worthy of happiness. I love you for that." "Alex, you've brought me to life and given me so much confidence that I never knew I had. I love you too, bird."

As we walked down the stairs for the last time and out to the parking lot, Pete and Jean were there to say their goodbyes. Jean hugged me and said, “Hey sweetie, you have a safe trip back home to Ireland and don’t forget about your American home. You’re always welcome to visit us anytime. You’re our Irish daughter now.” Then Pete came over to give me the biggest bear hug ever. “I’m going to miss those hugs,” I laughed as the tears started to roll down my face. Pete and Jean were my American parents. They were the kindest and most supportive people and I was going to miss them terribly.

As Pete and Jean drove off with Alex’s belongings in tow, it was time for the drive to the airport. Alex asked Tom to come along as she didn’t want to drive back alone. I didn’t think she would have the emotional energy to drive. We were both drained. Tom decided to drive and Alex and I sat in the back of the car, head on each other’s shoulder and holding each other’s hand. The drive to the airport was our last road trip together. Passing by the stores and shops we used to frequent, passing by the mall and passing by our go-to restaurants, I wanted to take it all in for the last time.

I didn’t want the car journey to end but then, all too soon, we had arrived at the airport. Everything was happening way too quickly. I wanted time to stand still and just stay in America. There were so many mixed emotions running through my head. Excitement about seeing my parents and James in a few hours but what I felt most was such tremendous loss. Leaving my best friend, my other half, my bird and not knowing when we would ever see each other again!

"Okay ladies, it's the end of the line," Tom declared and then realised it didn't sound too funny. "Sorry, I didn't mean the end of the line, line. It's just time to go. I mean it's time." Tom was trying his best to let us know that we had to say our goodbyes.

Standing at the Departure Gate reminded me of leaving Dublin all those months ago. Watching people leave loved ones and heading off on flights. I was one of those people again. Alex and I threw our arms around each other, holding each other and not wanting to let go. With tears streaming down our faces, for once, we had no words to say to each other. It felt as if we could just stand there for hours and let the world go by but we knew that couldn't happen. It was time.

"Bird, I gotta go," I whispered to Alex. "I know but I can't let you go. What will I do without you?" This was it. "You'll never be without me. I'm always going to be there for you. We are badass Mother Cluckers, remember?" After what felt like forever holding on so tight to each other, Tom came over to prise us apart. "Alex, you gotta let Cat go. It's time to board your flight, Cat." Even Tom had a tear in his eye.

We let our hands slip slowly apart, slowly to the fingertips until suddenly there was only air between us. Tom held Alex tightly as she reached out her hand like I was going to come back. As much as I wanted to, I knew I couldn't. I had to board my flight. My flight back home.

I held Alex's gaze for as long as I could and before turning the corner, I mouthed "Goodbye bird." Alex mouthed back "Goodbye bird." Then she was gone and I had to pluck up the courage to take my seat on the plane. Sitting on the runway with a tear-stained face and red eyes, I started to think of the special friendship I had with Alex.

When I first came to College, I thought that I would feel guilty for making new friends, like I was being disloyal to my old friends back home. Little did I know how special these new friends would become.

College friends are different than any other friends. You live with them. They see you when your make-up comes off at the end of the day and after a bad breakup when your heart has been ripped to pieces. They see the real you and tell you the home truths that no one else would have the courage to say. They see all the highs but they're also not spared the lows.

It's an interesting dynamic, these two sets of friends. One is a group of friends who have known you your entire life while the other is a group of friends who have come to mean more to you in six months than some people have in six years. With these friends, you have shared fun, laughter, sadness, tears and memories that will last a lifetime. You find yourselves telling each other the most private, intimate details of your lives. These are the people who know you best. They leave beautiful footprints on your heart and you are never quite the same again.

A shoulder to cry on, an ear to listen, a College friend is all of these things and more. These friends make days brighter and happier. They always find a way to make you smile even on your darkest days and you don't know what you would have done without them. My College friends are so special to me in so many ways. 'Friend' is a word so small, yet so large in feeling, a word filled with emotion, a word overflowing with unconditional love.

We may have our disagreements; we may have our disappointments; we may argue; we may have concern for one another. Friendship is a unique bond that lasts through all the trials and tribulations of life. A part of each of us goes into our friendships; our humour, our experiences and our tears. These friendships are foundations that are necessary for life. They smooth over the cracks and make us feel like we are the most important person in the world. I never knew that, when I came to College, I would find a friend that I could call my best friend. There are some things that you take for granted but to have a true friend is more valuable than the most precious gem of all. A true friend is priceless.

True birds of a feather who always flock together.

Cat and Alex's Playlist

1. Wide Open Spaces - *The Chicks*
2. Livin' La Vida Loca - *Ricky Martin*
3. No Scrubs - *TLC*
4. Dreams - *The Cranberries*
5. Believe - *Cher*
6. Walking on Sunshine - *Katrina and The Waves*
7. Are You That Somebody - *Aaliyah*
8. I Wanna Dance With Somebody - *Whitney Houston*
9. Can't Take My Eyes off of You - *Lauryn Hill*
10. Never Ever - *All Saints*
11. Girls Just Want To Have Fun – *Cyndi Lauper*
12. Save Tonight - *Eagle-Eye Cherry*
13. Dancing Queen - *ABBA*
14. Oops! I Did It Again - *Britney Spears*
15. You Make Me Wanna - *Usher*
16. Where My Girls At - *702*
17. The Boy is Mine - *Brandy & Monica*
18. Flying Without Wings - *Westlife*
19. Time of Our Lives - *Tyrone Wells*
20. Everybody's Free (To Wear Sunscreen) - *Baz Luhrmann*

Acknowledgements

Thank you to June Alexander of Temple Woman Publishing for all your help and support. June, when I think back to our first meeting to now having my book completed and published, I want to thank you for your expert advice, encouragement and taking me on this amazing journey of writing, editing, designing, publishing and launching my book.

Thank you also to Donna Laverty of Just Peachy Design for the fabulous book cover design. Donna, it has been a pleasure to work with you on the design and I loved every minute of it.

About the Author

Clare Gallagher lives in a suburb of South Belfast, Northern Ireland, with her son. When she is not writing in her journal, she is standing at the side of a football pitch rooting for her son's team or taking long walks up the beautiful mountains close by and catching up with friends.

Clare has worked in the Marketing and Events industry for over 20 years. She self-published her first book "Birds of a Feather Flock Together" in 2023 and has plans to start work on her next book in 2024 which Clare admits should be completed by the next millennium!

As can be seen in her writing, Clare values her dear friends who have supported her through the trials and tribulations of her life. With many friends living in America, Clare enjoys travelling to the States as much as possible and racking up those air miles!

Follow Clare at:

www.claregallagherauthor.com

www.facebook.com/claregallagherauthor1

www.instagram.com/claregallagherauthor

Made in the USA
Columbia, SC
02 February 2024